Fortune Giver

by

Tobin Rayne

Fortune Giver

Cover Art by *Jennifer Greeff*

The Wild Rose Press, Inc.
PO Box 708
Adams Basin, NY 14410-0708
Visit us at www.thewildrosepress.com

Publishing History
First Edition, 2023
Trade Paperback ISBN 978-1-5092-5189-6
Digital ISBN 978-1-5092-5191-9

Published in the United States of America

"So what do we do now about the case?" he asked.

I shrugged. I knew why he felt connected to this case; I felt a connection, too. "Not sure. Sounds like the police didn't take what I shared with them seriously; they seemed to have nothing new on the case."

I liked having Jack as a new friend.

"What if I tried to Read you again," I suggested, "but focus more recently—not going so far back this time? Maybe I could home in on Domino and what you saw with her."

He looked at me. "Not sure it's a good idea, but I'd like to get her out of my head."

"We could try…slowly? And my roomie's here, just in case."

He gave me a nod.

I got up and sat on the coffee table so I was positioned right in front of him. I was shaking already. "So you just sit there…and I'll go slow." I lightly touched the top of his left hand with mine. Feeling a slight tingle. I held my hand on top of his, almost hearing a buzz.

"I hear that," he said.

I reached out and touched his right hand, resting my left on his. I closed my eyes, took a breath. I thought of Domino with her curly, mahogany hair and animated smile. I could see Domino and her killer walking toward the woods, the perspective Jack had. Floating above the two, I needed to get closer. I clenched Jack's hands.

Dedication

This book is for everyone whose dreams and make believe world are far better than their real life. Thanks to my family and friends who encouraged, supported, and humored me—I appreciate you giving me the grace to do my thing.

Chapter One

I jogged west and downhill, slowly and methodically, knowing my run's path, assuring avoidance of gathering spots like busy weekend cafes and farmers' markets. The morning was brisk with intermittent wind and hints of rain.

The Sound's metallic ocean smells curled between the ebbs and flows of the breeze. I took in a deep and purposeful breath, then let it out slowly. I loved living in Seattle.

I had donned my personal armor—e-phones set to deafening white noise to ward off rogue pings, and specially designed gloves, taut on my hands, to keep me from unintentionally touching or sensing anything with my bare skin.

I used the headphones and low-conduction gloves as interference so I didn't hear or feel other's thoughts, making it easier to get through my daily run. My daily run was a necessity to clear my head and get ready for my clients and their mental barrage of feelings, thoughts, and contemplations, whether outright desires or ones of the more clandestine kind.

Luckily, I was off the hook for the next two weeks with no new or recurring clients booked. More time to stream animal videos and have occasional cyber-sex. Or in-person sex if I happened to be craving my usual, pre-screened physical hookup.

I was a certified life coach, which was laughable, as no real *coaching* was involved. I was able to Read and Push customers psychically down a better path. Because of my Sensitive skill, I had amassed a list of wealthy customers who paid well, allowing me to live the socially withdrawn life I preferred and I had grown accustomed to.

A life choice that permitted me to be reclusive and focused on avoiding random human contact and the associated health issues that often came with such proximity.

I was a Sensitive and one of several thousand other Sensitives with varying paranormal abilities living in Seattle proper and the Central Puget Sound Region. Few and far between, we often gravitated toward each other. Like my roomie and I had several years ago.

I trotted to the right, past my neighborhood of condos and apartments stacked atop businesses, another right past a micro-park with a mammoth Seahawks statue, past some e-billboards, and toward the fourth block of high-end dwellings.

An adorable couple with matching haircuts held hands on a bench across the street, staring at each other, lightly kissing, as I passed. As disgustingly sweet as it was, I longed for something like that. Something real beyond a roomie-vetted bone or online transaction.

I turned a corner and noticed a vehicle moving slowly a half block behind me.

The dark, high-gloss sedan with heavily tinted windows mirrored my path. It stood out in this neighborhood of mostly bright-colored, alt-fueled, autonomous vehicles, e-scooters, and e-bikes.

I took a left toward the industrial area flush with

micro-bottling and distilleries, the car still behind me. From what I could tell, it was a luxury e-cell town car and not the typical creeper e-van from the movies I streamed that followed lone female joggers into unpopulated areas to murder and dismember them.

I popped one side of my wireless headphone off, slowed my roll, and concentrated. I heard various thought pings, then worked to fine-tune random waves into close-in, internal conversations.

What I heard was not threatening in nature. It was desperate...and a bit annoyed. I stopped running, pulled my headphones down around my neck, and waited for the car to pull up beside me. I slowed my breathing and took in a long lungful of Puget Sound air.

The car came to a stop in the street near me. An electric buzz from the back-passenger window juddered down. I leaned in just a bit.

"Good morning." I already knew some of what the woman wanted from me—something about her son—but I was not exactly sure how she was going to approach it or any of the sordid details.

She had on a bright-blue, sustainable-silk-blend designer jacket and blouse and had salt-and-pepper hair in an attractive pixie cut. She wore engineered diamond earrings, similar to the ones I'd bought my roomie the last time I touched someone I shouldn't have and ended up in the ER. So I knew they were pricey.

The woman paused for a moment and seemed to collect her thoughts. Had I met her before?

"Good morning—I'm sorry we had to track you down like this," she said in a noticeably apologetic tone.

Although something about the way she said it made me think she *wasn't* sorry.

"But I *have* pinged your office and left multiple texts."

I smiled at her and nodded. "Yeah, I'm sorry about that. My business manager slash scheduler is on a much-needed vacation...which means there's no one to schedule and—"

She interrupted me. "Yes, that's what your office e-message said, but this can't wait another week. I need someone now, and I can assure you I will pay generously for your help."

I leaned in a bit more, careful not to touch the vehicle. "Money is not usually...the issue," I stammered. "It's...it's more about timing and appropriateness of the client fit and their needs...and..."

"Please. We've seen other specialists, and we need someone with your particular skills...and particular discretion...for my son."

I could never say no to anyone, which was why I was not the business manager. I blew out a breath. Part of my flyaway curly hair fluttered upward and to the side. "Um, how about...tomorrow at ten a.m.?"

I figured not too early or too late in case it went badly. Probably an easy one. How many problems could one rich kid have?

"Thank you." She held out her hand for a shake.

I eyed her hand and instead placed my gloved fist into my other palm in a respectful bow.

"OK, then." She retracted her arm and hand back into the vehicle. "We'll see you tomorrow morning."

I gave a half wave as the window went up and the town car drove away. My interest was piqued, and I was uber curious who the familiar-looking woman who'd tracked me down so easily was. Had she really been watching and stalking me? *Creep alert.*

My business kept a low profile and discerning clientele to better assure customer confidentiality. A random web search for my roomie's and my business brought up an interior design firm, which was also a legit side business of my roommate.

I guessed in business anything was available for a price. Who gave up the fact I was a psychic life coach? I knew it wasn't my business partner, Vee, as she was on top of keeping our work on the down-low so she could charge the fees she did for my specialized and uncommon services.

The high fees also afforded her an exotic and exclusive resort-island vacay, which was where she was off to for the next couple of weeks with her girlfriend.

Oh shit. I hadn't gotten the woman's name. I smiled. Again, that was why I was not the business manager. I assumed since they tracked me down jogging, they could just as easily find my office and had probably already staked it out.

I started back out in a slow jog to finish my run, stopping slightly and maneuvering around a street-cleaning box-bot picking up garbage and rinsing the sidewalk. Fucking robots. I would never get used to them.

I jogged back to my condo. I'd need backup plans in place for the next day since Vee would be out of town. I tried to ignore the fact that she'd be extra perturbed that I'd scheduled a session with a new client without her critical once-over and measured vibe.

When I got home, I took a shower, redressed, and called for backup. I dialed a familiar number.

"Howdy, Roe, what's up?" said a very sexy, drawled

male voice on the phone.

"Hey, Kel. You at work?"

"Yep, but saw it was you, and I was free. What's up?"

"You working tomorrow morning? I need a favor."

"Monday morning? That's a bit early for a hookup. But hey, I'm game."

"I need you as sort of a…chaperone for a couple hours. You free around nine?"

"Sure, I'll be there." He mumbled something to someone else. "Hey, my next client's here, Roe. I'll talk at ya later." He hung up.

Kel was my bestest eff buddy and a great friend. He'd started out as my roomie's fitness trainer, and she'd invited him over for a house call to help "strengthen my core" at the condo so I could avoid the gym.

During our first session, he touched my back with his hands to help me stretch. I braced for a bevy of thoughts, but nothing apprehensive came through. He was just a dependable, nice guy with low noise. And oh, so very attractive.

My roommate vetted him and told me she had a hunch we'd hit it off, and she was right. She's always right. Our multiple sessions turned from fitness into libidinous physical contact with no strings.

He was ever generous in bed, and we left it at that, providing me the occasional in-person shag I needed to decompress with no commitment. He also provided the occasional kick in the yoga pants I needed to stay semi-fit, especially with my proclivity toward all things donut.

I had been wounded in the past by a controlling relationship and had paid a physical price after spontaneous, one-off, casual encounters went wrong.

Because of my gift, I had to be extra choosy about companionship.

If the wrong pings got through, a night of debauchery ended in a days-long, killer migraine, or worse, a trip to the emergency room. A hefty price when trying to function in life, but a girl's gotta get laid, right?

After the last fiasco and before meeting Kel, I'd had to restrict my sexual activity to virtual-reality hookups. Nice, but a girl's gotta have real-life variety, too.

Tomorrow would be the first time I had asked Kel for a business favor, but I had also been meaning to call him for a hookup or two with Vee out of town. He was a good sport.

My most important relationship was with Vee. My roommate, my business partner, and my BFF soulmate. She also happened to be a Sensitive on the Healing spectrum and the one who'd rescued me from the hooks of a hellish boyfriend, bringing me stability, to my senses, and to Seattle six years ago.

I sure hoped she was having a relaxing and fun time on vacation. She really deserved it.

Chapter Two

After the call to Kel, I listened to a couple of e-messages from the office so I could get the client's name and do a bit of research to see what I'd gotten myself into.

Janelle Knight. Oh fuck. That was her? My new client? Nobody special. Only the matriarch of one of the city's wealthiest and most prestigious families. Shit. And double shit.

I knew she'd looked familiar. Vee was going to flip that I'd taken on such a client without her go-ahead. This could go so terribly badly, and clients like the Knights needed to be treated carefully.

"Well, you can't shove the synth shit back in the robot," as Vee would have said. I could only do as much prep as possible. I went online to gather what information I could find on the Knight family. The internet did not disappoint.

The Knights had four kids. One daughter and three sons. I made a guess that this was for their seventeen-year-old son. Probably wanted to know if he was going to get into Harvard or some other Ivy League school and how to steer him that way. Easy peasy, lemon squeezy. Research done.

I streamed shows the rest of the day, snacked on and off, and was ready to call it a night. I was even prepped for bed, already in my jammy pants, tank top, and signature crazy hair bun. I planned to binge-watch *cats stealing dog beds* videos and maybe a bit of BritBox before nighty-night. I heard my Ding video doorbell.

I peeped at my Ding viewer, and a strikingly handsome gentleman was at my door. I opened it, of course.

"Well, hello there." I waved him in.

"So, since you needed someone in the morning," Kel said, "thought I'd get a jump on things and just stay over to keep you company with your roomie out of town and all."

Kel was short and sweet, about my height, which was five feet eight, with dark-brown hair, muscular with chiseled features, green eyes, a southern accent, and a smile that could part rivers and other natural barriers.

"Well, why didn't I think of that?" I smiled at him, feeling the sweet sensation of anticipation. I shut the door, punched in the e-lock, and set a second and third e-lock. Probably overkill but I had to respect my intuition's need for isolation, security, and safety.

I turned around, and Kel was standing just inches away from me, his emerald sparkling eyes and our faces level.

"At your service, ma'am," he said in his mesmerizing drawl, tipping his ball cap just a tad in my direction. He was one hunk of a man, still wearing his Rock-Hard logoed gym training T-shirt, his large arms barely fitting, stretching tight around his biceps. His chest rounding out the front.

He had a short buzz cut, which on him looked hot in a boy-next-door kind of way. The boy next door with the super amazing physique I wanted to fuck.

He smelled clean with hints of musk and the

outdoors. Just his smell made my nipples erect with expectation, and a warm flush rushed from my head down past my breasts to my groin.

Kel was a sight and sense I relished in, knowing I would be able to relax, have fun, and just fuck since he was as much friend as lover. The fact that his silky voice made me instantly wet didn't hurt either.

I loved our casual, no-strings-flings policy, and I appreciated that he was an easy Read. When we were having sex, it was just that. Sex. His complete attention was on me and my body, which allowed me to focus wholly on pleasure, his and mine. Because I could Read what he was thinking, I already knew what he wanted, and he was cool with me showing him or Pushing what I wanted.

No real crazy kink like some past lovers. I was OK with his more conservative style, and I respected those boundaries. Mostly.

Sometimes, when he was training me, his focus would flash to sex, but a side-eye from me would get him back on track. Not that I didn't want to have him all the time, but the workouts were just as important as the sex to help keep me sane and in check.

Having him as my occasional bed buddy would not be forever. A time would come when he would fall for someone and our time between the sheets would end. But until then, this man was mine…but just in a total best-eff-friends way.

Kel reached his brawny arm up and fondled a piece of my flyaway silvery hair that had fallen out of my bun, petting it between two fingers before letting it go again with a light swish.

I grinned at him, taking in the sight of his body and

handsome face. Every inch of this man was tight, and thoughts about how we had pleasured each other in the past and what was to come sent charged chills up my spine.

I reached up and slowly snagged his Rock-Hard ball cap, then tossed it aside with a mischievous grin. I tugged my hands up and under his shirt and pulled him toward me, looking forward to having him deep inside of me hopefully multiple times throughout the night.

Kel's warm, taut skin looked like melted caramel and felt just as smooth. I always wondered if he removed all his body hair. Never thought to ask him. Never cared as long as I got to enjoy the glossy feel of him on top, beneath, and behind me on occasion.

I liked the way my skin warmed and slid next to him, his strong hands and rippled body parts meshing with mine.

I leaned in and brushed my lips against his, and he pulled me closer with a hand at the small of my back. His hand was warm and firm behind me. He looked at me and exhaled, his breath a mix of vanilla mint gum and protein powder.

He kissed me aggressively and ran his hands up my back, sending warmth down to my ass, which perked my nipples. I sighed breathlessly. He pulled my face toward him, using his tongue to explore my mouth.

My tongue touched his. He tasted just as good as he smelled. Like vanilla mint. A moan slipped from my lips, and he breathed out in response. I kissed him harder.

He grabbed my hair lightly and tipped my head back to kiss and taste down my neck to where my tank top started. He tugged a bit harder on my hair and tongued the hollow space just below my neck.

His wet lick ignited neurons from that hollow space right to my brain, headed through my spine, into my stomach, and slowly maneuvered down to settle and spark in my pussy.

I put my arms around him and used his velvety smooth and tight ass to pull his hips toward mine so I could feel his hardened cock. He let go of my hair, pulled my tank top over my head, and tossed it aside. It hit a nearby wall with a low ruffle.

My hands slid from his rear to the large rigid bulge in his pants. He was wearing joggers, and I could easily feel his stiff dick through his sweatpants. Gotta be one of my favorite feels.

He moaned when I put my hand on his cock and again when I shifted my hand down to his balls and clutched them lightly, kneading them ever so softly over his sweats.

He cupped my breasts, licking the tops and rubbing them, his wet mouth making me shudder. He circled his thumbs roughly on my nipples with a sharp pinch, which burned with pleasure and then cooled with relief as he took each nipple in his mouth to suck them.

I leaned into him with a moan, wanting him to continue. His warm tongue was wet and wonderful on my nipples. My lips parted with pleasure, and an "oh my God" escaped from my lips.

I reached under his shirt and ran my hands over his steel-like sculpted back. I could not get over how smooth his skin was.

On the way down his back, I snagged the bottom of his shirt with my thumbs, pulled his T-shirt up over his head, and dropped it to the floor. I ran my hands over his slick and rippled chest. His nipples responded with delight, perking up.

He pulled the ribbon on my PJ bottoms taut with a zip, and I felt them loosen and flutter down, sending a chill straight up to my clit. I stepped out of them, and Kel grabbed my ass and pulled me into him.

I could feel his rock-hard cock between his sweats and the thin layer of my panty fabric.

I undid his sweats in return and pull-pushed them down. He kicked them off. Several inches of his dick tip bulged from the top of his briefs, glistening with drops of arousal. I reached in and stroked his hard cock, the slick pre-cum making it slide and slip in my grasp.

He drew me forward by my head and kissed me fiercely. His and my tongue played and danced in each other's mouths, his hands kneading my bare ass underneath my panties, making me extra moist with tingling.

Kel had large, strong hands and a chokingly large cock. Impressive in both girth and length and he knew how to use all his body parts on me to make me come efficiently and frequently.

I put my arms around his back, kissing him, relishing his taste and the warmth of his tongue on mine. He took that moment to pull his briefs down in one motion. His cock stood at complete attention.

He continued to squeeze and caress my cheeks, pulling my body next to his rock hardness, its moist head touching and sliding across my stomach, making my cunt jealous of the attention.

Kel slid his hands up across my back and around to caress my breasts. My chest was heaving and my pulse racing. I could hear both our hearts beat in unison.

He reached down and cupped my pussy, my reflexes

bucking me toward him, my breath caught in my throat. A cry escaped my lips but sounded more like a three-syllable moan.

He moved aside my panties, and I felt a surge in my core when his fingers grazed my clit. I moaned loudly; he responded with a pleasured groan. He rubbed my clit, gently at first, then more purposefully.

I moaned again, and he slipped two fingers into my moist pussy. The feel of his fingers sliding into my sopping hole with gratifying ease was cataclysmic, my cunt pushing against him.

He plunged his fingers in and out of me rhythmically while holding on to my ass to pull me into his long, wet, finger-fuck thrusts. Harder. A high-pitched moan escaped from my throat. He quieted the moan with a full-mouth kiss.

He knew the perfect spacing and pressure I needed because I exuded what my body was saying directly to him via unmeant pings during sex. In other words, his timing was impeccable, leading us to come together easily, literally.

I smoothed my hand down his hard stomach and gripped his stiff cock, grabbing and rubbing it and then caressing his balls. I was imaging his fully erect dick already inside me, pulsing, pushing, pleasuring.

Kel put his hands on my shoulders, pushed me down on my knees and then onto my back on the tile.

The frigid floor was a sharp, shocking contrast to his radiating warmth, but the thought of fucking him soon warmed my body. I was shaking with anticipation, wanting him so badly.

He paralleled his full body on mine, settling down into a familiar fit. His highly muscled dead weight on top of me was centering.

He paused, looked at me, and winked, taking a few breaths before snagging my lips again with his, pairing his tongue with mine the way he knew I liked it.

His soft kissing grew more vigorous, and I returned his intensity. He lifted off me and moved down my body, his lips kissing and tasting my neck, breasts, nipples, and stomach.

His hands and fingers touched everything along the route down, my hips bending toward him, my throat breathing in and out in moans.

He made sighing sounds as he licked his way south, his tongue lingering on my uber-sensitive area between hip bone and the top of my bush. His heat and his breath on my skin made my body, my pussy, percolate toward his mouth.

He ran his finger around and inside the top line of my low-cut lace panties. He didn't take them off quite yet. The anticipation of having his tongue diving down drove me wild.

He kissed near the top where the lace began and ran his tongue across where the satin ribbon seam ended. I wanted to tell him *please*, but a moaning breath came out instead.

He slowly lifted and pulled my panties down and off, the weight of the fabric increased due to my wetness. I had my eyes closed but could feel him looking at me, waiting.

Please I tried to say again but couldn't, I only moaned with hunger, but I had already Pushed out my plea to him, and he was eager to comply. His lips slid again over my hip bones on both sides, licking as he went, and then he opened my legs wide and settled in between them.

Kel focused in on my clit. Lolling his tongue around with pressure, before taking me in his mouth and sucking. His combination of licks and finger-fondling my hole made me writhe on the floor, the frigid tiles moist with the heat of our libidinous activities.

I grabbed at his buzzed hair, trying to grip his head down toward my cunt. The sounds of his saliva mixed with my aroused wetness were waves lapping at rocks on the shore. Hypnotic and frothy.

He continued to douse my pussy fire with his liquid kiss, and when he parted my lips with his tongue and plunged it directly into my cunt, I cried out. His cock grew even harder against my leg.

"Fuuuuuuuuuuck." I moaned again with pleasure.

He used his thumb to roll over and circle my clit as he continued to dart his tongue in and out of my hole while sucking and licking down. I wanted to smash his face inside me so his tongue would go deeper. I pulled his hair. Oh fuck. I wanted him to fuck me. Bad.

I wanted his cock inside me. I moaned *please, please* out loud and in my mind's voice, begging him. He moved back up to kiss me, his lips slick and wet from my own arousal, his knees keeping my legs pushed open.

Kel knew I liked to be teased, so he rested the hardness of his cock just at the entrance to my pussy as he maneuvered his full weight of muscle and bone on top of me. Feeling his cock that close to my climactic zone drove me wild.

He pushed his enlarged cock against my pussy and waited for me to mind-beg him as my cunt released more juice to make the deep travel needed for his large dick easier. My wetness dripped on the cold tile, making the floor as slippery as my hole.

Kel intensified the pressure with his penis, his tip wedged between my lips until I couldn't stand it anymore. *Please. Fuck. Me. Now.* My mind and body begged.

He inserted his first several inches into my pleasure passageway, and my hips bowed toward him as he plummeted his cock all the way inside me. His huge dick filled my hole, causing my Kegel muscles to clutch down, pulling him in deeper.

His rock-solid cock hit the back of my box wall hard, making me catch my breath and my body slide on the tile. *Fuck me. Fuck me. Fuck me.* I infused in his brain, moaning loudly, pushing him toward his sexual climax.

His breath quickened, and he plunged his cock over and over into me. Again and again and again, squeezing by my G-spot and banging the back of my hymen's long-broken home. I was sooooo there, my vag canal contracting in vigorous spasms. I cried out piercingly in his ear, clawing at his back and probably leaving marks.

I came hard with a swift, pulsating buzz, and Kel exploded in the depths of my pussy. My body shuddered and bucked in continued orgasm, and he jolted and pulsed several more times before he moaned and collapsed on top of me.

Sweet holy fuck. His hotness heated the air around us.

He rolled to my side and onto his back. "Shit, this floor is cold on my ass." He rolled toward me, sliding from our fallen sweat and wet lovemaking.

"Uh, yeah, I know the feeling." We had skidded a couple of feet in our slick mess due to his hefty thrusts.

He grabbed my hand and kissed it, taking one of my fingers in his mouth, sucking it. He was always hungry after sex.

I got up, found my tank and PJ pants, slid them back on, and headed into the kitchen to heat up some food. Vegan, homemade mac 'n' cheese. Yum. One of the meals Vee had left for me. We ate in my bed and watched cat videos. Then we were ready for the next round of fun.

****

Monday morning came fast. Just like I had, multiple times the night before. Multiple.

Kel brought me a coffee made by Brewster, the nickname for my autonomous, intelligent brew system, after programming his own specialty beverage.

While I was not one to trust most robots, I had complete faith in my coffee bot's ability to make me a perfectly brewed cup of sustainably engineered Joe, every time. It knew what I liked, and I liked that it knew. I also had deep fondness, more like true love, for Sweepy. Sweepy was my autobot vacuum. Unless he was mopping, then I called him Moppy.

I gave Kel the lowdown of what my session today might entail and how I would need his help.

"So I never know after Reading or Pushing a new client if I might have a bad reaction," I told him. He knew that my job was half life coach, half medium—a bit of fortune-telling and a bit of fortune giving, but I'd never given him all the details.

"What kind of reaction?"

"Well, that depends. Sometimes nothing but a clear Read and a twinge of pain, but sometimes I get sick with a killer headache and throw up."

"OK, I think I can handle that." He paused. "Can

you Read me?"

"I Read you every time I see you, which is why I know almost everything about you. But I've never Pushed you. I'd be happy to try if you're game."

"What's the difference?"

"Well, I typically Read people first—I guess it's like Reading their energy and background, taking in hints of where they are headed next and what trajectory may be best for them. I get an overall picture of what they are all about, events in their life, and what they may need help with or need to change."

I continued. "And a Read can be different for everyone. Sometimes, I get snapshots of life moments, or I see what the client sees when they think of things. For instance, I may see a large closet and the customer running around and rummaging through things or a huge beach with multiple towers containing a customer's life events. Sometimes, I get an illustration of them centered in the middle of a storm. It depends on where they are coming from."

He looked a bit confused, but I could tell he took in and considered what I had just said.

"Then I take all of what I observe and recognize into consideration and provide a mental Push to move them forward in life, typically onto a more positive and rewarding life path. And that's about it."

I nodded and waited for mental receipt of his understanding. He nodded back at me. I motioned for him to sit on the couch, and I dragged one of the side chairs over to sit in front of him. I handed him my mobile.

"What's this for?" he asked.

"Well, you know the consent app we both thumb-printed before having sexual relations for the first time?"

"Yeah...but when you say it like that, 'sexual relations,' it sounds clinical and not much fun."

I ignored him. "Well, this has the same authorization language and includes customized legalese I ask my clients to acknowledge before I Read or Push them."

He looked at me, eyebrows raised.

"It's serious. I need folks to know that when I touch them, I can find out a whole lot about them—stuff they may not want me to know. They need to know their lives may change and it could have physical, mental, family, or financial repercussions on their life—so the language holds me and my company, VeRo, harmless now and in the future."

VeRo was the company Vee and I owned together, its name a combination of both our first names. It's also the name of Vee's interior design side business and the front for the work I did.

"OK," Kel said. He scrolled, scanned, put his thumbprint on my device, and handed it back. I looked to see it had been signed, then tossed the phone next to him on the couch.

I took his hands in mine, closed my eyes, breathed in, and concentrated.

I get glimpses of Kel with quick pictures fast-forwarding, some rewinding. I see him running at Green Lake. Working with clients at the gym. In his Ballard apartment doing planks and push-ups. We're having sex the night before. In his apartment again. He's fashioning some kind of apparatus with large body bands. He draws a contraption on drafting paper. I look inward. His mind is full of knobs and dials, like a clock's insides. A rusty clock...

I laughed out loud. He tensed. I grasped his hands tighter. I breathed, went farther in.

The inner workings again. I visualize wiping, buffing, and moving levers, and the parts start moving slowly. I virtually brush off the cogs to clean them. I chisel off the rust. The parts begin to work faster and are at full speed. All systems go.

I let go of his hands. The twinge of a slight headache was forming. I clenched my teeth, breathed in, held, and released.

"Have you ever thought about going back to college?" I asked him.

"Not really." He looked at me like I was nutty. "I was never good at school."

"You need to go back and study human performance engineering. You should no longer have trouble with school."

"And that's it? That's my Read?"

"Yes, that's a Read and also a Push. I just Pushed you to go back to school and told you what to study."

He looked at me and gave me his best *you're bullshitting me* smile. "And people pay you for that?"

"They sure do. And a lot for it. I won't charge you, though." I put my fingers in his hair, grabbed, and pulled lightly down, giving him a coy smile. "You can pay me in other ways."

"Well, I'll do *that* for free." Kel winked, then stood up and went to retrieve another cup of coffee for us while I showered and dressed for the day.

I made us some toast and fried eggs, from uncaged and organically fed hens, of course. Vee had written a note on the egg carton. *Yummy! Full of protein!* As if I didn't know eggs had protein in them. Well, now I did.

Chapter Three

Kel and I headed downstairs. I made sure to grab another cup of coffee and snag my gloves of protection to put them on. I remembered to have Kel thumb-sign a confidentiality agreement, too, in case he met the client. Vee would have been proud.

My client was prompt, knocking on the office door at 8:55 a.m. When I opened the door, it wasn't who I'd thought it would be—well, definitely not the seventeen-year-old son of the Knight family. This client was closer to my age, which was twenty-four.

I didn't need an introduction as I recognized his face from being plastered all over the online tabloids. This was Jack Knight. The middle brother.

"Hey, I'm Jack," he said gruffly and held out his hand.

"I'm Rogue, co-owner of VeRo coaching, and this is my assistant Kel. And I don't shake hands," I said unapologetically.

Kel smiled an apology for me, leaned over, and shook Jack's hand.

"And this is for you," he said groggily, handing me an e-reader.

I looked down. It was the consent app already downloaded, with what appeared to be slight tweaks where I needed to sign, too. I'm sure the Knights' lawyers had gone through the language all weekend.

I quickly scrolled and looked for fatal flaws and that the important signatures were there. I e-signed as well, knowing they probably required confidentiality as much as I did. I file-jumped the docs onto my mobile device. Vee would be doubly proud of me, checking the signatures *and* keeping a copy.

"I thought your mom was coming, too?" I asked.

He shook his head and shrugged. "She's waiting for me in the car. Probably to make sure I made it in here." He yawned wide, stretched his arms out, and looked me up and down with a doubtful and disbelieving smirk.

Most of my new clients were like that. At first. I smiled and took him into the coaching room. I asked Kel to hold back to keep the session private. I wasn't worried about this guy as he seemed harmless, and I didn't get any initial unsettling pings.

"So how does this work?" Jack sighed and ran his fingers through his unkempt hair.

"Well, I have you sit there"—I motioned toward the vegan yellow leather couch, with huge throw pillows— "and I sit here." I sat on a matching wingless chair stationed in front of the couch.

His beard was disheveled, and he needed a haircut. He also smelled a bit funky, like he had been binge-drinking, sweating, and playing vids all night. He needed a shower. Maybe a detox.

I looked down at the reader again and browsed through what was written about Jack's background. I could only assume his mom had filled out the e-form for him.

"Failure to launch?" I questioned, looking up from the e-reader toward him.

"I guess so. Can we get on with this?"

"Listen, Broody McBroodster, you sound bored and impatient," I acknowledged. "I realize this probably wasn't your idea, but I'd like you to know you can trust me as I have a ninety-eight percent approval rating."

He rolled his eyes at me.

I was only kidding about the percentage. I had a hundred percent approval rating. I put the reader on the table and slowly took off my specially designed, ping-protection gloves. "May I take your hands?"

He nodded. His hands were hot and moist. Probably because he was annoyed, nervous, or had vodka sweats. Or a combination of all three.

I could already feel pulsing from his hands, like static electricity building. I leaned forward, tilted my head down, took a deep breath, and concentrated. I took in another breath and blew out.

OK. Failure to launch. I'd need to go back. Way back.

Sounds of kids playing. There's a lake. Light-colored clothes. Running around. Laughter. Barbecue. Grungy water. Sound of speed boats. Sulfur. Fireworks. Summer. Warm breeze, humidity. Breathe. Sink deeper. Breathe.

Taste. Corn on the cob, potato salad. Iced tea. My skin. Hot sun. My feet. Hot wooden planks. Jump into the cool water. Gurgling underwater sounds. Giggling. Bubbles. Kids everywhere. Brothers. Sister. Cousins. Mom. Relaxing. Peaceful. Breathe. Deeper. Cool water. Sounds fade. Then alone. Swimming. Splashing. Underwater. Voices. Garbled. Sputtering. Pull back. Underwater. Drowning. Screaming. Pull back. Gulping. Help. Bodies floating. Rotting. Held. Down. Gagging. Trapped. Seeing. No. No. Get back. Putrid. Feeling. No.

No. Get back. Head burning. Searing. Pain. Shhh. Shhh. Blood. Flesh. Pull back. Pull back. Shhhhh. No breath. Hands. On fire. I'm on fire. Shhhhh.

****

I squinted and opened my eyes slowly. So slowly. Oh fuck. It hurt. I squeezed my eyes closed. I hurt all over. I heard voices. Noises. Sick. Nauseous. Couldn't move. *Fuck it. Don't move. Back out. Back out.*

****

"Hey. Hey? Heeeeeeeyyyyy?"

I heard a soft drawl as I stirred and recognized Vee's voice. I opened one eye very slowly and then the other. My head throbbed. I tracked my pulsating eyes across the room slowly. So slowly.

Vee was smiling at me, sitting by my bed. I was in a hospital room.

"Welcome back," she said.

I tried to give her a smile, but my dry lips painfully stuck to my teeth. *Ugh.* My teeth felt fuzzy. My throat was on fire.

She picked up a cup of water with a bendy straw for me to drink. I drank a couple of sips. That was better. The water felt cooling and soothing on my dry throat. Her face looked worried. She looked like she had been crying.

"Shit. How long was I out?" My voice was deep and raspy. I didn't sound like myself.

"Seven and a half days." She looked relieved and angry at the same time. She started to cry and put her head down on my bed.

Wow, seven days. I hadn't been totally out of commission from a Read for a couple of years and never for that long before. I tried to pat her head and noticed

25

that my hands were bandaged. "What the fuck happened, exactly?"

"*Jack Knight.* That's what and who happened." She sniffled.

I sort of remembered him coming to the office and sitting down with him. Then a blur. "Where's Kel?" I remembered that I'd had him in the office with me.

"He's OK. He's the one who called me. He said you were with a client, and it was as if you got struck by lightning. Both of you. Jack, too."

"What? Both of us?" I had never made a client sick as far as I recalled.

"Yeah. You both have third-degree electrical burns on your hands—that's where we are now. In the Knight Hospital derma and burn unit."

"Please tell me you didn't have to cut short your vacation with Josie." I knew by her look that she had.

"You owe me. You owe Josie." She seethed. "You owe us both a big apology."

"I'm so sorry. I thought Jack's Read and Push'd go fine. He's from one of the wealthiest families in the city…"

"Yes, and that's why I vet them first—rich kids have the most messed-up lives of anyone!"

I looked around the room. From a window reflection, I could make out I had my head bandaged, too. I shook my head. What had happened? "Can I have a mirror?"

"I don't think you want to see. Part of your face is burned, and your eyes look worse than they did last time you did this to yourself."

"Give." I reached out for the compact mirror I knew she had in her purse.

"All right, but you're not going to like it."

I carefully grabbed the mirror with my bandaged hands, wincing a bit as I did. She was right. My eye sockets were badly bruised—the whites of my eyes were more bloodshot than I've ever seen them. Part of my forehead was bandaged.

"Good news is the doctors said there will be minimal scarring on your hands and forehead," she said. "You got treated here right away, and Knight is the top burn center in the country."

She sounded like a frickin' advertisement.

"They slathered on some quick-healing honey-gel and grafted pseudo-fish skin onto you."

I took a last peek in the mirror and looked down at my hands. I'd never had burns before, just migraines, bloody noses, and bruised and bloodshot eyes. Maybe Jack and I *were* hit by lightning? I gave Vee her mirror back and looked around the room.

My industrial noise machine was at full bore, its protective gray body plugged in by the door. I'm sure Vee had brought it in and probably requested a room in an isolated section of the hospital.

Flowers were everywhere. I hadn't noticed them. Typically, my nose was my other keenest sense, which Vee called my super-sniffer power, but I couldn't smell them. I couldn't smell anything.

"Who brought the flowers?"

"All kinds of people. Me. Josie. Josie's folks. Kel. Tiana. Neighbor lady. Mystery lady. Mr. and Mrs. Knight…Jack…"

"Which ones are his?"

She pointed to a large rainbow bouquet with a *Get Well* kitten balloon. *Fuck you, Jack, and your cheery balloon and screwed-up life.* I was pissed at myself for being stupid in accepting him blindly as a client and Reading him without Vee's nod.

She had been able to help keep me safe for years by using her Healing gifts to assess anyone I was going to touch. Well, safe enough, until I got wild and made a stupid decision to go all half-cocked for a tryst, or full-cocked, depending on how one looked at it.

I laughed out loud a bit, which was painful on my scratchy throat. My giggle resulted in a serious look from Vee. Well, at least *I* found myself funny.

The last time I slept with intentional, unsanctioned strange, I wound up in the emergency room with a killer migraine and a nosebleed from hell. Hence the expensive gifts I had to buy Vee as an apology each time I fucked up or fucked down without thinking. She was gathering quite the collection of fine jewelry.

Today she was wearing the pair of sorry earrings I'd bought her. The same pair Janelle Knight had worn when we met on the street.

But I had been so good for a couple of years, ever since she hooked me up with Kel. Which was the whole reason she probably introduced us so I wouldn't go looking for it elsewhere and make a mistake. I looked over at her. God, I loved her, and I felt bad she had such a worried look.

"What did you see? With Jack, I mean?" Vee said, concern in her voice.

"I don't remember." I didn't want her to know that hints of what I'd seen during Jack's Read started darting back into my senses. Bubbles at a lake. The taste of corn on the cob. The smell of rotting flesh. Bodies floating, looking at me, reaching for me. I didn't like those feelings, and I couldn't shove back the panic that welled up.

"I think I need to rest now," I said with a choked voice and looked away, not wanting her to see my fear-filled eyes. I reached for the pain-relief drip that I knew had to be there somewhere. I pumped it into oblivion and concentrated on the white noise of nothingness.

Chapter Four

I woke up and opened my eyes, still wary of any quick movements. Jack Knight was sitting in my hospital room, scrolling on his mobile.

He was a dazzler, for sure. Dark-brown wavy hair, honey-hazel eyes, and finely carved features. He looked like a Knight—a much younger version of his father and grandfather who were both severely handsome men from what I'd seen in photos. Was that a smile plastered on his face?

I didn't recall thinking how striking he was when I Read him, probably because that's not where my mind was at the time. He cleaned up good. Really good.

He glanced up and gave me a grin that flashed an amazing smile. Teeth bright white. Like a shark. Right before it bit someone's arm off.

"Hey." He lowered his device. "Just happened to be at the hospital to check my burns and thought I'd check in on you."

I looked at him warily and noticed he had similar bandages on his hands. He seemed comfortable and refreshed.

"Hey," I said back.

"So, not exactly certain what happened back there, but wanted to make sure you were still…" He paused.

"Alive?"

"Still OK and on the mend."

"Yeah, I'm OK. What do *you* think happened?" I asked him as I hoped he'd remember more.

"Don't know…it was wild, right? You grabbed my hands, and at first, I felt nothing, but then I saw and felt glimpses of our lake house—in the summer like I was watching an old slide show, and it was warm, and my family was there…"

Jack was looking up and to the left.

"It was a great memory. Or at least I think it was a memory. Then I heard static and bubbling sounds. Pictures floated and disappeared, and I was back sitting on your couch. You had a super-tight grip on my hands, and then you let go, fell on the floor, and passed out or something. And then I felt my burned hands."

"Hmmm." I looked at him skeptically.

"Then I got your assistant, and he called 9-1-1."

"Do you still think I'm bullshit?"

"Oh God, no. You definitely have something. Not sure what, but something."

He was animated, which was a far cry from the *meh* Jack I had Read. His appearance was clean-shaven, and it looked like he had showered and changed his clothes from stinky sweats to business casual. He seriously seemed like a different person.

So perhaps I had helped him after all, even though I didn't have the chance to do a true Push. He got up to approach my bed, and I flinched.

"Too soon?" he asked.

I nodded.

He backed away. "Well, just wanted to stop in. I think my mom got her money's worth, anyway—at least it got me to shower, get out of the house, and start some work at the Knight Foundation. Apparently, I'm

31

supposed to be a board member. No more Broody McBroodster…"

"Did I really call you that?" I asked, even though I knew the answer.

"Yeah, but all is good. I even stopped by the office to have lunch with my dad last week and sat in on a couple meetings. I thought he was going to have a heart attack." He beamed.

Compared to last week's angst-filled entrance, Jack's new giddiness was unnerving.

"Can I see you again? To get another Read?" he asked.

"Yeah, that'd be a *no*. The first time didn't go so well, so…no," I replied with a sarcastic smirk.

"Yeah, that first one was crazy, right? Well, OK. Glad you're alive." He waved slightly, moved the kitten balloon bouquet closer to my bed, acknowledging it with a head nod, and walked out. I hoped to God I hadn't created a giddy monster.

Stupid balloons. OK, so I liked balloons. They were cute.

As soon as he left, Vee came back in, hopefully to take me home. "Was that Jack Knight? What'd he want?"

"Apparently, he wanted to share. Fucking chatterbox."

She frowned, probably at the negative way I said that. I was homesick, grumpy, and fearful that the industrial noise-cancelling would lose its efficacy and start letting in stray thoughts. Plus, I missed my comfy pillow and fuzzy coverlet. I was still in pain, so I tapped the button for more sleepy juice and settled back into a stupor.

****

My medical team cleared me to go after a couple more days, and Vee came to take me home, which was a huge relief.

En route, I stared out the window, curious how I had gotten myself in so deep with Jack Knight's inner thoughts. Something outside on the sidewalk caught my gaze.

A black-and-white dog was sitting at the intersection, waiting patiently as if ready to cross at the signal like he was floating there. The dog was big but still puppyish. I wondered what breed he/she/it was—maybe some hound mix? Super cute.

The dog followed the car with its gaze and turned its head toward us when we passed. When I glanced back, the dog was gone. I couldn't put my finger on it, but I had a peculiar feeling about the pup.

Finally at home, all I wanted to do was sleep. I was amazed at the progress my burns had made, allowing me to remove my hand bandages. Thank goodness for modern marvels of medical advancement and Knight Industries.

I still had a big bandage on the left side of my forehead. Vee had cleared my calendar for the week so I could rest up. God, I loved that woman. I was so glad she hadn't had to be alone while I was out of commission, and I did owe her and Josie, her partner, for cutting their vacay short.

Josie was at our apartment when we got there and gave me a nod. I liked her, and she was good for Vee. She was good for me, too, as Vee fretted less about me when she was around. Josie owned a trendy fitness clothing line bearing her namesake and hooked us up with a variety of fashionable workout gear, which was a win-win. I was growing to love her, too.

She had come into our lives five months ago, wanting to get a Read. She was in search of answers to her troubled marriage. I Pushed her and suggested she find what made her happy and to look where she hadn't looked before.

When I came out to retrieve my next session, Josie and Vee were deep in discussion about music and Healing.

Two months later, Josie was divorced and a perpetual fixture in our apartment. I was happy to get the athletic wear hookups from Josie's company for sure, but especially grateful to see Vee happy and in love.

"You look, like…really great," Josie said with a semi-smile on her face. A gorgeous face, speckled with striking freckles from the tropical sunshine she'd been able to get, even though my actions cut their vacation short.

"Thanks." I tried to smile and walked away but turned back slowly. "I *am* really sorry I messed up your trip. I'll make it up to you," I promised. Josie was another person whose presence didn't ping me with random reverbs and noise, which was a relief.

That's why Vee always checked clients *before* we took them on. She somehow knew within a few minutes of meeting someone if they were a good fit. Typically, she didn't accept other Sensitives as clients as they could cause the most potential damage to my brainwaves. I was thinking that was what had happened with Jack. He must have been a Sensitive of some type.

I walked zombie-like to my room, dropped on the bed, and hugged my pillow and soft blanket, ready to down some z's. But my dreams wouldn't let me rest.

I peer from someone else's eyes, from their perspective. I'm walking with a dark-haired girl. No. A characteristically young woman. She is chatting me up, glancing up at me as we walk. Explaining something. I can't quite hear it all.

I look down and see my arm. The arm is masculine. The woman has just taken my hand. She laughs, and we seem to be headed into trees. Some wooded area. She is saying something about herbs...medicinals... She has a large pink crystal on a silver chain around her neck that swings back and forth as she walks, her face animated. Oh, she must be a Healer, *I think.*

She points forward, and I see my hand drop hers while she is telling me something. She is still looking away, motioning toward something, and then I see my hands grab her around the neck. I am wearing purple latex gloves. When did I put those on? She can't yell. My hands are taut on her throat. So tight, and I can't let them go. I can feel her silver chain pinching the flesh between my grip and her neck. The latex smell is exhilarating; the rubber texture makes it easy to keep my hold. She is turning blue and makes a rasping sound. I am busting her windpipe. It gives way with a snap and a couple of clicks. I feel a sick, euphoric rush. Pull back. Pull back. Pull back.

I sat up vertically, in mid-crawl out of bed, one foot already on the floor to escape. My pillow and blanket tossed across the floor, my top sheet to one side, and my fitted sheet yanked off the mattress with my struggled acceleration. A loud sob escaped from my lips.

That was a tremendously real dream. I looked around to make sure it had been a dream, my heart bursting with a million booming beats. I felt severe pressure on my neck and a crippling spasm in my clenched hands. Was I just choking myself?

My sob was amplified enough to wake my roomie. Vee called my name in the dark from her suite across the apartment.

"I'm OK," I barked back.

My hands were shaking, my body shivering. I tried to breathe slowly in and out to calm my racing pulse and stifle further sobbing. I'd heard that people got pernicious infections from burns, so maybe that was it? It had felt like a fever dream.

I went to fix my bottom sheet; it was soaking wet, my top sheet the same. The foul, tangy smell of terror sweat hung on them. *Ew.* I snagged my blanket and pillow and headed to the couch, hoping a change of scenery could calm my nerves.

That dream had been so real, but it couldn't have been real, right? My mind still raced, but my heartbeat was now at a more acceptable pace. I needed to calm myself even more.

I breathed in through my nose and out through my mouth, counting to ten slowly, wanting to push out the sickening, lingering panic keeping me from slumber town.

I slowly started to relax, talking myself out of having another night terror.

But this time sleep was generous, gifting me with the rest of a dreamless night.

Chapter Five

I woke up feeling surprisingly energetic and mostly without pain the next morning. I wasn't quite ready for a full-on run but needed a walk to clear my mind. Especially after that mess-with-my-head dream last night.

I glanced in the hallway mirror while passing through and had to stop and backtrack to look closer. What the fuck?

Fresh bruising marred my neck—thumb- and finger-shaped on both sides. A couple of different patterns caught my eye—a thin, elongated, chain-like, raised welt and a small, half-inch mark on the mid-right side. I had no idea what to make of it. I threw a scarf around the bruising. I needed to think.

I took a slightly different way, wanting to avoid the farmer's market, which would be in full swing today. Yes, always best to avoid crowds.

I was a block away when I noticed I had forgotten my headphones and anti-Read gloves. How could I just forget the two staples of my morning routine? A daily routine I'd had for years? I must have been all out of sorts. Plus my mind kept going back to last night's dream.

I rounded the corner to head back when I saw the same black-and-white dog from...was that just yesterday? That couldn't be a coincidence. I went to cross the street toward it, briefly stopping for an e-microvan to cross, and when I looked, the dog had gone.

This was some really funky juju. I was not one to test fate. I went home and back to bed.

Vee popped her head into my bedroom and told me she was going to SensiCon happy hour with a group of her friends and asked if I needed anything. I shook my head. I just wanted to sleep all day.

I woke up after one a.m., my mobile buzzing me awake.

"I need to talk to you," the voice said. It was Jack Knight.

I didn't ask him how he'd gotten my personal mobile. "So talk."

"No, I need to see you in person. Something weird is happening. I need your help."

"I'm not sure I'm in any condition to chat. You know my eye sockets are busted—do you know what that feels like? You obviously know what it looks like when you saw me in the hospital. It's not pretty."

"I think a woman was strangled…killed." He sounded out of breath. "A Sensitive…"

I got a bit light-headed, and my heartbeat quickened. "I'm listening."

"I had a dream…or a vision…and…" He sounded distracted.

"And?"

"And she's standing at the foot of my bed…right now. She's looking right at me." He did not sound as scared as I thought he might. He sounded more confused and frantic.

"Is she real?"

"Um—yes. I think. Not a person. But a real dead

ghost. She has dark, dead eyes and black-and-blue marks around her neck."

My hand went up to my neck, the scarf still on. "Is she wearing a pink crystal on a chain?"

"No, why?"

I blew his question off. "OK. You can come over, same location as my office, but up the outside stairs— but I swear to God, if you fuck with my head again, I will be that ghost haunting you." I hung up the phone.

Music and laughter came from Vee's side of the apartment. They must have been back from the convention.

I walked out of my room and down the hall, and a naked guy staggered out of Vee's room, headed toward the bathroom. I shrugged, figuring I'd ask about that tomorrow. Wait. It was tomorrow. To each his or her or their own.

I asked my Brewster, my auto-brew, to make me a hot beverage of engineered coffee.

I opened the front door before Jack could knock or ring and wake up my roommate from sleep, or whatever she was doing or *who* she and Josie were doing in there.

"Come in. Just please don't touch me," I warned him.

"OK, I don't want to touch anyone or anything—I had to *walk through her* to get out of my room."

I assumed he meant the spirit who had visited him.

He handed over his tablet, scrolled down, and pointed to the bottom right of *Seattle e-Times*. It read *Woman's Body Found Near Golden Gardens*. Apparently, someone murdered wasn't as big a deal as Boeing's pilotless cargo plane, which filled the top screen.

I glanced at the story and then thumb-jumped to 4b and saw a picture of my dead woman. The one strangled from my dream. Identified as Domino Treasure.

I plopped down on the couch with the tablet. I was nauseous, and my head was pounding. "So she's the one from your vision?" I didn't tell him I had seen her, too.

"Yes. I was floating above her, watching a man choke her. I couldn't see his face, but I know what he was wearing. Then I woke up and saw she was in my room."

"And you want me to do what with this information?"

"You could go to the cops."

"And tell them what? You saw some dead woman maybe murdered in a vision, and now she won't leave you alone?"

"Um, yeah. Don't the police use Sensitives all the time now to solve crimes?"

"How should I know? Why don't you go to the cops, then?"

"Because everyone knows my family and the fact I can see ghosts can't get out."

"Oh, but it's OK for me to talk to the police like a dumbass at two a.m. when I didn't see what you saw?" I'm not sure why I kept the fact that I had a dream about her, too, from him.

"Then what do you suggest?" Jack asked.

"Well—" I thumbed through the e-news. "—you contact this guy, Detective Greg Falco, who is lead for the case, and tell him what you think you know. Do it anonymously." I pointed to the detective's quote from the story about the dead Sensitive.

Jack was looking at me.

"Fine, I'll do it." After a couple of clicks, I found the detective's instant message and chat platform. *Hmmm.* And a photo. Too bad he's a cop. Yummy. I could just imagine what I'd see if I Read him.

—*Det. Falco—U don't know me but I may have some info re: the Domino Treasure homicide. I am a homebound Sensitive, so coming into the station is not an option. Chat back at your earliest convenience if interested—a Concerned Citizen—*

I read through it again and hit send. Almost immediately the detective pinged back.

—*Concerned Citizen—I'm intrigued. Can we meet? Det. Falco—*

"Wow. That was fast. Now, what?" I said.

"Uh, meet with him?"

Then another ping from the detective.

—*I'm at the precinct—looks like it's in your neighborhood. Seems like you're up—can you stop in?—*

What part of *homebound Sensitive* and *coming into the station is not an option* did the detective not get? He pinged again. Jack read over my shoulder. Rude. But he smelled good. Yes! I had my sense of smell back!

—*Or I could come by there?—Det. Falco—*

Shit. I didn't want him coming here. I looked at Jack and then heard a laugh from Vee's room. And I had no fucking idea what was going on in her room, or what potentially illegal activities or substances might have been going on or consumed in there and might still be on the premises.

Sensitives tended to lay it on heavy with the still illegal medicinals, and I didn't want to bring the police into what could be a sticky situation.

I glanced in the living room mirror by the sofa. I was

a train wreck, bruises around my eyes and a small stuck-on head bandage. I was glad I had the scarf on so Jack couldn't see the black-and-blue choke marks.

The way I looked, Detective Falco wasn't going to want to shake my hand, let alone touch me, so I should be safe. And at after two in the morning, the precinct probably wasn't crowded. I'd bring my sense-reducing arsenal, my specialized gloves and headphones, just in case.

I texted back.

—Yeah, I'll come there. Give me fifteen.—

I asked Jack to drive me since Vee and her friends were otherwise occupied. I put on my gloves, turned up my headphones, and leaned as close to the passenger door as possible in Jack's two-seater for the ride there.

Expensive, all-electric sporty cars were too elite to have proper back seats apparently. *Sheesh.* At least he didn't have a town car and driver.

Chapter Six

Detective Falco was right. I lived close to his office. Like five minutes. When we pulled up, I saw the dog sitting on the curb out of the corner of my eye, but when I looked to the right, no dog. What's with the dog omen?

"So…I'll wait here?" Jack asked, the car stopped but not parked.

"I guess. You think it'll take a long time?"

"No idea. Never been to see the cops before."

Me neither. I got out of the car and walked up to the large glass doors. Jack had already shared details of what he wanted Detective Falco to know. The doors were locked, but I heard a buzzing as they disengaged, and I walked in.

The detective met me in the hall. "I'm Detective Greg Falco; you are?"

"I'm Rogue Hunter," I said, pulling down my headphones as he reached to shake my hand. I shrank back.

He looked at my gloves. "You don't shake." It was a statement and not a question. He nodded as if he understood and led me back to his open-concept cube farm. He was in plain clothes.

"Thanks for coming, I've been working all night, combing online resources for the cases I'm working on—when I got your message. Have a seat." He pointed to the chair by his desk. He seemed to be one of only a handful of folks in the office. Which was good news for receiving limited pings.

"Were you in a car accident or something?" He looked at me and gestured to my face.

"No. Job-related injury," I replied, and he nodded.

He then looked at me for a long time in silence. It was uncomfortable. Making it worse was I couldn't Read him. At all.

"So is this how interrogation works? You stare at me, and I just…" I questioned.

"Well, you mentioned you were Sensitive, so I figured you could read my mind."

What a royal dick. I'd been dealing with disbelievers like him my whole life. Two could play that game. I just stared at him with a wry smile.

God, I really couldn't Read him. Maybe if I took off my gloves? Fuck that, who knew what miserable thoughts I could drum up from touching things at a police station. So we sat there and stared each other down.

He had a medium, athletic build, quite tall, dark hair, slight curl to it, and had amazing, amber-flecked eyes. He probably started the day clean-shaven, but since it was after two a.m., he had the dark shadow of a beard coming through. He was quite attractive but seemed to have a perma-scowl fixed on his face—he hadn't smiled once since I got there.

I was sure he had the role of bad cop down pat. I guessed if I was a cop who had to deal with mayhem day in and day out, I would have a tough time smiling, too.

"Hey, Greg, how's it hangin'?" some guy said as he approached also in plain clothes.

I was assuming another cop.

"Just trying to interview a concerned citizen," said

Detective Falco.

I couldn't tell if he was being sarcastic or matter of fact.

"This here's Rogue. She has important information on a case I'm working on. This is Detective Bruce Barrow."

"Hmmm," Detective Barrow murmured, moving in front of me, looking me up and down, resting his gaze on my chest for a few seconds too long. He brushed his hand past my knee.

I tensed up.

Then his gaze worked its way up to my face. "Looks like someone's done a number on you," he said with a salacious grin.

I grimaced as we locked eyes. "I ran into a door," I answered back quickly, trying to be tough, even though his close proximity made me cringe. I wasn't anticipating his next move, which was odd since I was a Sensitive.

He grabbed hold of my chin with his hand and tilted my head up, keeping my gaze. I quickly grabbed his wrist to yank it down; it was surprisingly firm so took a couple of tugs to pull it down. But it was too late.

I just wanted him to let go. I had already connected and managed to Read and Push him in my panicked state. Something changed in his eyes. I flinched and shoved my chair back, almost knocking it and myself backward. He backed off.

"Well, have fun, kids," he said, sounding unsure. He had a confused look as he turned, smiled uncomfortably at Detective Falco, and walked away.

Asshole. Motherfucker. Now I was just pissed. I'd come down here to help. Not to be fucking insulted by the detective and disrespected, visually assaulted, and touched by some fucking pig.

"Sorry about that," Falco said flatly.

I looked at him and shook my head. "Sorry about that?" Rage boiled up, my neurons firing. "How sorry? Like sorry you've been his friend since the academy? Like sorry he got promoted to lieutenant before you and was a superior asshole about it?"

I stood up and leaned toward his desk, whispering angrily, "Like sorry you had his back when he was fucking sex workers in his squad car as a recruit? Like sorry you let him lie for you when you pummeled that teacher selling drugs to kids? Like sorry…"

He held his hand up as if he was trying to silence me.

I was just getting started. I leaned in closer. "Like sorry he fucked your ex-girlfriend? Oh, that's right. She wasn't your ex-girlfriend at the time he fucked her. I'm sure he's sorry about that, too…"

He raised his hand defensively again. I stopped talking, knowing I had just crossed a line. The few people still in the office across the room were looking our way.

I had a headache. I had to throw up. I reached over, snagged a trash bin from the side of Falco's desk, and puked twice.

He held out a box of tissue. I nodded for him to put the box down at the edge of his desk. I grabbed several to wipe my mouth. I snagged a couple more to catch the tears. Fuck. I hated myself when I dredged up shit like that. He might not have any feelings, but I sensed every miserable ounce of them.

"How's that?" I finally said, trying to be smug, but

my voice choked. "Is that *Sensitive* enough for you?"

He paused as if in thought, nodded, and seemed to refocus on the task at hand. "Well played," he said without a pause and continued, "So what have you got for me?"

I had to take a couple of breaths to calm myself and make sure I wouldn't puke again. "So I saw the picture of Domino..."

"You knew her?"

"No...but that's her name, isn't it?"

"That's *one* of their names."

"I just saw her photo in the paper and realized I had a dream about her the night before. It's going to sound weird, but I was the killer, in the killer's body, and saw him, me, strangle her. We had been walking to go see some medicinal plants, or..."

"Herb garden," he finished for me.

"Yeah. She went with him willingly; they may have been friends? Or dating? And he just reached up and strangled her." I reached over and vomited again, then grabbed two more tissues.

"Does that happen all the time?"

"Sometimes, but my roommate is a Healer, so it doesn't usually get to this."

"Your roommate?"

"Yeah, I get bad headaches from when I do Readings, and she can usually prevent or head off a really bad one."

"So you do read minds?" he questioned. Was he trying to lighten the conversation?

"Listen, I didn't come to talk about myself," I said, annoyed. "I came to talk about Domino. I know what the killer was wearing."

"Go on." He looked ready to write in a small black digital note-taker but turned on the record-and-auto-type feature instead.

"He wore black tactical cargo pants, pockets everywhere—the ones you get at sporting goods stores. Dark-gray leather boots, untucked dark and a light-gray striped collared shirt—the quick-dry kind—and a puffy gray vest. He had dark hair and was wearing aviator glasses. His stuff looked new and top-of-the-line."

"So you saw all this in your dream?"

"Not exactly." I hesitated. "I also have a *friend* who sees things. For some reason, we are seeing the same thing but from different perspectives. My friend saw what happened from a distance. I just saw them walking to the garden, what *she* was wearing, her braided silver chain necklace, and the choking…"

"Necklace?"

"Yeah, Domino was wearing a large pink-hued crystal on a long silver braided chain."

He snagged a portable cooler from under his desk, opened it, and pulled out a large, clear plastic bag. "Did the chain look like this?" He pushed a bag with the word *Evidence* on red tape across his desk.

God. Just like old crime scene investigation reruns. I watched a lot of cop shows online.

I didn't touch the bag; I couldn't. I peered into it. The chain had what looked like pieces of something embedded in it. *Domino's skin.* The chain was the one I saw.

"Yes, that looks like it—but it had a large, light-pink silver-wrapped crystal hanging from it. In my dream, the necklace was swinging when she walked. The chain dug into her neck when he choked her. He probably has a mark on his wrists."

Falco looked up at me and seemed surprised, maybe because I had that detail. "We think the perp may have taken the necklace with him but dropped the chain along the way. The chain was found in the parking lot of the larger park a few hundred yards away from where she was found. It had her DNA on it. That seems careless. The perp left few clues at other scenes."

"Other scenes? There's more?"

"Yes, Domino is the third Sensitive found dead in a month in the Puget Sound area. The other two looked like drug use, but I have my doubts."

I was dumbfounded—why wasn't this in the news? Why was I just hearing about this now?

Falco interrupted my thoughts. "We didn't find a crystal, just a stretched and broken silver loop hanging on the chain. Something may have been attached to it."

I nodded.

"So it was your roommate who *saw* the killer?"

"No, not my roommate. She's a Healer, not a Seer or Intuitive. My friend is more like a Seer. They see ghosts, and they bring them visions. I'm going to keep his or her name…anonymous."

"OK, I respect that. Anything else."

"Yeah, the perp might be married. In my dream, I *was* him, and when I looked down, I saw a wedding ring through his gloves. Thicker band with distinct rippled markings." I hesitated and exhaled. "Wait, I can show you. *This* happened the same time as my dream." I slowly untied the scarf I was wearing to reveal my neck.

"You can see where the ring was"—I pointed to the rippled welt—"and where the chain dug into her skin closer to her collarbone." I put my fingers on the thin, now-raised line. It was sensitive to the touch. "I know it sounds far-fetched, Detective, but I think I acted out part of my dream and choked myself in real life."

Detective Falco looked at my neck, his eyes wide, and shook his head. "OK, so now I *have* seen everything. Mind if I snap a photo?" He sounded skeptical.

I shrugged, nodded, and he pulled out his mobile and snapped a couple of pics. He then looked at his note-taker again, scrolling up and down.

"Domino didn't have bruising near her eyes or a head injury." He looked at me with skepticism.

"Yeah, those came from another Read. Sometimes, instead of throwing up, I get bruises or swelling or debilitating headaches." I kept it at that. "Can you tell me about the others?"

"I can't really discuss ongoing investigations, but I don't have much to go on at all...unless you have potential evidence in those cases?" He looked at me for an answer.

I shook my head. "But does one of them have a large black-and-white dog, large spots, short hair, docked tail, about this high?" I held my hand to the height of his desk. I thought it was worth an ask.

"Uh." He scrolled through a few pages of his notes. "No dog, why?"

"I've been seeing this dog around everywhere. I thought it may be related."

Falco's phone started blowing up with pings. I retied the scarf around my neck.

"Sorry, something's come up," he said, looking at his phone, and stood up. "Thank you for coming in. I'll call you if I have any questions." He pinged his e-business card to my mobile. "Please contact me if anything else pops up."

I accepted his contact ping. I didn't give him mine, but he's a cop so could easily get it.

"Appreciate you coming in," he said dismissively.

I got up, turned, and walked out without a backward glance. *You're welcome*, I thought to myself.

Outside I looked around for the dog. No dog this time. I walked toward Jack's car and saw someone sitting next to him. When I got closer, no one was there.

I tried the door; Jack unlocked it. Safety first. I looked down at the seat before sitting, lightly patting it and feeling its smoothness. I could sense *something*. A presence of some sort. I sat down.

"So how'd it go?" Jack asked.

"What? With Detective Iceberg in there? I'm not sure. It took a bit of wrangling to get him to listen, lots of uncomfortable silence, and I'm not sure he believed me…and…and… Was a ghost just sitting in my seat?"

"Yeah, you saw her?"

"I did for a split second, and I can feel her essence. It smells like evergreens."

"Domino is still very confused," he said gloomily. "She's angry and upset."

"Listen, Jack…" I wasn't sure how to say this to him, so I just started. "I haven't been upfront with you." I reached my hands to untie my scarf. "I dreamt about Domino, too. I saw her strangled, and I was the murderer. I did this to myself while sleeping." I pointed to the bruising around my neck and the welts. "I just didn't know it was real until you showed me her photo. I don't know why I didn't tell you. I'm sorry…"

He looked at the bruising and marks around my neck but remained quiet. I didn't know if he was upset or just contemplating.

"So why us?" he asked. "Why did she come to us?"

"I don't know, but the detective said that she is the *third* Sensitive found dead in as many weeks."

"So now what do we do?"

"I don't know. Wait, I guess." I shrugged.

Jack shrugged, too, and started the car. We sat in silence the rest of the way to my home.

I wasn't sure what we should do next. We'd already gone to the police. I didn't know why Domino had shown up in our dreams and why her ghost was still trailing us. All I did know was that it was late, I was tired, and someone was killing Sensitives in Seattle.

Chapter Seven

I had a rough go the next morning. No amount of engineered coffee could kick my focus into high gear, and no number of pastries could chase the sinking feeling I had about last night's interaction. Talking to the detective had been a waste of time and energy.

"Hey," Vee said, entering the kitchen. "How'd you sleep?"

"Didn't get much sleep, but apparently, you and your entourage didn't either," I said with a knowing smile.

"We met some new friends at SensiCon last night. We seemed to hit it off."

"*Obviously.* I already ran into Naked Guy last night. It wasn't a formal introduction, but I did see his dick, so we're old friends now."

"Oh good, that's…that's…fuck…um, that's Hank." She seemed to have quite the trouble finding his name in her brain. "And I thoroughly vetted them before they came home with us."

"I'll bet you did." I added, "Jack was over last night."

"Jack Knight? What's up with you and him?"

"Nothing like that. We do seem to have some Sensitive connection or something. We both had a dream about the same dead woman, and now her ghost is following him. I've seen her, too."

Vee didn't look shocked at my revelation, just a bit hungover.

"And," I continued, "since I had no idea who was here doing who knows what in your room, Jack talked me into going to the station to tell some detective about what we saw in our dreams."

"And?" She sounded surprised probably because I rarely left the house, except to go on my runs, without her forcing me.

"And nothing. Let's just say it didn't go as planned. The detective sort of blew me off—that is after being a royal dick, insulting me as a Sensitive, and letting his lieutenant friend touch me, which made me barf. And I dredged up a bunch of dark secrets about him."

"Did you take it too far?"

I nodded and shrugged. "He sort of deserved it after being such a shit."

Vee then seemed to focus on the bruising on my neck. "How the fuck did that happen? You know what? Never mind. I don't want to know." She programmed a cup of Joe, then gave me a side hug and kiss on the face. "I bought you some fresh green juice. It's in the fridge."

I scowled. Damn Healer.

"Drink it. It'll help you get better." She squeezed my hand and then walked back to her room.

My mobile pinged; I jumped. It was Jack. Didn't this guy have any other friends?

—*Coffee? I'll pick it up.*—

—*Sure. Mondo iced chai. Dirty 3X.*—

—*Dirty XXX? J*—

—*Yeah, chai with three shots espresso. And a donut. Any kind.*—

I showered and washed my hair. I looked in the

mirror, placing my fingers on my waterproof head bandage that I should be able to remove soon. My hair was a mess. I needed to call Tiana to get some serious hair help and major brow threading.

Tiana was one of my besties. She was also my hairdresser, aesthetician, and one of my initial Reads when Vee and I first moved to Seattle.

Vee had a sharp business acumen, and when we arrived, she'd focused us on turning both our special skills into successful careers in the Emerald City.

Vee had already started contracting out her design and healing skills but had the idea for me to offer complimentary Reads and Pushes with guaranteed success rates. Customers who found success due to my coaching agreed to provide a portion of their first year's profit.

Not all customers I Pushed found monetary success; some led to much-needed happiness, life contentment, or uncovered health issues and, in a handful of cases, fulfilled parenthood hopes. In these cases, the clients would provide in trade an equally valuable offering.

Tiana's case was a win-win scenario. She found success, and I got top-notch salon care from someone I trusted and who didn't make me ill from being around them.

When I first met and Read Tiana, she was a struggling actor working part-time at a low-end barbershop. I Pushed her to keep creativity close to her heart, pursue her love of glamour, and lean into current pursuits to find profit in being a stylist to the stars. And Tiana did just that.

Tiana's fast-tracked local fame as a stylist for the wealthy led to her prosperity, huge payouts, and a running referral of high-end clients for VeRo Industries, the company my roomie and I formed together.

Due to Tiana's success and her connections, we hatched a booming business within the year, despite multiple days when I was out of commission with headaches.

Early on, we didn't know how to discern between clean Reads and those that would make me sick. Not until Vee comforted me after a particularly bad spell and I inadvertently Read and Pushed to her did she have the ability to sense, somehow, if I would have a bad reaction to a particular person or not. She'd been my skilled screener ever since.

Today, Tiana was trading for a Read to help her decide in what locations she should expand her Seattle boutiques. I loved bartering with her because getting soothing facials and amazing haircuts for Reads was a worthy exchange. Plus, she made house calls, so I didn't have to go to Capitol Hill.

Tiana and I had a brief text exchange.

—*Ugh, T! It's Rogue. I need some serious pampering.*—

—*Free tonight at nine p.m. You game?*—

—*Yup, T. See you then. Miss you!*—

—*:) MYT!*—

I lounged on the couch to wait for Jack and to think over a plethora of things. About Domino. About ghosts. About the dream. And about Falco. What? Why did that jerk just pop into my head? Then Jack popped into my head, and I knew he was at my door.

I opened the door for him with ample room for him to breeze by. He set our drinks on the coffee table and sat in one of the comfy chairs, upending a fashionable throw pillow.

Jack had dark circles under his eyes like he hadn't slept for days.

"Brought the latest news," my apparent new BFF said as he leaned across the coffee table to hand me his e-reader. It was open to the latest *Seattle e-Times* article brought to us by free city Wi-Fi sponsored by Filstroms, the neighborhood outdoor store per a large e-ad.

No New Leads in Case of Murdered Sensitive, it read. *Hmmm*. Seemed like I had given the cops new leads the other evening.

Ungrateful dick. I laughed at myself, seeing what I'd done there…dick…detective…lingo I'd drawn from the vintage cop shows I often binged. Good thing *I* thought I was funny.

Jack laughed, too. Which was odd, since it was an inside joke in my own head. I scrolled down and saw the mention of two other Sensitives found dead. No flags had been raised because their deaths looked accidental and drug related. I looked up at Jack.

"So what do we do now about the case?" he asked.

I shrugged. I knew why he felt connected to this case; I felt a connection, too. "Not sure. Sounds like the police didn't take what I shared with them seriously; they seemed to have nothing new on the case."

I liked having Jack as a new friend.

"What if I tried to Read you again," I suggested, "but focus more recently—not going so far back this time? Maybe I could home in on Domino and what you saw with her."

He looked at me. "Not sure it's a good idea, but I'd like to get her out of my head."

"We could try…slowly? And my roomie's here, just

in case."

He gave me a nod.

I got up and sat on the coffee table so I was positioned right in front of him. I was shaking already. "So you just sit there…and I'll go slow." I lightly touched the top of his left hand with mine. Feeling a slight tingle. I held my hand on top of his, almost hearing a buzz.

"I hear that," he said.

I reached out and touched his right hand, resting my left on his. I closed my eyes, took a breath. I thought of Domino with her curly, mahogany hair and animated smile. I could see Domino and her killer walking toward the woods, the perspective Jack had. Floating above the two, I needed to get closer. I clenched Jack's hands.

I am back in his view, the scene playing out in slow motion. Even her speech is slowed. I need to see what Domino is seeing. Then I am her, full of life, excited, moving forward, but decelerated. I look at the man I'm with, and I see his eyes. They beam a frenzied look, then turn black as he brings his hands around my neck. Tight. Choking. Confused. Disbelief. Chaotic.

"Let go." I struggle, but I can't produce a sound. I pull at the hands, clawing them. They won't budge. I crane my eyes down to see a wristwatch left uncovered by the purple latex gloves. Gold with little circles and dials on it…a man with multiple arms? The face counts, "Tick, tick, tick, tick." It is deafening. It is louder than the adrenaline pumping hard and fast in my veins. I smell latex and then a vanilla, saffron, sandalwood scent. Rich. Earthy. A man's cologne? God. It is wonderful. Then I smell blood as my eyes black out and the squeezing hands cause my capillaries to explode.

I was kneeling on the floor when I came to. Breathing evenly, almost peacefully. The taste of blood ripe in my mouth. I was suddenly sick. I bolted up, just made the edge of the kitchen sink, and vomited. Shit, I'd need to bleach that.

Jack looked at me, searching my face; he seemed eager and not worried. He could barely contain his enthusiasm. I glared at him from the kitchen, then snatched a paper towel to wipe.

"What'd you see?"

I exhaled with a long, slow "whew…" I had to think. I snagged the trash bin under the sink and walked back to sit on the couch near Jack, keeping the bin nearby.

"I saw a watch, a dark-brown, leather band, gold face with one of those perpetual calendars. The dude on the watch looked like that Da Vinci poster drawing with the arms," I said, "but the strongest sense was the smell. Once I got past the rubber smell, the guy was wearing some nice-ass woody-vanilla-smelling cologne, gotta be expensive as hell, and almost soothing."

"Hmmm." A slight recognition glimmered on his face for a moment, then it disappeared. "Is that it?"

I nodded. "Yeah, just the watch and the smell. I saw his eyes, but that's all I saw of his face. They were jet black."

"You should probably share it with your cop BFF."

"With Detective Cold Front? Yeah, I don't think so. He doesn't like me much."

"It's new information; maybe it could help narrow down the search."

"I'll think about it." And I would, just not for another several hours or so. I needed to sleep badly. I popped a couple of extra-strength pain relievers from the kitchen, swung my legs onto the couch, snagged a throw pillow, and crashed, my head resting on Jack's lap.

****

I had no idea how long I slept, but when I woke up, Jack was gone. But he had left his ghostly friend who was translucent and half sitting, half floating in one of the chairs, looking at me. Domino.

I reached my hand up and grabbed my phone off the coffee table. It was six p.m. I dialed Jack.

"Hey, I was just having the best nap," he said, yawning loudly. "I guess Domino decided to leave me in peace for a bit."

"Great for *you*," I said. "That's because she is sitting here, staring at me."

"Really? Hmmm, should I feel jealous?"

"Funny. I *am* going to contact Detective Falco. We're missing something, and the new clues *could* mean something. She's here for a reason."

I hung up, looking forward to more verbal abuse from the detective. That I seemed so dang comfortable with a spirit sitting just feet away from me also felt weird. I tried not to look at her as I dialed Falco at the station.

"Miss Hunter," Detective Falco said. "To what do I owe the pleasure?" He seemed to have me programmed into his mobile. That was a good sign, right?

"I have some new information I think may be important to the Domino case."

"I'm listening."

"The guy was wearing a watch with a brown band and a gold face with a perpetual calendar and chronograph, and it had a Da Vinci Vitruvian Universal Man drawing on it...and yes, I did Gyzmo it." I pinged his phone a snapshot of what the watch looked like.

"And by 'the guy,' you mean Domino's killer?"

"Yep."

"Well, Rogue, that's quite some detail and quite the expensive watch."

I fluttered when he said my name. I *liked* this guy, and I barely knew anything about him. Plus, wasn't he an a-hole? "He also had a distinct smell on him, I think cologne or body fragrance? It was vanilla, honey, woody smell—rich and earthy. It smelled amazing...and expensive."

"So the killer smells amazing *and* expensive?"

Was he fucking with me? "Yes. Like many Sensitives, I have an additional heightened sense. Mine happens to be my sense of smell."

"Hmmm. OK," he said like he wasn't paying attention.

"Are you getting this down, or am I just wasting my time?"

"I got it. This could be important information. Tell me about this sense of smell. I haven't heard that one."

"Yeah, I can Read and Push people, but I can also pick up smells from a mile or so away...gasoline, blood, paint, seaweed, donuts..." I drew out that last item.

"You want to go get donuts?"

The prickling of a blush stung my cheeks. Was that a real proposal? I stumbled to answer, so he filled the silence with another question.

"You assume that since I'm a cop I like donuts?"

"Yes," I blurted, finally able to speak.

"Yes, you assume I like donuts?"

"No. I mean, yes. *No* to assuming you like donuts but *yes* to going to get donuts with you." I sounded like a dumbass.

"Donuts for dinner?"

"Why not?" I took a quick look at my phone screen. It was dinnertime. Donuts were good for any meal, right?

"Donuts are not in my repertoire. Gotta keep my calories down."

"Oh…OK." I deflated. The conversation had just gone downhill.

"Anything else?"

"I like tacos, too." I was hoping to keep the dinner conversation alive.

"I meant anything else on the case?"

"No, but I'll call if I remember anything else."

"Thanks." He hung up.

That was an odd conversation if I could call it one. I mean, who didn't like donuts? I loved donuts and was OK to trade calories for the sugar rush. And I was OK being kind of chubby. Whatever. And why the fuck was I still thinking about him? I couldn't stand that guy, right?

I had forgotten Domino's spirit was in my apartment and nearly jumped out of my flesh when I looked up at her fading in and out. "What?" I demanded. She didn't answer.

Chapter Eight

Domino's presence urged me to do some old-fashioned detective work, and I had a couple of hours before Tiana came over to cut my hair, which meant using search engines to find information on Domino myself. Detective Falco could pound sand for all I cared.

Domino was a well-known professional sex worker in town. She was classy and charged a lot for her special services. Kind of like me. Well, except for the classy part. I did charge a lot for my special services. A handful of Domino's online ads were still up, which made me sad.

Was the fact that Domino was a sex worker the reason why the cops weren't taking it seriously? I thought we had gone beyond that when Seattle completely reformed policing and legalized sex work in the late '20s.

Vee and I were early supporters of sex-worker rights and legalizing their job choice. The forward-thinking atmosphere was one of the reasons we decided to move to Seattle.

Really, why was it anybody's business who chose to fuck whom? So what if someone wanted to get paid to get laid. It's strictly a business transaction. And by the looks of the ads, it was a good business for Domino.

"Why were you killed? And who killed you?" I said out loud to Domino's spirit. She didn't answer.

＊＊＊＊

Tiana was a bit late but well worth it. Her essential oil scalp massages were to die for.

"Hey, Tiana, what do you know about men's fragrance?" She was a freaking wealth of knowledge about almost everything, so I thought I'd ask her a couple of questions about the case.

"What do you want to know?" She continued rubbing my head, me perched on a counter stool near the sink for easy wash-and-rinse access.

"So, I know you said nothing shocks you, but I've been seeing…I still see…a spirit who was killed by a man potentially wearing a really amazing fragrance…and I'm hoping to track down the scent." Domino clearly floated to my right between the floor and ceiling.

Tiana went on rubbing my scalp, then paused perhaps in thought. "Well, men's fragrance is not *my* thing, but I have an ex who works at Harald, a perfumery downtown. I'll bet he could help you. Ask for Jerome."

I nodded slightly, her expert fingers still working oils into my scalp. The lavender, citrus, and vanilla aromas mixed and mingled, ebbing up my nose and my psyche. I squinted my eyes and could see Domino to my far right. She seemed slightly faded.

"What about men's high-fashion watches?" I asked as Tiana began to wet my hair.

"Well, you're in luck. My sister works at Hellebores Boutique at Northgate. Go see them. They sell exclusive watches in the Kraken rink atrium. She once sold an Auto-cad Chronograph Elite to Brock Bresnick after the Seattle Kraken won the Stanley Cup—she made a twelve-K bonus on that one watch." She was a huge sports fan.

I took mental note of her suggestions as she started shampooing my hair after a quick rinse. "What about expensive outdoor wear? The guy wore fancy tactical pants and vest."

"Really." She took a quick break from the shampoo to give me the eye.

"What?" I said sharply.

"Honey, you have one of the best outdoor fitters two blocks from here—Filstroms."

"Oh, yeah…I don't get out much."

"Well, Rogue, you really need to, or life's gonna pass on by." She rinsed and then began to condition my hair.

"Duly noted." I squinted again to my right. Now I was positive that Domino was more translucent than before. She was barely there.

When Tiana was done cutting and blow-drying my hair as well as threading my brows, I felt wonderfully refreshed and a bit back to normal. Well, normal for me. My hair looked great. My brows within limits. And my resident ghost had dissipated.

I hugged Tiana as she left.

"Something's different about you," she said.

"Uh, yeah," I joked. "No more unibrow."

"No, something else. You seeing someone new? Romantically?" she asked with a curious smile. Although not Sensitive, Tiana was good at reading people.

"Nope, no one new besides a ghost, a black-and-white dog figment, an emotionless cop, and a strictly platonic new BFF—definitely no one romantically."

"Hmpf." She gave me a disbelieving look, then

hugged me again and left.

It was late, and I had a plan for the next day. To Read and Push my two early morning clients and then go poke around. I thought I'd take Tiana's advice and try and get out more. The thought of going out in public in unfamiliar territory both exhilarated and scared the hell out of me.

I spent the evening watching dog videos and web searching anything I could on Detective Falco. Damn. I was really crushing on him.

I found dozens of articles about him online. He'd only been with the Seattle Police Department for ten years but had saved multiple lives, including people from choking, drowning, and burning in crashed vehicles. Wow. He did seem to be a magnet for disaster.

I also did some more searching on other Sensitives who might have been killed recently. I saw slight mentions of several suspicious and overdose deaths in and near Seattle in the past two years. Most were sex workers, four labeled as Sensitive. I had no idea what to make of it all.

****

After seeing my morning clients, I still felt keen on trying to get out on my own. Filstroms was closest, so I went there first. It was raining hard, so pings were down, and I put the car on auto-drive since I rarely drove. Filstroms had just opened, so the store was practically empty, which was a relief.

I had my specialized gloves and noise-canceling headphones set to a 1990s White Zombie album. Classic devil music. Rock on.

I asked a salesperson behind the counter for help instead of randomly combing the aisles and was directed to hunting and fishing apparel. Had no idea there was such a thing.

Holy shit! How many pairs of tactical pants could one store hold? Apparently, a lot. I concentrated on the black ones. I focused in right away on one rack. *Those* were the pants. A quick look at the price tag said I was right thinking the killer's clothing looked expensive. Four hundred and eighty seven dollars. Made from platinum?

The killer had good taste and would want the brands to match, so I knew the vest would be close.

"Well, hello," a voice said behind me. "Fancy meeting you here."

"Way to sneak up on a person." I recognized the voice, my heart jumping from the scare and pitter-pattering for other reasons. Falco was probably the only person who could really sneak up on me. I tried to be aloof, moving clothes around the rack and not looking up at him. "Thought you just lurked around your office, waiting for evidence to fall into your lap." My heart tried to calm itself. "I mean, someone's gotta do some police work around here. Am I right?"

God, I sounded like an idiot.

I handed him the pants, turned to my right, sorted through a rack quickly, and pulled out the twin to the killer's vest and the shirt.

"This is what he was wearing?" Falco asked.

"Yep, I figured you could get the UPCs and then the store can check how many were sold and who bought them and at what time, and maybe there's closed-circuit video or something." I said that very quickly and then looked up at him for a response. Yep, still as handsome as ever.

"This isn't a streaming series," Falco said.

"It's not?" I laughed nervously. "Then why can't I stop watching?" OMG, I wished I could stop myself from blabbering.

"The store won't just give up the information. We need a warrant, which we can't get without specific, actual evidence, not just a feeling…or a dream sequence. I'll need more."

"Then why are you here?" And then I knew. "You followed me."

"I did, but only because I wanted to ask another question about donuts."

He smiled at me, and I nearly vaulted out of my skin. That smile launched him from being quite handsome to *holy shit fuckable*.

"So I'm assuming your next stop is…" he asked, as if expecting an answer from me.

"Um, a high-end watch store at Northgate?"

"That's not exactly where I was going with this, but, hey, you're psychic, so I'll follow your lead."

I couldn't tell if he was being facetious. "Not psychic, just Sensitive. And it was my stylist who told me about the watch store. She's not Sensitive; she just knows a little about everything."

"So want to rideshare? Better for the earth and traffic congestion."

I nodded because I couldn't talk. This guy made me nervous for all the right reasons. Or all the wrong reasons. I wasn't sure which.

Detective Falco took phone pics of the clothes and the tags. We left my car in the lot and took his. It was a compact, green, semi-driverless electric car. It was cute and peppy, and we arrived at Northgate in no time. It was still raining hard. Bad for my hair but good for no to low pings. We got out of the car to find the shop while the car self-parked.

The watch shop was tucked in near the hockey arena, next to several high-end stores. I had never been to the mall before. Just the parking lot. Too much crowd noise, too many pings. The mall was fairly empty, except for a small pack of mall walkers. We walked into Hellebores. A snazzy shop. And definitely pricey.

Tiana's sister was not working. Instead, salesperson "Haley" was there to greet us.

Falco handed her a business card and showed her the watch photo I had sent him.

"That's a nice watch," she said as she walked us to a case and opened it. "The band comes in brown or dark-gray luxury sustainable leather." She slid the watch off its display.

She proceeded to strap it on Detective Falco's wrist, touching his arm in the process. A little longer than necessary, I thought. He turned the watch so I could see. I nodded. It was either the same watch or very similar.

He handed the watch back to her as she wrote down the model number and other relevant information. The price was six figures. For a watch. *Sheesh*. She also had written her name "Haley" with her direct mobile and a winking emoji. Not a fan of Haley, I pouted in silence.

"Where to next?" he asked as we walked back to the car and got in.

"Harald. Perfumery. Downtown."

The car's navigation picked up the location instantly and started driving there. OK, so another robot-like thing I loved was the driverless cars. So convenient.

"So should I call her?" he asked, smiling.

"Call who?" I knew exactly who he was talking about.

"Haley. The watch gal."

"It's a free country." I looked out the window. Was he trying to mess with me? Could he tell I was a tad jealous?

As we neared downtown, the rain stopped completely, and I started to pick up more and more rogue pings. I put my headphones on and turned up the sound.

The outside noise was really loud, and it was nearing the busy lunch hour. So many people. Too many people. Some louder than others. I panicked.

"I can't. Could you please take me to my car? It's too…loud."

"Change directions, back to Filstroms," Falco said, and the car took the next tolled ramp back onto I-5.

I could feel the pings lessen.

"You OK?" he said.

"I'm trying not to throw up in your car. I have a…migraine. Sorry."

"No need to apologize, I can check the scent shop later."

We got off the freeway, and I thought I saw the black-and-white dog on a corner for just a moment, then it was gone. By then the headache was bad, and Falco was nearing my house. We must have driven by one or several people with negative pings. I texted Vee that I was sick.

"Can you drop me off? I'll program my car to drive back later."

Falco helped me to my apartment and into the waiting care of my pissed-off roomie. She glared at the detective. He shrugged an apology. So much for getting out more in the world.

The bright side was I'd gotten to hit two places without getting too sick. I felt that's progress, right? I guessed for most of it, I'd have to stick to online detective work.

Chapter Nine

I was able to sleep the rest of the day and felt pretty good when I woke up. It was still early, and the weather had turned into heavy rain. Perfect for a noiseless neighborhood jaunt. I'd forego the run and just fast-walk. I put on my raincoat, headphones, and gloves.

I saw my car back on the street, so either Vee or Detective Falco had programmed its return or brought it back from the Filstroms parking lot.

I found myself walking toward the police station. I couldn't get Detective Falco out of my head. I planned on turning around but saw what looked like the backside of a dog just rounding the corner away from me. I started a slow jog and tried to catch up. Then I was running and splashing water all up and down my clothes. I circled the corner, but no dog.

A horn beeped from behind me. A familiar green car pulled to the curb.

"Hey," I said as the detective rolled down the passenger window. I pulled off my headphones and threw back my raincoat hood.

"You feeling better?" Falco asked.

"Much better." I leaned in. "Are you still following me?"

"Pure coincidence. I was headed into work. I checked out the perfume place."

"And?"

"Hop in."

I sloshed into his car.

"Wow. Did you leave any for the salmon?" He nodded toward my soaked clothes.

"Barely." I tugged at my raincoat so it wouldn't get stuck in the door, water spurting everywhere. "I was chasing a dog."

"OK. The same black-and-white dog also following you?"

"Yep." I could smell a familiar scent already, sniffing inside his car.

"Here." He handed me a business-sized card embossed with an angel and some text. A hot naked angel with muscles.

I sniffed the card. I immediately flashed back. "That's it! That's the smell." I kept sniffing it. Taking it in, trying to remember more.

"You were right about the cologne being expensive. It's called Mortis Lux—which is *Death Light* or *Light of Death* in Latin. It sells for three thousand six hundred dollars an ounce."

"Ouch. That's steep." I breathed in and couldn't stop sniffing the card. "Might be worth it. Did that salesperson try and pick you up, too?"

"Yes, but he was not my type," Falco said, smiling at me.

I reached over to give him the card back, and I brushed his hand with mine. Couldn't say it wasn't nice. It was. Even just for a moment. I looked up at him, and he met my gaze. I looked back down at my hands. We sat in silence.

"So," he said. "What I really want to know is…"

"What?" *Please be about going out for donuts.*

"What in the hell did you do to Lieutenant Barrow?"

"Who?" I asked, confused.

"My buddy Bruce…Detective Barrow. You met a couple weeks ago?"

"Oh…yeah…" How could I forget? I still felt cringy from that interaction with him.

"He is *not* the same guy. Right after he came over to talk to us, he immediately took a leave of absence and was back in today acting like…not his old asshole self."

"I didn't mean to Push him; it just happened. He touched my face." Guilt surged through me.

"No, I think folks in the office would actually thank you. He was a complete assclown and made work difficult. Now he's going around making amends. Weird, but refreshing."

I didn't know what to say at first, so we sat in silence for a few seconds.

"Did he apologize…for…the stuff he did to you?" I asked.

"Yes. He texted me several days after, and we met for dinner. He apologized for all the shit he did. He even brought up stuff I didn't remember. He was a real douche."

"And?"

"And what?"

"Did you forgive him?" I was hoping if he forgave Barrow, he'd forgive me.

Falco shrugged. He fiddled with the fob control dangling by his coffee cup in silence. Then he looked up at me again. "Your abilities—your Sensitivities. They're powerful." It was sort of a question, sort of a statement.

"Yes, that's why I'm careful. I try not to touch people without consent. I've hurt people…" I didn't want to continue. I didn't want to dredge up a past that I barely remembered to someone I barely knew.

"Well, I'm just saying I think you did Bruce a solid, Pushing him, or whatever you called it."

I shrugged and looked down. He touched my shoulder, and I looked up at him.

"I'm not kidding. He seems like a decent guy now. He was volunteering for a senior center yesterday. On his own time. You should feel good," he said. "Except that he calls me a lot now, just to 'talk things through.' "

I laughed out loud at that. Falco and Barrow *talking things through*. That's funny. Then I looked at him. "I'm sorry I dredged up that stuff on you. It wasn't right. I shouldn't have said…"

"The truth?" he finished for me.

I nodded.

He continued, "Well you certainly did Read me."

"I actually didn't Read you. That was all Detective Barrow's Read."

He gave me a questioned look.

"I can't pick up anything from being near you. Nothing. I haven't met anyone I can't Read at least a bit, especially when sitting close." I wasn't sure what this guy was doing to my brain waves, but I over-enunciated the last word, "close," making it sound awkward and loaded.

He nodded and looked like he was mulling something over. "So you do that—Read people—for a living?"

I nodded.

"You do seem to have a lot of clients."

"OK, so now you're spying on me, too?" I smiled, excited by the thought.

"I *am* a detective, you know."

"Yes, I'm well aware of that."

"So how do you do it?"

"What?"

"How do you Read people?"

"Well in the case of your friend, *he* touched *me*. But mostly I sit across from my clients and connect through touching their hands. It's very intimate." I enunciated the last words.

"Hmmm."

"Do you want me to try and Read you?" I offered. "You'll have to e-sign a consent."

"Sure." He sounded not so sure.

I took out my device, scrolled through my apps, and handed it over to Falco.

"Where do I sign?"

"I actually need you to read it."

He took a couple of minutes reviewing and then thumb-printed my app.

"Thanks." I took back my phone and pocketed it in my coat, then zipped it in. I then wriggled out of my sticky raincoat and shoved it behind me in the seat. I noticed the car windows were foggy. "So turn toward me. May I have your hands?"

It was an awkward angle, but he put his hands out, and I grabbed them lightly, my thumbs resting on the top of them. I closed my eyes to focus. *Breathe.*

Touching his hands gave me a warm and enjoyable prickly sensation that started in my fingers and slowly melted up my arms into the rest of my body. The connection wasn't a mental or psychic one. Just a physical one.

I really couldn't Read him. But I did like touching

his strong hands. I opened my eyes and looked up at him.

"Anything?" he asked.

"No, sorry." I was still holding his hands and let go slowly. "But the bright side, or dark side, depending on how you feel about it, is that makes you a Sensitive."

"A Sensitive? Really? I don't think so."

I could still feel the tingle where his hands had touched mine. "Yeah, but I've only read about that Sensitivity. There've been folks who don't ping right away for me, but never a complete block."

"So you've been trying to Read me this whole time?"

"Uh-huh." I nodded, probably smiling at him like a nut. What was it about this guy that made me flitter with excitement? I was curious if he had additional senses running on all cylinders like most Sensitives.

Falco's device pinged; he looked down and then back at me. "Hey, I gotta take off. Can I drive you home?"

"Sure." I nodded.

He pulled away from the curb and drove me the mile home.

"Thanks," I said as I was reaching for the door.

"We really should go get donuts sometime."

"Now *you're* reading *my* mind. You're on! This weekend?" I did not want him to have room to pull out of the donut excursion but hoped I didn't sound desperate.

"Uh, sure."

I half waved, and he drove off. What did "uh, sure" mean? Oh God, he'd been joking about donuts, and I'd made it all date-like and uncomfortable. I couldn't win with this guy. I was tired still from the early-day headache, so I went into my room to lie down.

My phone pinged. Jack was calling. I gave him an update on my day and that I had done some investigation on my own, coincidentally met up with Falco, and found out more about the case, including what clothing, watch, and cologne the killer might have been wearing.

I also told him I tried to Read Falco but didn't get anything out of him.

"Wow," Jack said, "I'm impressed you got out of your condo and did some real cop shit."

"Yeah, I know, right? I mean, I can't stay cooped up and isolated all the time."

"You're right, Rogue, and it seems you may have done more than just cop shit. You may have been doing a real cop, too."

I could sense him grinning on the other side of the call. "No, it's not like that…" I stammered, then stayed quiet.

"OMG. You really like this guy." Not so much a question as a statement.

"He's OK." I was thinking about Falco.

"Whatevers, keep me posted—" He broke off. "Oh, crap. I gotta go…headed into a board meeting. Talk to you later." He hung up.

"OK, bye," I said to no one and put my device down. Jack was right. I guessed I really did kind of like Falco. What was it about him that made my thoughts crawl toward images of him?

The way Falco said my name. God, he was super-hot. I felt guilty because Domino's murder was unsolved, the killer still out there, but I couldn't stop thoughts of Falco from entering my brain. Mostly thoughts of wanting to fuck him. I was terrible.

I half tossed, half hopped out of bed, not being able to nap. I was hoping a shower would cool me off and help me focus on anything but Falco.

But as the water flowed over my hair and down my body, I thought about nothing else.

"Falco." I whispered his name, enunciating the F sound and the K. Wondering if he was thinking of me. Like I was of him. Maybe he was showering, too? Maybe he touched himself while he said my name?

He exhilarated me. Excited me. Turned me on. Fired up my best body parts, made my brain react, my chest heave, my pussy tingle. I could hear his voice. Feel his breath on me, his lips saying *my* name.

If I hadn't already been in the shower, my panties would have been soaking wet.

"Falco." I loved the way his name sounded on my moist lips.

I leaned back in the shower, my shoulder blades on the heated ceramic tiles, imagining him in there with me. Kissing me. Touching me. Pleasing me. About to fuck me. I took a deep breath.

What did he feel like? What would it be like to have him inside of me? Fucking me. Rocking my world.

I closed my eyes, touched my fingers to my face and to my lips, and pretended he was there tasting me, feeling my soft, wet skin.

I touched down my smooth neck and chest lightly, then squeezed and fondled my breasts with both hands in measured and forceful grasps like I hoped Falco would. Even with the heat of the water, all the steam, my nipples were erect.

I reached down and touched myself, spreading my legs slightly, my feet sliding out with ease. Water flowed down my front, over my breasts and stomach, and between my legs, between my vulva lips. I was wet from the water and slick AF from my own wanting.

The steam shower filled my lungs with a wet moan, mist floating all over my body.

I rubbed my index and middle finger on my clit, lightly at first. I said his name again. "Falco." I rubbed harder, my other hand massaging each of my breasts, one at a time.

My breath came out in gasps. I rubbed myself harder, imagining what he would look like standing there in my shower with me. The thought made my pussy pulse. My legs wanted to spread even wider. I wanted him to fuck me. I imagined him ready to fuck me.

I used my other hand to grasp my pussy as I hoped he would, my middle finger entering my hole while rubbing my clit with the other. Oh fuck. This was not going to take long.

I rubbed harder and shoved my finger up inside myself while my hips gyrated toward my hand. "Oh fuck." My voice was raspy as I breathed in more steam.

I moved my finger in and out, inserted a second finger in the next thrust, and I burst with climax. I came hard. And again. Hard. *Fuck. Fuck.* My breath caught. My heart raced. *Fuck.*

The steaming water caressed my body as I finished coming. Moisture dripped down the shower tiles. Moisture gushed down my legs.

That man made my body feel things, do things, I wasn't in control of. I didn't want to control. I dried off, threw on a long tank top, and lay in my bed.

Well, at least that little release could help me nap. And nap I did.

Chapter Ten

I fell asleep longer than I thought after my much-needed self-love session when my device chimed at ten p.m. It was Detective Falco.

"Hey," I said sleepily, still thinking about my Falco-fueled shower masturbation.

"Hey, Detective Barrow is on his way to your place. I know it's late, but can we borrow you for an hour or two? We found the dog."

"What? The dog? Yeah, I'll be ready in five."

Falco hung up, but his intense tone already made me forget all about my earlier shower activity focused on him.

Holy shit. The dog.

I dressed, put my still damp hair up in a loose bun, left Vee a note, and ran down to the street. Barrow pulled up a minute later in a large hybrid monster-like truck. Figured.

I got in. "So where's the dog?"

"Detective Falco is onsite at an investigation," Barrow said. "He asked me to get you. The dog's there. He's assuming it's the dog you've been seeing."

"OK, I'm only getting in and going with you because of the dog. Just don't touch."

He drove away. We had gone two blocks when he let loose. "Look, I'm so sorry the way I treated you the other day. That was not OK, not acceptable. I shouldn't have spoken to you like that, and I should never have touched you."

I didn't say anything, just listened.

"I have been an asshole most of my life, and you showed me that." He was talking fast. "I'm not sure what happened, but I'm grateful for the Push. That's what Detective Falco called it."

I still did not say anything.

"Again, I'm so sorry. If I can make up for it, just let me know. I've got a lot of making up to do." He got on the Digi-wave to let Falco know we were on our way with a ten-minute ETA.

I nodded at him, still not saying anything. I've Read and Pushed jerks before, but none had made such a...what would I call it? A recovery?

We drove for twenty minutes and pulled into a neighborhood. Police lights were flashing, and yellow *Do Not Enter* tape was strung around a residence.

Falco met me as I came out of the car. I gave him my best *what's going on* look.

"So I don't know if it is the dog, but it matches your description—black and white, short hair, about so tall," he said, holding his hand up to his waist, "and the fact you seem to have some connection..."

"Where is the dog?" I could already smell dog and a strong rusty smell. Blood. It was so strong it was as if it were injected directly into my nostrils. I retched a bit, tasting bile and blood on my tongue.

"The dog's in there," Falco said, "protecting its owner's body. It's a big dog and has a menacing growl. We've been waiting for animal control to tranquilize it, but they haven't arrived yet."

I was quiet, trying to take it all in.

"Rogue, I'm not sure why I called you, just a hunch you could help." He put his hand on my shoulder. "Just be prepared. It's a mess, lots of blood. We need to process the scene as well as take forensics off the dog."

I nodded as he handed me a couple of booties to cover my footwear and latex gloves to cover my own gloves, which was weird, but I put them on anyway.

"Wait." He took the small hair scrunchy out of my messy and loose bun, put his hands through my hair, pulled my hair up into a tighter knot, and refastened it.

Any other time it might have felt erogenous, but I had to shove those thoughts out of my head. I looked at him.

"What? Hair gets into everything; gotta put it up. Don't want to shed DNA." He nodded toward the house and handed me a dog leash.

I took a couple of deep breaths. What I noticed most of all was no pings. No overwhelming thoughts. Not just from Falco. But no pings from anyone. Even with a dead body nearby. This was new.

Falco led me through the house and then steered me to the middle of the home. There, on the floor, was a woman's dead body and right next to her, a large black-and-white dog.

Because of the amount of blood, it was difficult to tell where the woman and blood ended and the dog began. A bloody reusable shopping bag and a bright-red tennis ball lay on the floor.

The dog deep growled a warning that softened to a pitiful whine as I approached. An overpowering scent of metal filled my nose. I forced myself not to gag and just concentrated on the dog.

"Hey, buddy," I whispered. It was the dog I had been

seeing. I felt like we knew each other, and I had no fear. I knelt on plastic that had been laid out and called the dog, holding both my hands open.

"C'mon, pup, come here," I said softly. I leaned down to get lower.

The dog started crawling toward me, responding to my calls, its docked tail slightly wagging.

"It's OK, c'mon, pup."

It got closer and crawled past most of the blood and spatter. It was covered in dried blood, its short fur matted in multiple spots.

"Are you hurt, buddy? It's OK, it's OK."

The dog came the remaining feet toward me, and as I sat up from my elbows, it leaned on my knees, almost like it was collapsing with relief, smearing coagulated blood on my pants on the way down.

I looped the leash over its neck and made soothing humming noises as I patted it on the head and neck with my gloves. The dog's butt and tail wiggled back and forth.

I felt and looked for injuries but didn't find any. All that blood must have been the woman's.

With the dog distracted, the team took the photos and processed the woman's body, taking her away to the medical examiner.

"Her name was Sophia Brooks," said one of the detectives.

I whispered and patted the dog as the team worked to gather evidence from its paws, fur, and mouth. I hoped it had bitten the motherfucker who did this to its owner.

"I'm so sorry, bud," I said while the team was taking photos and combing out its fur. "You're such a good—" I looked down. "—girl, such a good girl."

Her sweet, clipped tail was wagging crazily. One of the investigators handed me a stack of wet wipes so I could clean the remaining blood off of her.

Two of the investigation team were talking. They said the woman's air conditioning and humidifier had been put on manual and cranked high, so body decomposition and blood-curdling had slowed. The poor pup had been lying with her owner for a day or two and had been found by the housecleaner who saw the mess and called police.

Falco was looking at the fireplace mantel. "Hey, Rogue, is the dog wearing a collar?"

"No." I looked at the dog's neck where I had looped the leash. I was still on the floor with her but had repositioned my legs, so I was off my knees, the dog between them, head resting on my upper thigh.

"Hmmm. We haven't found the collar that's in these photos yet," Falco said. "Dog's name is Lyla."

Lyla perked up her ears.

"Is that your name? Lyla?" I said to her. "That's a beautiful name for a beautiful dog." She was so sweet. Sophia had definitely loved this dog while she was alive. The place was a dog mecca with toys and beds and treat canisters all over.

"Detective," said a woman off to the side, "the neighbor's home."

Detective Falco looked at me, and I gave him a thumbs-up, so I assumed he left to talk to Sophia's neighbor.

My mobile buzzed in my pocket, but I ignored it. Who would be calling me at one thirty or so in the morning? Probably Jack.

They were done with the dog, but Lyla seemed so

comfortable I didn't want to get up. Detective Barrow was off to my right.

"Detective," I said, and several heads turned my way. "Barrow."

Barrow came toward me.

"Hey, would you please snag some water for the dog? I don't want to get up just yet."

He brought a bowl of water to where we sat and put it down. The dog immediately drank all the water without standing up. She was a thirsty girl.

Lyla and I sat for a few more minutes, then I stood up to take the dog out.

"We're gonna need those," one of the forensic team members said.

"What?"

"Your clothes," she said, "for trace blood, hair, and fiber, just in case. You should have suited up."

I looked down at my blood-smeared lounge pants and shirt. She carefully took off my rubber gloves, bagged them, and handed me a police-branded sweatshirt and pants. I quickly changed right there, and she helped me stuff my clothes in a large evidence bag with the gloves.

"Taking the dog outside," I said, and she motioned toward the booties. I picked up each of my shoes one at a time so she could grab them.

I took the dog out into the front yard. She peed forever.

"Good girl." I patted her head.

"So is this your new best friend?" Falco asked from behind me.

Lyla wiggled her butt and went in for a pet.

"Yes," I said toward Lyla in a high voice. "My new

bestie." I moved her a few feet over and sat on the lawn.

Falco petted her head and deep-scratched her neck. She seemed to like him. I didn't blame her. I liked him, too.

"So I talked with the neighbor. He is not able to take her since he is leaving on a trip tomorrow," he said. "We'll have to wait for animal control."

"Can't I take her? Just until we connect with Ms. Brooks' family. She seems to like me." I smiled and petted the dog's head.

"Yeah, it'd be like a foster. I'll check with my chief on it to be sure it meets protocol." He turned to walk away.

"Hey."

He turned around.

"Thanks for calling me; I was meant to find the dog, you know."

He shrugged, nodded at me, and walked off.

"I know, right? He's a cutie, just like you." She seemed to nod in agreement and wagged her tail.

Barrow came out about twenty minutes later. "Hey, Chief said OK to you taking the dog. Falco asked me to drive you home."

"OK." I'd been hoping Falco would drive me home. I got up and took Lyla out the back gate to the front. The yellow police tape was still up, lights still flashing. It remained an active investigation. I pulled my phone out. I had been there for hours.

Jack had left me a couple of texts wondering where I was.

I opened the back of Barrow's quad-cab truck and motioned for her to jump in. Someone had put dog supplies in the back seat, including two gallon-sized plastic bags of kibble, plus a blanket and a couple of toys, including a programmable micro ball-tossing bot. Always wanted one of those. But never had a dog. Always wanted a dog, too, but not like this.

"Falco had those put in there," Barrow said.

I nodded and got in the car. I felt surprisingly comfortable sitting by Barrow on the trip back to my house. Maybe because I'd already Read him, and he seemed to have changed. No skin-crawling bad vibes, just comfortable. It was a different feeling altogether than when we'd driven a couple of hours earlier.

Chapter Eleven

I texted Vee that I was coming home with a dog. She replied OK, so I'm not sure if she was chill with it or not. We had never talked about getting a pet.

"Thanks for the ride," I said as Barrow parked in front of my condo.

He made a motion to help me.

"I got it, thanks." I grabbed Lyla's leash, rolled the food bags and toys up in the blanket, and carried it like a sack. Barrow waved a goodbye. I waved back.

When I got home, Vee was sitting with Josie on the couch.

"This is Lyla," I said.

"She's so big," Vee said. "And so cute."

Lyla wiggled over to her. Vee and Josie both petted her and then looked at their hands.

"She's still kind of sticky," I said. "I wiped off most of the blood, but she needs a bath."

Their eyes got wide.

"Long story. You need a bath. Don't you, girl?" I led the dog back to my bathroom and filled the tub. I put the blanket, toys, and robot on my desk and shook out some dog food in a snack bowl already in my room to give her. I put it down for Lyla, and she ate a little.

I gave Lyla a bath. Had to use people shampoo and I hoped that'd be OK until I could get her puppy shampoo. I dried her with a couple of big towels, making sure to clean off any blood traces or water left on her. She looked clean and smelled nice.

"Gyzmo," I said, "order healthy, high-end dog—or puppy—food and an assortment of fun toys for a big...very large dog."

Gyzmo bleeped in acceptance.

I looked down at the sweats I was wearing. I shrugged—they were damp but not bad—and hopped into bed. Lyla hopped in right next to me. I checked my phone. Shit. Jack had been trying to call and texted multiple times.

I texted Jack back, taking a photo of the dog already sleeping and sending it to him.

—*What? Is that the dog you've been seeing?*—

—*Yep. She's a sweetie.*—

Jack called, and I picked up.

"You up?" he said. "I'm walking up your front steps. Can I come in?"

"Uh, sure." I hung up. He didn't sound good.

"Stay," I said instinctively to Lyla. She didn't move and was snoring lightly.

I let Jack in. He looked like shit. Large, dark bags had returned to his eyes.

"You didn't call me back. I haven't slept." He ran his fingers through his hair and shook his head like he was trying to clear it.

"I'm sorry, Jack. The detectives brought me out to an investigation late. The dog's owner was killed and..."

"Domino's back," he interrupted, "and I think she brought others with her...lots of others. They were back in the darkness. I think I'm cracking up." He sounded crazed and was visibly upset.

"I'm sorry. I thought you were done with ghosts."

"So did I. Is the dog back there?"

I took him to my room. Lyla looked up for a moment and then went back to sleep.

"The dog's big," he said. "What kind is she?"

"Yes, she's huge, and her name is Lyla. I have no idea what kind of dog she is." I looked at her. It didn't matter, though. I was already in love.

We both stared at the dog in silence for a few moments.

"I don't get it, Jack. I saw the dog first a week or two ago—before her owner was killed." I started to cry. "How was I supposed to prevent it?"

He shook his head. "I don't know, Rogue."

"There was so much blood." I sobbed, my nose running freely. "I had to wipe dried globs of it off the dog with wet wipes."

Lyla woke up briefly, turned in a circle on the bed twice, repositioned herself, and lay back down. Jack handed me the tissue box on my desk.

"I'm sorry you're seeing ghosts again. And sounds like more than just Domino?"

"Yeah, they were trying to talk to me all at once," he said. "Made the mistake of doing some imported elicits with a couple of my companions earlier, so thought I was having a bad high, then sobered up, but Domino and someone else appeared…closer and louder."

"What are they saying?"

"To be honest, it sounds like one of those old-time radios from a movie where someone is switching between stations, so I only get pieces of multiple conversations."

"We're missing something. There's gotta be a

reason."

"I have no idea, but one of the spirits, not Domino, stood near the kitchen during our family dinner tonight in the big house. It was fucking surreal."

I just shook my head.

"Can I just stay here tonight? I don't want to be by myself."

I nodded. Both of us slept on either side of the dog, with the lights on.

I am leaning over a woman on the ground and watch as she stops struggling and the life leaves her eyes. I am sick and thrilled at the thought. A short, shrill laugh escapes my lips. My hand is on a large knife, embedded in her stomach, and I am still pushing hard. I hear something behind me, a door opening and a "goodbye," and a door shuts, and then a dog growling and attacking me. My adrenaline is on high, and I body-slam the dog, knocking it over. The knife propels out of the woman's gut, blood spluttering and glugging onto the floor. It comes back at me, but it is slipping and sliding on the bloody floor, still trying to bite me. I grab a reusable grocery bag with handles and put it over its head, trying to tighten it. Then I see its collar, the tag tinkling as I pull it down to the floor. Lyla *the tag reads; it is in the shape of a bone. "Fucking dog," I say. I quickly unsnap her collar with my free hand, pull down on the bag, push her to the ground, snag the knife with that hand, and run for the back door. She shakes the bag off and follows and almost catches me, but I shut the door quickly. I hear her barking and barking. I laugh. I look down at the collar I took.* Whew, *I think,* that was close. "What a pretty collar," I say and make my way through the backyard and out the gate.*

I woke with a start, panting, and with a deep sadness.

Jack woke up, too, and looked right at me. "You freaking saw that, too?"

"The dog?"

"Yeah, a dog was attacking a guy, and there was blood. I was floating in a house, watching a dog growl and bite at someone, and I looked down, and I saw my body lying there. It wasn't me, though. I was *that* woman, and I was dead, and that man had stabbed me, and blood was oozing out."

I looked at him and then down at Lyla. She was breathing fast, and her legs and body were moving, twitching, and I could hear quick whines from her. I laid my hands on the dog and breathed.

I like car rides. The wind is nice. I'm going home. The lady opens the door in front of me. I pad through the door, and someone is fiddling with my neck. I hear a high-pitched "goodbye," and the door shuts behind me. I am happy to be home. I run through the house, grab a tennis ball in case my mom is home. Something isn't right. I can smell something is off. I run into the living room, and there is someone in there with my mom. I growl, drop my ball, and jump between them, trying to get him away from her. I try to bite him, and he bumps my whole body and tosses me aside. I run back, trying to scare him away. My paws keep slipping, and I am trying to bite him, and he pushes me. He puts something over my head, and it makes it dark, and he pulls me down by my head and reaches in and takes my collar. Then he lets go, and I shake the thing off my head, and he runs for the back door. I chase him, and he shuts the door on my nose. I bark and bark and bark. I am wet and sticky and smell like my jingly collar. I try to shake and shake and shake.

I go over to my mom, and she is sleeping. I pick up the ball and put it by her so when she wakes up, she'll play ball with me. I wait and wait and wait by my mom and sleep some. And then the lady with the bucket, who I see sometimes, who gives biscuits, comes in, but I growl at her. Then a bunch of people come in, and I really growl at them. They scare me. My mom is still sleeping.

I sobbed loudly and took my hands off the dog. Her breathing was back to normal, and her body had stopped twitching. She woke up briefly, stood up, stretched, shook her fur, moved to my side of the bed, and let out a big sigh as she lay back down. She started snoring immediately and seemed restful.

Jack got up, went out of the room, and came back with some items he put on my desk. He handed me a glass.

I was dehydrated. I took a big drink and coughed and sputtered. I was not expecting that. "That's fucking vodka." I swallowed, trying to clear my burning throat.

"Yeah, needed to take the edge off." He took a couple of big gulps. "What the fuck did we just see?" He sat back in my bed.

"I don't know. Similar perspectives to last time. Me as the killer, and you floating above watching but also her. I *saw…experienced* what the dog did. Oh God, that dog loved her owner." I started sobbing again. I was turning into quite the crybaby.

I put the glass up to my lips and just chugged, gagging the vodka down. I needed sleep and didn't want to think about anything.

I didn't have room on my side anymore because of a sleeping dog, so I walked around to the other side and motioned for Jack to scoot. I sidled in next to him, put my pillow down by his chest, and snuggled into him. I was still sniffling, and he handed me a couple more tissues.

"Thanks for staying." I hiccupped.

"Thanks for having me." He shrugged down, one arm over my back.

I felt a tingle of electricity from him but no crazy pings so settled down. The vodka did the trick, and I was off to dreamland. Hopefully good dreamland and not scary-as-fuck murderous dreamland.

Chapter Twelve

"Wake up, sleepy-head. You have a visitor," my roommate said.

"Who? Jack?" I mumbled.

"No, your detective friend is here."

I looked around. Maybe Jack had gone home? "What time is it?" I looked at my phone. *Sheesh.* I'd slept in until past ten a.m. I had a couple of unread texts from Detective Falco.

Lyla was still fast asleep, lying on her back with her legs up in the air, one ear flopped forward and one back. I patted her tummy, her fur soft, fuzzy, and warm. Vee had already left my room.

I went out into the living room. Detective Falco was there chatting with my roomie. I smelled them first, then spied the open lavender box of donuts on the kitchen counter.

"Good morning, Rogue." Falco grinned. "You said something about donuts this weekend...so thought I'd hand deliver some."

Not exactly what I'd had in mind as far as a date, but hey, donuts. I looked skillfully at the selection before grabbing a fluffy one with pink frosting.

Vee glared at the donuts.

"It won't kill you to eat one," I said to her.

She gave me a dirty look, snatched a maple bar from the box, and scurried off to her room.

I noticed Detective Falco was not partaking in donut consumption, but he was smiling at me. I think. Hard to tell with this guy.

"Not hungry?" I said.

"Not really, just came to check in on you and see how the dog's doing."

"She's good, still sleeping. I slept OK after a couple nightcaps. Was going to call you anyway and share some new insights; might be helpful, or not, to the case."

"Go on."

"So I had a dream that I was the murderer, like with Domino? But it was after he already stabbed her and the dog came in."

He nodded.

"This time I felt his feelings...heard his voice. He was excited over the killing. Lyla tried to bite him, and he pushed her off; he called her a 'fucking dog.' He took the knife with him."

"Anything else?"

"Yeah, I also Read the dog," I said cautiously as I wasn't sure how he would take it. "Lyla showed me she had grappled with the killer. A man wearing a hat and sunglasses and gloves. She had slipped all over the blood, and he put a bag over her head, took her collar, and then got away out the back door."

"You Read the dog?"

"Yeah, I just did it without thinking. And my friend was there as well, floating above the murderer and Sophia and Lyla, watching. The killer was dressed differently, all covered up, pants tucked in boots, sleeves tucked in gloves, hoodie on, cap and large glasses." I let out a quiet sob.

"Your friend saw it, too?"

"Yeah, he stayed over last night, and we had a similar dream or vision or whatever...a flashback."

"Him?" Falco said, raising his eyebrows and giving me a side glance.

"Um, yeah, my friend..." I raised my eyebrows, too. "Oh, not like that, we didn't hook up or anything...strictly professional."

"Whatever floats your boat." He shrugged and looked down.

Hard to tell with Detective Iceberg, but was that a hint of envy in his voice?

"Is that it?" He looked up from his e-screen, taking notes.

"Um, yeah." I thought. "Oh, the hat was a black baseball cap with a drug name on it...the one that cures opioid addiction? No OD..."

"NoODxone?"

"Yes, that's the one! Does that help?"

"Not sure, but I'll look into it. And I'm gonna need my sweats back."

"These *yours*?" I pointed to the charcoal-colored SPD sweats on my body. "Feel free to take them anytime." *What is wrong with me?*

"I'm assuming they'd need to be washed first." He sounded a bit repelled.

Just when I thought I was warming up to him. "Roger that, Officer, sir," I said smartly while saluting, a remnant gesture from the time I'd spent at military religious reform school in the Midwest.

Falco rolled his eyes at me and left. Geez, there was no joking with this guy.

I went for the box of donuts and polished off another one. Then took two more. Took another.

Lyla came out of my bedroom, stretched, a deep down dog, and hopped on the couch.

"Good morning, sunshine." I rubbed her ears, gave her half the donut, and we snuggled on the couch to watch cats stealing dog beds.

Jack texted.

—I'm still seeing ghosts. Can I drop by?—

I was about to answer his text but knew he was already at the front door. Lyla's ears perked up. Maybe I should just register him for his own entry code?

"This time," he said, bounding in and handing me his e-reader, "it made the front page."

Murder in Seattle. Well-known arts curator, benefactor found dead.

I read the headline twice and then clicked on the live story link.

Peppy yet ever-so-serious reporter, Olivia Oliver, popped up on-screen. "Police were called in last night after a woman was found viciously stabbed and murdered in her own home. She was identified by neighbors and family as a well-known art curator and contributor, Sophia Brooks. Investigators are combing through evidence and talking to neighbors and friends of Miss Brooks for any clues in her brutal killing. You'll find the latest on this case and other breaking news, right here on KING 5. This is Olivia Oliver, reporting."

I scrolled farther down on the e-reader. "So Sophia wasn't in the same line of work as Domino, but the killing *felt* so similar. It's gotta be the same guy."

"Yeah, I don't know. So similar. Gotta be the same guy." Jack paused and swallowed in a couple of gulps, then sat on the couch. "And Miss Brooks...Sophia? She was known to my family; she started with the Knight

Foundation when she was just out of school. I didn't recognize her in my dream. Too much blood. But I haven't seen her in, what? Fifteen years?"

"I'm so sorry, Jack. Is she the one…"

"Haunting me now?" he confirmed, nodding. "Yep, she has been hanging out since early this morning. That's why I left here early. I needed to let my mom know. They used to be best friends."

"Used to be?"

"Yes, they had a falling out. I don't know the history, but I know it's a sore subject between my folks. I had to let my mom know she was dead…and that I could see her."

"Wait…you told your mom…that you see ghosts?"

"I did…and about which ghosts I've been seeing."

"And?"

"She was very quiet…took my hands and looked at me. She didn't seem surprised and then just hugged me tight and told me some stuff from when I was a kid. It was an odd exchange. Then my dad came in, and she got chatty and changed the subject."

"Maybe she needs to process."

"Or wants to keep me being a Sensitive secret. Not sure my dad or the rest of the family would approve."

"Maybe." I shrugged. "My adoptive parents thought my Sensitivities were the work of the devil, so they tried to church it out of me and sent me to a strict boot camp. I feel lucky I survived that bullshit." It hadn't been all bad, I guessed. I'd also picked up my potty mouth and some great military lingo from my time there.

Jack smiled at me. "What about your bio parents?"

"No idea. I think my adoptive parents tried to erase all records. I haven't found out anything about them, even with major DNA advances. I don't think about them much." Not sure why I'd just lied to him about that as I thought about my real parents all the time.

"That's a lie." He laughed. "You know I can read your mind?"

"Really?"

"Sort of. I knew just then; you were lying because your eyes told me so."

I lightly punched him in the arm.

"Ouch. No need to resort to violence," he said playfully.

"I'm sure they'll come around...your folks." I smiled. "You're their golden boy."

"Yeah, and I guess I've always been this way...well, at least when I was younger. My mom said I had always talked to people who weren't there. I told her I talked to her dad and was able to tell her things I couldn't know. She said everything changed when I almost drowned at our lake house."

I nodded at him to continue.

"I was clinically dead for a few minutes, and my uncle brought me back. My mom said I didn't see ghosts anymore after that. At least I didn't talk about them. She said I was troubled and distant ever since, not her sweet little boy anymore. She said she could see a difference in me now...almost like the old Jack is back."

"Hmmm, I wonder if something about the almost drowning caused your gift to be suppressed, and maybe when I Read and Pushed you, it came back...with a vengeance."

He shrugged and nodded.

I was comfortable around Jack, and so was Lyla as she stood on the couch, stretched, and then repositioned herself over his entire lap.

"I guess you're not going anywhere for a bit." I petted Lyla on her face.

"She's sweet."

"I know, right? I hope I can keep her."

We sat in silence for a couple of minutes.

"So…what do we do now?" Jack let out a breath.

"Well, I already shared the new info with Detective Falco…except for the ghost part."

He gave me an anxious look. "You didn't share the drug name on the baseball cap, did you?"

"I did, why?"

"I'll just need to give our PR folks at Knight Industries a heads-up just in case it gets in the media that the killer was wearing a NoODxone ball cap."

I nodded. "Sorry, must rouse the sleeping giant." I patted the dog. "Lyla's gotta pee. C'mon, girl."

Lyla hopped off the couch and followed me out the front door.

Chapter Thirteen

I walked down the condo stairs and noticed a patrol car parked in the street. I walked over to the grassy strip near the car and waved.

The uniformed cop rolled down her window. She looked about twelve.

"Hey." I smiled at her. "How's it going?"

"Good morning, Rogue. I'm Officer James, and I'm the lucky rookie short-straw winner slash weekend morning shift casing your place."

"My place? Really?"

"I don't make the assignments; I'm the newbie. But let me know if you need anything."

"Sure thing—let me know if you need to use the restroom." I pointed to my office on the ground floor. "There's one downstairs. The code is 9-8-1-1-5."

"God, no wonder Detective Falco has me watching your place. You don't pay much mind to security. You didn't even check my ID."

"Well, I guess it's good, then, that I can read your mind." I smiled at her, waved, and took Lyla back upstairs. Why did Falco have cops watching my place?

"Hey, Jack?" I said when I came in. "Was that patrol car sitting out there when you came up?"

"Uh, no. But Detective Falco was," he said slyly. "I gave him a wave on the way up."

"Hmmm." I drew out my m's.

"I think he *likes* you."

"Yeah, I don't think so. He thinks we slept together."

"But we did sleep together." He grinned, scrolled down his e-reader, and then activated the *cats stealing dog bed*s video stream.

I gave him a weird look.

"What? It's my favorite stream. That and BritBox."

"OMG. We *are* connected." I shoulder bumped him on the couch and settled in with him and Lyla to mindlessly binge.

Not sure how much time had passed but I heard the familiar ping of my phone.

I pulled myself away from Jack's e-reader and read the text on my phone. Jack was sleeping.

—Hey. Going out to interview folks. Want to tag along?—

It was Falco.

Tag along? Who did he think he was? He thought I'd just drop whatever I was doing to follow him around while he interviewed folks?

—Would love to!— I texted back. I'm such a sap. Could I have been any more excited or obvious? Apparently not, as I had already grabbed my jacket and lip gloss and was halfway down my stairs when he texted, leaving Jack napping on the couch with Lyla.

—See you in five.—

I tightened my hair in its already messy bun and waited by the curb. *Too desperate*? Uh, yes. But I didn't care. Something about that detective had me intrigued. Maybe because I couldn't Read him. Not knowing all the thoughts in someone's mind was a turn-on.

He pulled up in his little green car, and I jumped in.

He winked at me when I got in, making my pulse skyrocket to 170, at least. I was also feeling pulses in areas besides my blood. Lady boner alert.

"What's wrong?" Falco asked. He could probably hear my heart pumping.

"Nothin'." I hoped I hadn't said that last part about the lady boner out loud, playing it cool, trying to get my heart rate down within normal levels.

"We're going to reinterview a few of Domino's co-workers to see if there may be any connection—they may recognize Ms. Brooks' photo."

We headed south down Fourth Avenue, took a left, headed to I-5, then a right on Corson Ave., and drove by the larger-than-life cowboy hat and boots. I'd always liked that landmark. Someone had scrawled in large lettering *Prevent Dark of Knight* with black paint on part of the boot. This was one of the many anti-big pharma, anti-Knight family sentiments seen throughout the city. This one was tame.

"So...what's up with the Knight family?" Falco asked.

"Hmmm?" I was curious when he'd made that connection. Probably when Jack waved at him this morning.

"Well, I know you've been spending time with Jack Knight, and Ms. Brooks was well known to the family and around town. I figured you talked about it."

Ah. That made sense why Falco would station a uniformed officer at my place. Either he was worried about me or spying on me. Or both.

"Jack said that Ms. Brooks had been a family friend—used to be his mom's best friend."

He nodded.

"There's nothing between us, me and Jack. We have a connection, but we're just friends."

"You don't have to explain anything to me. It's none of my business."

"OK."

"He's a good-looking, eligible bachelor who…"

"I thought you said it was none of your business?" I smiled at him.

"Just making conversation."

"Oh, of course. What about you?"

"Me?"

"Yeah, *you're* a good-looking, eligible, yet emotionally unattainable bachelor." I teased him a bit.

"Emotionally unattainable?"

"You heard me."

"OK."

Falco drove in silence for a bit. Then he looked over at me, and he was grinning. "You said I'm good-looking?"

You have no idea. I just smiled at him.

We drove up to Hatty's House and parked. It was still early in the day, and half-a-dozen glowing digital moving portraits were perched on individual verandas outside the structure. Motion-picture billboards advertising the variety of workers available at Hatty's House. A digital potluck for any desire.

Hatty's was an immense, Craftsman-style mansion with dispersed Victorian flair thrown in that looked like it had been built in the early 1900s but was a modern structure. The facility was designed specifically for the owner-operator sex professionals who lived and worked there. I had visited the home on occasion.

Before it opened several years ago, Vee had

scheduled a time to tour it when it was still vacant so I could see her handiwork with minimal pings. She had helped the owners design the home's interior pro-bono in her spare time when not babysitting me and my clientele. Vee was quite the artist.

Several of these safe, working homes had popped up in industrial areas after sex work became a legal and profitable profession.

The house was named after Hatty, a sex worker killed and dumped in SODO back in 2027, sparking riots and legislation that led to sex-worker protections and eventually its legalization.

Falco got out, and I sat in my seat, waiting for a barrage of thought-pings. Nothing. Was he rubbing off on me? *I wish.* But I wasn't hearing anything, which, for a typical person, was a good thing. For me, not so good as I made a career of it.

I got out of the car and shot him a worried glance.

"You OK?"

"Um, yeah…that's the problem."

He gave me a confused nod.

We walked to the front of the home and were greeted by bouncers. One looked just like hottie and former actor-turned-governor Jacobi Jones. Was he part of the available menu?

The other one nodded at us and tipped her ball cap at Detective Falco. We went into the lobby, which was immaculately designed and laid out to increase worker safety and clientele comfort.

"Well, good morning, Detective Falco," said our host, dressed in a shiny burnt-sienna dress with a metallic, gold scarf.

I gave Falco a sideways glance.

"Hey, Sugar, and this is Rogue."

She looked me up and down and smiled. I had met her during Vee's tour.

"You're Vee's friend," she said.

I nodded and smiled at her, keeping my hands behind me. She was stunning, and I instantly felt calm. Sugar was an Emitter.

"Welcome again to Hatty's House, Rogue," she said.

Falco gave me a sideways glance. Sugar walked us down the hall and took us to a cozy room with a fireplace and a couple of couches for sitting. I read the sign to the right of the fireplace.

Sensitive Emitters in use.

This signage was standard practice for businesses that employed Emitters or other Sensitives. Emitters were Sensitives who could exude or emit particular feelings onto others. Clubs, bars, spas, hotels, and bordellos employed these Sensitives to create warm, soothing, or exciting mental environments for customers.

Sugar Emitted calm and comfortable emotions, which was a great skill to have when running a brothel, putting the customers she greeted at ease.

Falco, of course, was not affected. Just my luck I'd gotten this man into a house of desire, and he felt nothing. Perhaps this was the reason I wasn't receiving any pings.

"So you're here to talk about something connected to Domino?" Sugar said, leaning toward us.

"Yes." Falco took out his note-taker, looked at it as if he was scrolling, then handed the digital pad to Sugar. "Do you recognize her?"

"Yes, she was the woman who was just killed. I saw it on the news."

"Did she look familiar to you from before?" he asked.

"Yes, I know Sophia from somewhere, but she is not a customer here. I know her from somewhere else." She paused. "But I can't recall, exactly, when or where I've met her."

I wasn't sure if it was Sugar's Emitting skills, but I believed her. Maybe if I could touch her?

"Did you ever see her with Domino?" Falco asked.

"Not that I remember. Were they killed by the same person?"

"We're not sure." He took his digital screen back. "We're—"

"I can help. I can try and Read you." I didn't mean to blurt.

She nodded.

"You don't have to," Falco said. "She's a Sensitive." He sounded worried.

"No, I'll be OK." I moved over to where Sugar was seated and asked her to give her digital OK on my phone.

I could feel sparking as soon as I touched her hands. I closed my eyes. She was easy to Read. I immediately saw what looked like screen-shotted events rolling backward through time. I skipped by something, rewound, and saw Sugar and Sophia Brooks in a group photo together. I let go of her hands.

I had no headache or nausea coming on due to the Read, which was out of the ordinary, especially for reading a powerful Sensitive.

"You both met at the Knight Foundation Celebrating Cures gala," I said. "You were there because of an invitation from the mayor for your volunteer work in finding a cure for herpes strain ten after multiple mutations."

"Yes! That is where I met her," Sugar said. "Such a wonderful woman…she volunteered for multiple causes. But I'm not sure she and Domino were acquainted."

"That's what we're trying to figure out." Falco leaned over to Sugar, showing her his screen. "Does this vehicle look familiar?"

"Really? A black, high-end e-SUV with midnight-tint windows?" She looked at him, eyebrows raised. "Our customers park dozens of large hybrid vehicles like that every day in our lot. While it's legal, our clientele still want to keep some semblance of anonymity."

He smiled at her. "If you would share both these pics around with my contact info, I'd appreciate it. It's all we have to go on at this time."

She nodded, took out her device, and tapped his to transfer the info onto hers. She gave him permission to ask the other workers if they recognized the photo, vehicle, or anything else about Domino. He came up empty.

"Well, don't be a stranger," Sugar said while seeing us out, looking directly at Falco, then at me. "You either, Rogue. Perhaps we can trade your services for Hatty services?"

"I'll keep that in mind." I smiled at her as we left.

Rain was ricocheting off the parked cars as we jogged to Falco's vehicle.

"So…" he said once we were seated, "sounds like you have been to Hatty's before."

"Yeah, I was on a tour several years ago and met Sugar."

"Well, you made quite an impression on her."

"I could say the same for you, Detective Falco. Visit the house often?"

"Strictly for business, I assure you."

"Oh, no need for assurance. You're a consenting adult, and it's legal, so no judgment."

"You have an interesting angle on life, Rogue."

I loved the way he said my name.

"You're different," he added.

Did he just say I was *different*? "OK, I'm not sure how to take that."

"Different in a good way. I like you."

He just said it. He liked me. But did he *like* me, like me?

"Well, I *like* you, too." I looked at him. It started to pour buckets, and the drops were making a loud tinning sound on the car roof. *Saved by the rain.*

He engaged his car's push start, pulled out of the lot, and took a right to head to my place. But instead of turning to take me home, he went straight on Fourth. "You hungry?"

"Always hungry," I assured him. I texted Jack to make sure he was OK staying with Lyla. Falco drove a couple of miles down Fourth, took a left on Madison Street toward the waterfront and a right on Alaskan Way, and parked mid-block across from Ivar's, one of my fav old-school delivery places.

"Fish OK?" he asked.

I nodded at him, and we got out of the car, crossed the street to Ivar's, and ordered at the window. I ordered the lab-made fish option. The rain had calmed into a mist.

We found seats in the covered section outside

overlooking the Sound. We ate our breaded filets and fries in silence, dipping in the world-famous tartar and occasionally tossing a fry in response to the lone seagull's food solicitation.

The salty deep-fried potatoes mixed with the sauce were tangy and tasty.

The silence, besides the gull's gawking cry, was comfortable. But obviously, I had to fill the space by talking.

"So I meant it when I said *I liked you.*"

"OK." He seemed to be thinking. I let him think.

We inhaled our meals. He got up and tossed his remaining fries to the thankless bird. One bird had multiplied into eight. I remembered they used to have bots that would scare away the seagulls, but hooligans kept hoisting them into the Sound for fun. Damn vandals.

I got up and sorted our trays into the large mulching bins. When I turned around, Falco was in front of me.

"Wanna walk a bit?" he asked.

I nodded, trying to down a monstrous nervous lump in my throat that formed due to his closeness.

The rain had let up, and we headed south toward Petty-Officer Park. We got about half a block when the torrents started up again with fist-sized raindrops. We bounded to a nearby enclosed Metro bus stop.

The enclosure was made of thick, clear acrylic and had a water view. I stood near the rail, looking over. Only a few boats were out on the Sound. The foot ferry was just taking off for Bremerton, and another ferry was headed in from Vashon Island. No one else was around.

"This is one of my favorite views." Falco's voice was right behind me.

His body heat on my back and his close presence

was overwhelming. He had one hand on the rail in front of me, leaning to one side. I turned around slowly to face him, and my breath quickened.

"Hey," I said, "thanks for the grub."

"Hey," he said back, "you're welcome."

I looked up at his face and into his dark eyes, which seemed to waver in color between intense hazel and sparkling honey, glinting with a warmth.

I hadn't seen much light in his eyes so far, but right now, so much for Mr. Unemotional. His eyes were fucking mesmerizing. I could almost Read him with those eyes.

And maybe it was just the lunar energy of the Puget Sound horizon egging me on, making me feel daring mixed with the intense pressure in my veins just being so close to him, but I dove right into those eyes and got lost. I wanted him and I wanted him bad.

I went for it, and in one graceless move, I leaned in and full-on kissed his lips. I closed my eyes. His lips felt firm and tasted like the french fries we'd just shared, salty yet sweet with savor. So sweet. The taste of sex. I wanted to part his lips with my tongue but noticed he wasn't moving.

I stopped, opened my eyes, and looked at him. The color still sizzled in his eyes, but he just stared back at me. Maybe his heat wasn't aimed at me. Had I mistaken passion for something else? Oh fuck, had I just crossed the friend zone uninvited?

My breath stopped in my throat. My pulse stopped. Time stopped. I was uncomfortable and felt a strong urge to get out of there. The salty kiss was replaced by a distressing bile taste.

I shook the shock off with a twist and ducked under

Falco's arm to leave. I was going to need to call for a ride out of pure embarrassment. For a Sensitive, I sure as hell had just read *that* situation wrong.

He gently caught the back of my arm with his muscled grasp, stopped me, and in the same swoop, leaned down and kissed me back. His lips pressed so firmly against mine I had to inhale him in fully, making me dizzy.

My full breath and pulse shot back with a vengeance, but time remained static. I couldn't tell if the beating I heard was the rain above my head or just my heart banging out of control.

He grabbed me by the waist and pulled me in close. His fingers tightly entwined in my clothes, and where his skin met mine, it felt like fire licking at my flesh.

He pulled me in even closer. I stayed locked on his lips and grabbed the back of his rain-wet hair to steady myself with the other held firmly on his shoulder. His tongue and my tongue meshed; our mouths opened to each other. We fit together.

I could feel electricity between our lips and could almost hear the crackling of static. He kissed me more fervently. Behind my eyes, hundreds of star-bursting impulses exploded in my mind. And those stars aligned with the planetary orgasm already bubbling up from my core.

I was anticipating a celestial wild ride. The cadenced tempo of our kissing in line with the Sound's waves washing up at the pier's edge. Within his embrace I felt planets converge, my milky way giving way to a frothy foam as his sensual touching and tasting made my panties soaked with passion.

His hands moved off my waist and enveloped my

entire presence. My body, eager, responded to his touch as the rain thundered overhead.

His musky scent mixed with the saline air of the Sound was intoxicating. Our tongues continued to explore, and I tugged his groin in close so I could feel his hardness against me.

He reached up and cradled the back of my neck firmly, then pulled my chin to the side to devour my neck. I sighed with pleasure. I moved my hands over him, wanting to be within him. Wanting him to be all the way inside me.

I pushed up against him and felt his hard cock through multiple layers of clothes. I wanted to get down there and devour him. Entwined so tightly, we were one person at the bus stop.

The rain stopped rattling overhead, and we were encased in a large, translucent box of foggy windows. Our heated activity revealed as the vapor ran down the sides. The air was moist with precipitation, and I was wet with anticipation. I needed him inside me.

"Let's get out of here," I said, wanting to savor the moment by continuing somewhere more private.

He nodded at me.

With the rain break, Falco grabbed my hand, and we headed back to his car. He soul kissed me one more time before he opened my door. I was ready to do him right there in his car. Fuck public indecency. It would be worth it. All my body pistons were on overdrive. I wanted him. Bad.

We drove back to my place, and I could barely contain my breath in my throat. I wanted to taste the rest of him. I rushed out of the car.

"You coming up?" I said through my open car door,

wanting to get back to what we had been doing at the bus stop. But a lot more, and with a lot less clothes on.

He didn't answer, and he didn't get out of the car. I waited, thinking he didn't hear me. I leaned down to look through the door opening, and he was staring straight ahead. I was uncomfortable.

He kept looking forward, and I shrugged at him, wanting him to say something. When he did answer, I wasn't expecting his reply.

"Rogue, this isn't a good idea." He leaned my way but didn't look at me. "I've got a lot of…background work to do tonight…and this week…"

I stood and stared through the passenger door in disbelief.

What the fuck had happened between five minutes ago at Pier 54 and now? How the fuck did he go from having his tongue down my throat, his hands on my ass, and wanting more of me to *oh, never mind, I got work*?

Oh fuck. He fucking changed his mind, and I looked like a confused, desperate dumbass standing there. He continued with more reasoning about his busy work, and I slammed the door on his further explanations.

I trudged up my steps, punched in my door code, walked through the door, and slammed it without looking back. I dropped, slug like, onto the couch. What had I just done wrong?

I replayed the scene over and over in my brain as my body recalled every touch. I wasn't sure I'd ever wanted someone so badly in my life. The feel of his hand on my back between my untucked shirt and my pants was a sensation I wasn't going to soon forget.

What a fucker. At what exact point had he lost interest in pursuing something more carnal with me? I just sat there and contemplated what in the fuck I'd done or said—or hadn't done or said—to make him go cold.

I got up and poured myself a glass of whatever Vee had up-front and center as part of her recently set-up cocktail caddy. I wolfed down half the glass of the amber liquid, the alcohol fumes sneaking up from my throat and out my nose. A sweet and strong hint of pistachio with a creamy caramel feel. *Yum.*

I poured and wolfed down another half glass. *Double yum.* Probably one of the pricey seasonal artisan specialties from the corner micro-distillery. I figured if anytime was the right time to drink exorbitantly priced craft brandy, it was now.

I planned to make the best of it. I sat on the couch contemplating once again my terrible decision-making skills when it came to choosing a bedmate. A flaw that I'd thought was solved when I stuck only to people Vee vetted for me. I guessed I'd just fucked that one up, and now I was paying the price with sad face.

"And I didn't even get to sleep with him," I whined out loud to my glass of booze. I must have been a bit tipsy as my speech was slurred and my eyes felt noddy. But I couldn't get him out of my thoughts. And I could still smell him on me. He could've been my new favorite scent, but he'd gone and ruined it. What a downer.

Chapter Fourteen

"Jack had to leave right after you took off," Vee said, coming in from the front door with Lyla. "He asked me to tell you. So I just took baby-dog on a walk."

I was on the verge of tears. She looked from my face to the glass of brandy in my hand, grabbing it from me. She shook her head at me. I tended to heavy day drink when something was amiss with my emotional state.

"What happened?" She touched my shoulder, true concern in her eyes.

"I have no idea. We were kissing, and then he's saying he's busy."

"Wait, you and Jack?"

"No! Me and Falco," I said in an impatient *catch-the-fuck-up* tone.

"What the fuck, Rogue? Falco?" she said with her *what were you thinking* sneer back at me.

I shook my head, and the tears appeared and rolled down my face. I had never cried over anyone, not even my dead ex-boyfriend, which was a whole other story.

God, I was hella confused and embarrassed. Vee put the brandy glass on the kitchen counter, took Lyla's leash off, and hung it up. She sat on the couch next to me, put her hand on my knee, and gave me her best worry face.

I leaned in for comfort and sobbed harder. Lyla jumped up and sidled herself halfway onto my lap, putting her wet nose under my arm.

"Rogue, it's OK." Vee pulled my head into her shoulder.

"I fucking hate him."

"No, you don't, you just can't Read him, so you didn't see this coming."

"I told him I like him…then I kissed him…then he kissed me back and more. Then we headed back here, and he said he had work to do. He wouldn't even get out of the car. He confused the heck outta me." I sniffled.

I had no idea where to put this feeling, so I canceled it out as quickly as I could. I had learned to compartmentalize at an early age and was skilled at keeping my emotions at bay, especially the feelings I couldn't define or ones that made me too uncomfortable. I needed that skill now.

I swallowed my cry hiccup, and maybe it was the liquid courage I had downed, but I talked myself into substituting that shit feeling with anger, because being pissed-off was the best feel to shake being pathetic. I hugged Vee hard, got up, and patted Lyla on the head.

"No use crying over spilt guy." I wiped my nose with my shirt.

"That's the spirit, Rogue. And that's why *I* sleep with gals…well, mostly."

"I'm going to bed," I mumbled under my breath and shuffled to my room, Lyla close on my heels.

"And no more emotional binge day drinking!" Vee yelled after me. "It's not good for your body, mind, or soul."

She was right. It didn't solve anything, just helped me forget for the moment.

I lay on my bed, and Lyla grabbed her organic rubber ball from her ever-growing mountain of toys and lay on the bed next to me, gnawing it for a chew every few seconds. The sound of the rubber on her teeth was unnerving yet rhythmic. Just having the dog there made me feel tons better.

I couldn't catch any z's. My stomach hurt, and I was befuddled about how I'd gotten to this point with Falco. Why in the holy hell had I kissed him? I kept replaying the scenario in my mind, and the thought of being in his arms made my face flush and sent other red-hot feelings to my groin area. I refused to cry. I refused to cry. I refused to cry. Repeating it didn't help.

What finally helped me sleep was the remaining bottle of vodka Jack had left on my desk when he was over last. Had that been just last night?

I knew Vee would not condone excessive depressive drinking, but I didn't give a shit at that point. I downed multiple shots in succession to kill being awake.

****

I woke up thanking the gods it was Sunday, so I had no clients to face that day. I hadn't fallen asleep the night before even after the first few shots. I'd kept thinking about Falco so downed another three shots. The guy's emotionally absent and an a-hole for leading me on, yet thoughts of him kept my brain ransom.

I took a quick look at my week's appointments. Two clients most days but a whopping four on Thursday. Must have been a full moon this week. I was planning on staying in bed all day, but Vee wasn't having any of it.

"You know the saying, 'When you tumble off that hover board, you gotta brush yourself off and get your butt right back to balancing again so you can move forward.' "

"Why are you *so right* all the time?" I whined at her.

I had to get up and take Lyla for a walk, and then Vee made me do hot yoga for two hours.

I might have cried a bit, but sun salutations did that to me. Lyla did some down dogs with us. I don't think Lyla would call them that, though. She'd probably just call them downs since she's a dog and all.

Lyla, Vee, and Jack made the week semi-bearable with walks, yoga, and ghostly updates. I entertained myself with the dog's ball-bot and watched it interact with Sweepy and Brewster. They pinged out secret robot language. Probably coordinating to kill all humans. I did need to come up with a catchy nickname for the ball-bot. Maybe I'd call it Ballsy. That could be a good name.

"You probably freaked him out, Rogue," Jack said when he came over later in the week, bringing me a chai and an almond croissant for comfort. "Us bachelors are skittish creatures."

"Don't defend him." I pouted.

"Bright side is you didn't do the nasty with him and regret it."

"Yeah, there's that. But I *wanted* to and totally would have." I gave him my best sad face. "And still would," I said quieter.

"From what you told me earlier, you can just head your sad face and ass over to Hatty's and *get some* in exchange for a Read."

I smiled at him, remembering Sugar, the hunky former-governor look-alike bouncer, and other beautiful creatures at the house. I was tempted.

"I'm meeting friends out tonight," Jack said. "Wanna come?"

"No, I'd rather mope here, feel sorry for myself, and do nothing."

"Suit yourself, but I'm going to go have some fun. Sure you don't want to come with us and enjoy the night?"

I shook my head and waved to him as he left to savor the single life while I stayed at home and wished I'd just stuck with virtual relationships and the one-offs with Kel and never tasted Falco.

****

While the next week swam by, I felt a bit underwater and did my best to concentrate on my clients to make their lives better. I had not heard from Falco.

On Sunday, I awoke with multiple text pings and my doorbell ringing. I dragged myself out of slumber to open the door. It was Jack.

"They caught him!" He shoved his e-reader toward me. "They have a suspect in custody."

"Will you take Lyla out, please?" I grabbed his reader and scrolled through the news while he snagged Lyla's leash and led her out. I clicked on the KING 5 link.

Olivia Oliver burst onto the screen, a monstrous umbrella covering her perfect hair, the wind threatening to upend her hair and umbrella. "I'm bringing you breaking news, exclusively from KING 5. A suspect in the brutal murder of Sophia Brooks has been arrested and is currently in custody. Police were provided an anonymous hotline tip leading to the arrest of the suspect. Police are holding back on identifying the subject, as it remains an active investigation. I'll be back live as the situation and investigation unfold. For those of you who knew Ms. Brooks or who were fans of her work, the Knight family is hosting a memorial at the Knight Library of Knowledge on the UW campus this afternoon where we will be bringing you live coverage. You'll find the latest on this case and other breaking news right here on KING 5. This is Olivia Oliver, reporting."

Hmmm. Who'd been arrested? I scanned quickly through some earlier reports on the murder but didn't find much.

"Apparently, your boy-toy Falco *has* been busy," Jack said as he brought Lyla back up from her potty break, "and you've been too pouty to call him and get the latest gouge."

"He's not my boy-toy, and shouldn't he be calling me?"

He sat on the couch, let out a guttural sigh, and rested his head in his hands. "I had no idea they were close to arresting someone. Maybe my ghosts will go away?"

"Ghosts? As in multiple? Still?"

"You'd be surprised." He ran his hands across his face and through his hair. "They've kept me up for a week."

I looked up at him then. I had been enveloped in my own issue and didn't bother to *see* him.

Jack looked abysmal, his usually animated eyes and golden glow replaced by midnight crescents under his eyes and a chalky, pallid tone. I could feel his unnerved exhaustion.

I leaned forward, put my hand in his, and gave him a hug without thinking. His hand was frigid, his grasp clammy.

Then I saw what he saw. Ghosts. Dozens of ghosts. All talking or humming or moaning. Everywhere in his mind's view. I dropped his hand. "Oh fuck, I'm so sorry,

Jack. I didn't know it was that bad."

He shrugged. I had been a shitty friend not to notice.

"Can I nap on your couch…now? The ghosts don't seem to bother me much at your place, almost like I have more control over them here."

I nodded and tossed him a furry blanket and fluffy pillow for warmth. Those comfort items always made me feel better, and maybe they'd do the same for him.

What he'd said made me think. He was right. The level of indiscriminate pings had gone down the last few weeks ever since Lyla came home with me. My Sensitivities seemed to be more under control.

"You know what, Jack?" I looked over at him, but he was already asleep. I'd tell him my theory about the dog another time. I was pretty sure Lyla was somehow able to block or center extraneous pings and thoughts.

I had heard about specific breeds of dogs, cats, and even horses being conduits for Sensitives, either enhancing, absorbing, or blocking psychic abilities. Maybe Lyla was one of those dogs.

Lyla looked up at me.

"You a Sensitive dog?" I said to Lyla, patting her head.

She went toward my bedroom, turned around, and stopped.

"What? You think I need a nap? Yes, you *are* reading me." Lyla and I headed to my room to sleep for a few.

Chapter Fifteen

When we woke up, it was dusk. Jack was gone. I decided to take Lyla on a little walk-run. I needed some exercise. Lyla was a good running partner; she anticipated my rights and lefts and navigated me away from large puddles or other crap, literally, I shouldn't step in.

Before I knew it, she had steered me toward the police station.

"Dang it, Lyla." I slowed down our jog, giving the dog a glance. She tipped her head up and gave me her best *who me?* look.

We were near the front entrance of the station. The place was a madhouse. Media was all over the place, and multiple detectives and police were milling about, some armed with long guns.

At that moment, I knew Lyla had something to do with me not hearing rampant and random mind pings. Only when I homed in on someone specifically could I hear their thoughts.

I saw Detective Falco and Barrow leading a man out of the precinct and into an awaiting vehicle. News cameras were trying to break through the protective line, and onlookers were chanting.

The prisoner was wearing a dark-gray jumpsuit, his hands zip-tied in front of him. His eyes looked wild. This was the suspect in Ms. Brooks' and Domino's murders.

And apparently on the hook for other Sensitive murders as well.

The multiple protestors had signs that read *Sensitives are people, too!* and *Stop sex-worker crime!* denoting the belief that crimes against Sensitives and sex workers weren't taken seriously enough, I was sure.

The prisoner briefly looked at me through the crowd, and we locked eyes. Our minds collided with a thud.

"Help me," the prisoner's voice said so loudly inside my head it made my veins sizzle.

My breath caught in my throat, petrifying my body. I couldn't swallow or move but could taste bile buildup in my throat. I stood there, watching him in the dark vehicle. I could barely hang on to Lyla's leash. I was touched by the prisoner's confusion and utter helplessness.

He felt vulnerable, hopeless, and unsure of what was going on and how he had gotten into this predicament. I didn't know what to do with his thoughts. I slumped back against the retaining wall, slid down, and hit the cement hard. Lyla sat down and leaned into my collapsed body.

Detective Falco and a couple of blues drove away with the prisoner.

Detective Barrow looked down as he was walking back into the building. "Hey, Rogue, you looking for Falco?"

I didn't answer him right away. I was out of breath. "No, Lyla decided to take me for a walk, and we ended up here…apparently to see the media circus."

"Yeah, that was crazy. Want coffee or something?"

"Yes, I think so."

He held his hand out to me. A true test. I grabbed his

hand for balance, picked myself up off the ground, and consciously tried not to pick up thoughts from him. Nothing. I let go of his hand and followed him into the station, Lyla in tow.

"She's getting bigger." He gave Lyla a head pat.

"You think, so?" I looked down at Lyla and smiled. "I'm not sure how she could get any bigger—she's monstrous as it is. No offense, Lyla." I scruffed her head with both hands.

"So I'm sure Falco told you the details on this guy?"

"No, we're really not talking. He's been so busy, and so have I."

"I can't share much with you, but we got a tip on a guy, and the details provided gave us means for a warrant, so we were able to search his belongings. The NoODxone ball cap was the clincher. It had blood spatter that matched Ms. Brooks."

"You sure? He just doesn't seem like the murdering type."

"How so?"

"Well, he seemed rather harmless, not the type of psycho who gets off on strangling or stabbing someone. Just a feeling." I felt guilty that what I told Falco about the ball cap might have resulted in this guy's arrest.

"Hmmm, you sure? Evidence typically doesn't lie."

"All I know is that what I Read off him was a far cry from the guy I saw kill two people."

Barrow's phone rang. "It's Falco. I've got to take it." He moved several feet away so I could not hear the conversation.

I eavesdropped without thinking, pinging into his thoughts.

He mentioned I was at the station and asked Falco

what was up between us anyway, to which he replied, "Nothing." Like the thought of him being interested in me was preposterous. Jerk. Barrow asked if he was sure, and Falco said of course he was sure. Whatever.

They talked a bit about the case, so I jumped out of Barrow's mind and out of their conversation. I wasn't meaning to spy. OK, so I *was* meaning to spy.

"So...how's Falco?" I asked Barrow after he hung up.

"Fine. He is signing paperwork at mid-precinct for the transferred prisoner."

I nodded.

"So I've got to tie some things up. Should take me about fifteen minutes. You wanna stick around, and then we can grab a bite to eat?"

"Uh, sure, I guess...like a date?"

"Well, yeah, why not?" He looked at me. "You gotta eat, right?"

"Yeah, gotta eat," I said after him.

Weird. I hadn't thought of him in that way, but he was boyishly handsome, and his recent revival made him a nice guy, so what the hell? It's not like I was going to get any action from Falco who was distant at the least and disinterested in me at the most. Talk about mixed signals.

Lyla and I waited around for Barrow to finish making a few calls, then we left in his truck and went to 13 Coins in Pioneer Square. Lyla stayed in the truck. She was tuckered out, probably from all the excitement earlier at the station.

Barrow made small talk at the restaurant, and I nodded and smiled. I wasn't into it. I kept thinking about *Falco*.

"I'm no mind reader," Barrow said, "but I can tell you're distracted. Everything OK?"

"Oh, besides you arresting a killer that doesn't fit the vibe and the fact that I am interested in someone who couldn't care less about me? Other than those two things, I'm OK. Everything's great." God, I sounded like a bitch.

"I knew it," he said excitedly. He didn't seem the least bit intimidated by my unfavorable attitude. "When I asked Falco on the phone if you guys were a thing, he said you weren't, but I guess I should have asked you."

"Well, we're definitely not *a thing*."

Our food showed up, so I was able to stuff my face without saying anything else. Barrow's new demeanor was pleasant, and he was nice to look at, but he wasn't Falco.

"Well, I'd like to keep you as a good friend, if nothing else," he said between bites. "You know I'll always have your back after what you did for me. I was a miserable person. And miserable to be around."

I smiled, nodded at him, and downed more of my eggs Benedict. We finished our meal with a random conversation about sports and weather.

Barrow took me and Lyla home.

Chapter Sixteen

I flipped on my e-reader to watch more coverage about the case and the media conference. I of course replayed video portions that had Detective Falco in them. Even though he wasn't into me, I still liked looking at him.

Falco's media brief included that the arrest was based on DNA evidence found in the arrested person's belongings and placing the accused at Ms. Brooks' home as well as the suspect having connections to Hatty's House and Domino.

He also noted that they were still looking for any additional information, so if anyone saw something or knew something, even something minor, they should please contact the station's tip line.

I scrolled down to get more information about the accused and to do some more self-sleuthing. His name was Drew Baltimore. He was an unhomed navy veteran and a musician who often played at local bars and festivals, which helped supplement his VA benefits and what he made as a street musician.

Last year, Drew was invited to play with bands during the Bumbershoot and Sasquatch Festivals. He seemed like an interesting character. Not a murderer.

One posting said he had past issues with traumatic stress and fugue states. He had been exposed to biological weapons while serving in the military, which was the cause of his, and thousands of other veterans', ongoing psychological and other health issues.

The article said Drew had an arrest record for minor infractions. His parents said he was a free spirit who had never been violent and was never formally charged with anything.

He was described as a creative genius but also as a lost soul who would often go into states of amnesia. When he had one of his memory lapses, he would wander aimlessly but harmlessly until he eventually ended up at the VA for treatment.

The police had taken him in for vagrancy on occasion in the winter, mostly because they knew him, and if it was bitter cold, they worked to get him *three hots and a cot*. Then they'd call his folks to pick him up.

I wanted to know more. I knew this guy wasn't a killer. I could feel it.

"Vee," I shouted to my roommate, "will you watch Lyla? I'm going to take the car out."

"Uh, sure...wait...you're taking the car out?" she said. "You got sick last time...what's going on with you?"

"I don't know, but since Lyla has been here, I am getting *better*."

"Getting better? Do we need to find another livelihood?" She smiled.

"No, I'm still reading clear as day, but I'm not getting sick because I can be more selective with pings—it's weird, but I think it's got something to do with the dog."

"Hmmm, OK then, let's talk about this later." She gave me the side eye and called Lyla into her room.

Vee was getting just as attached to Lyla as I was.

Which reminded me I needed to follow up with Falco, or the station since he wasn't talking to me, to see if anyone from Ms. Brooks' family had a claim for the dog. Not sure what I'd do if I had to give her up. Maybe run to Canada with her?

I drove away and wasn't sure what I wanted to accomplish on this mission. I *did* want to go back to Hatty's and poke around.

I parked in their lot and maneuvered my way through a smorgasbord of large, black, parked e-SUVs with tinted windows. Sugar had been right about all the vehicles looking the same. I made a screenshot of Drew's photo so I could ask questions about him.

My brawny and beautiful bouncer greeted me at the door. I told him that I was hoping to talk to Sugar about letting me chat with some of the folks there. He radioed inside and got the go-ahead.

"Typically, Sugar keeps customers' info confidential, but she said you'd find out anyway," the actor-governor doppelgänger said, smiling and revealing amazing-pearly whites. "So whatcha got for me?"

I showed him my screenshot of Drew.

"Drew is a regular customer. Don't remember having issues with him. He is polite, professional, and he tips well. When he was having one of his memory fits, he was a little off but never aggressive. He didn't go in, would just wander by, and we'd vape and shoot the shit for a while. The guy wasn't even a smoker and definitely not a killer."

"OK." I nodded and made mental notes. "Thanks." I went into Hatty's and met with Sugar.

"Drew was a sweetie, came by here every couple of months," she said. "Visited Heidi or Domino or both—

God, he was crushed when she died, cried in Heidi's arms when he found out. I don't know about Ms. Brooks, but there is no way Drew would hurt Domino. Even when he was not himself, he was never hostile, always easygoing. From what I read about how Domino and Ms. Brooks died, that's just not him. I told the detective the same thing."

"Falco?" My heart skipped as I mentioned his name.

"Mmm-hmmm." She drew it out. "Wish that man would come around for non-police business. But not sure I'm his type." She frowned. "I've thrown a lot of good vibes his way, but he isn't having any of it."

"Yeah, I don't think I'm his type either, but can't say I didn't try."

"Well, as I told you before, if you ever need some love, you can come here and get it anytime."

"Duly noted. Guess I've been holding out for him."

Sugar just gave me that *been there, done that* smile.

I left Hatty's and drove to the station. I called Falco from police reception, but he didn't answer. I called Barrow, and he met me.

"What's up?" Barrow asked.

"Wanted to talk about the case…about Drew Baltimore," I said. "I don't think he's your guy."

"OK, Falco's around here somewhere, and he's lead on this case." He pivoted his head around, probably looking for Falco.

The great thing about offices made of mostly glass was I could see through the walls.

"There he is." Barrow pointed.

My pulse raced and my breath caught at the sight of him across the atrium in another glass-walled room.

Falco glanced our way, gave Barrow a questioning

look, and stared right at me. Then he averted his gaze like I hadn't been there. Barrow walked to meet him in the hall. They conversed for a few minutes. Falco glanced at me once more, then nodded his head and walked the other way. I felt rebuffed.

Barrow returned to his desk.

"So what's up?" I questioned.

"He's in the middle of interviewing Mr. Baltimore's folks right now," he said. "Drew is back in the station for more questioning, and Falco let him see his folks."

"So…what, I wait?"

"He told me to take an informal statement."

"Really? Maybe I should make an informal appointment?" I was irritated and hurt.

He didn't answer me.

"You know what? Tell Falco, *informally*…to forget it." I walked away from Barrow's desk, shaking my head. Why did Falco insist on inventing new ways to make me feel rejected and hurt? I bit my lip to stop the tears. But they popped up in my lower eyes, and my nose started to run. I hurried down the hall, unescorted.

To my right, I saw Falco in one of the adjoining halls through the glass. I took a quick right down the next passageway.

Two blues were leading Drew out of a room. I stopped and followed them, piggy-backing on their access. They led him into another hallway and waited for an elevator. They were talking and joking with each other, not paying attention to their prisoner. Drew looked at me in a daze, and I took the chance, reached out, and brushed my hand firmly down his back.

It was just a brief touch but enough to know he didn't do it. He was being set up. So much was running through my head I had to get out of there and think. I snuck back out of the hallway.

I drove home and took Lyla for a long walk. I thought about the info I'd taken from Drew. Although I hadn't gotten his permission, I felt the situation warranted my decision to Read him without consent.

Drew had no idea why he was being targeted or why someone would plant DNA evidence. But I had the feeling Drew was more intricately connected with the murders than even he himself knew about.

While Drew loved Domino, he didn't seem to have a recent connection with Sophia Brooks, although he somehow knew her, and the police had found his DNA in her home and her DNA in his belongings, including a NoODxone cap, spattered with her blood.

The evidence would be difficult to fight. Drew was just as confused and had no alibi as he had recently begun a fugue bender and his recollections were sketchy. Barrow had told me they couldn't find any closed-circuit video to speak of, which was odd in this society of recording *everything*.

When I got home, I searched online for details on how and why evidence was mishandled or planted, hoping to find some correlation or way out for Drew being arrested. I had no idea who was murdering Sensitives and who had murdered Miss Brooks, so I was not sure where to begin.

I texted Falco.

—*Drew didn't do it. I'm positive you have the wrong guy.*—

I checked my phone for the next couple of hours. No response from him. Figured.

135

Chapter Seventeen

Vee and I ordered dinner delivery, and I tackled a load of laundry, listening to streaming desert metal, hoping my mind would be mesmerized into thinking of a way to get Drew out of his predicament. I was stumped.

It was late, and I was ready for bed, putting away laundry, still mulling over how I was going to prove Drew's innocence. Should I try and go directly to the station again? Would anyone even believe me?

No response from Falco on my earlier text. No surprise. Fucking ghoster.

Deep in thought, I heard a knock at my bedroom door. I hadn't sensed any visitors, and Lyla didn't perk up to alert me. That meant the one visitor I couldn't Read. Falco.

"Yeah?" I said.

It *was* Falco.

"Hey." He wandered into my room, shutting the door, like he fucking owned the place. But his voice sounded hesitant. "Vee, uh, your roomie, said you were in here...said I could come to say hello."

"So, 'Hello.' You said it," I snapped, putting my last laundered pair of socks away and slamming the drawer. "Now you can go." My voice sounded harsher than I had wanted it to. I was taken aback at how upset I still was.

When I stood back up, he was looking at me, his dark-copper eyes intense. Blazing and fierce like that day by the pier before his police-work excuse cock-blocked me.

I stepped closer to him in a challenging stance, fired up, choked up, and elated from him just being there. His body gave off sex fumes meant to asphyxiate my better judgment. His presence sent my pulse racing and the blood rushing to multiple parts of my anatomy, some lower than others.

God, I still wanted him. His rugged smell was a drug I wanted to breathe in and lose myself in. My vivid recall of how his masculine aroma melted and mixed with the ocean scent of the Sound from our make-out session by the pier was so strong I could taste it.

I was immediately wet, my nipples erect with arousal. Why the fuck did his mere existence do things to me I couldn't explain? I wanted to not like him, not want him. Why couldn't I talk myself out of falling for him?

My room was dim and lit only by my bedside table lamp, so I had to look deep to search the copper color in his eyes for any thoughts or indications on why he was there.

Besides his eyes' flaming, metallic intensity, I found nothing behind them, but I was speechless just the same. His effect on me was potent.

"Rogue, look, I'm sorry." His voice was in smooth rhythm to the blood pulsing in my ears, my core." I just…" He hesitated, but instead of finishing his sentence, he stepped forward and pulled me toward him.

His touch brought up an acute mix of uncertainty and desire. His thirsty grasp on my waist said he wanted to drink me in just as much as I wanted to devour him. I looked up at him with a confused glance. Where the hell did this just come from?

I was about to protest. I needed him to explain himself. But I didn't get a word out.

He stopped my questioning with a full kiss. A fucking kiss for the record books.

Forceful at first, then light, then forceful again. My mind was slow to react, still waiting for the rest of an apology, but my traitorous body gave me away and pulsed toward him, taking whatever he dished out and swallowing it whole.

My mouth, with its turncoat memory, unlocked and opened in response to his osculation. My lips pulsating, parting, and delivering back to him, lip flesh to lip flesh. My tongue seeking his out and his obliging with equal exploration and unbridled fervor.

Slow down, I told myself. *Stop and embrace the pre-fuck. Sense and savor each touch, each graze. Enjoy it as fleeting, like sunshine during a Seattle spring.* I chose to slow the flow and ebb to relish in the now.

The taste of Falco's lips was less salty than the Ivar's french fry taste from before. A much sweeter, magnified flavor. Maybe because I'd been longing for his lush lips again. His same tight lip pressure my masturbation muse for the past few weeks. It's almost embarrassing, but it had gotten me through. *OK, Rogue. Focus.*

Falco flopped his jacket off onto the floor with a muffle and lifted me onto my dresser, the variety of items on top shoved toward the wall, most falling to the floor with several rattles and a scraping thud. The thud was probably my white noise machine, which luckily had an extended warranty.

The hard slickness of the furniture top made my ass

slide back and then forward as he grabbed my waist and tugged me toward him, forcing my crotch into his. I wrapped my legs around him, pulling the core of my being against him, clinging. I hated to be clingy, but what the hell? I didn't really want to give him the chance to pull away this time.

I untucked my way beneath his dress shirt, feeling his slim, athletic build. His warm, firm skin sparking desire. He shivered. Because I couldn't read him, I hoped it was with desire. All signs pointed to *yes*.

I unfastened his necktie and slicked it off with a muffled slide. *God, I'd like to blindfold him with that while going down on him for the first time.* I appreciated that he still dressed nice for work. I hadn't yet seen him in his formal cop uniform. Not sure I could stop from tearing it off him if I did. Hoping that'd be a scenario saved for another day.

I slowly unbuttoned his dress shirt, and my mind wandered. I had to lean in to focus on the feels, the sights, the tastes, the sounds. Because I couldn't Read him or know what he was thinking, I had to concentrate to stay in the moment.

Stay out of your head, I kept telling myself. *Just keep your attention on the things you can sense.* My breathing, his breathing, what his lips were doing, what else I was looking forward to him doing with those lips and vice versa.

I didn't want to get ahead of myself and jinx it like last time, so I stayed *there*, tasting his tongue on mine, his lips around mine, mine around his. Appreciating the sensation of my saliva comingling with his, relishing his warmth and the wetness.

His taste and his smell. Hints of warm cocoa and

whiskey on his breath and…something I couldn't quite put my taste buds on. Whatever it was, I wanted to savor his flavor forever.

I undid the last button on Falco's crisp, tailored shirt and pushed the top of it down over his shoulders with a crinkle. I slid my hands over his skin before flinging the shirt aside. He shuddered and took in a breath.

Then it was my turn to take in a breath. Holy shit. I knew he was fit, but fuck. He was sculpted and tight underneath, a magnificent specimen under wraps for far too long. I looked up at him, his eyes still aflame, my eyes reflected in his.

He traced up the sides of my thighs, and my pussy fluttered like a bird, taking off. He slid his hands around to my ass, lifting my paper-thin tank slightly to touch bare skin on my lower back. My flesh was molten, his touch melting into it, bringing roughness and silky smoothness into infused warmth.

He slid me off the dresser so my feet were on the floor. Because he had about six inches in height on me, I tipped up on my toes and snagged his lips in a kiss with mine. He started kissing back and then stopped. My mind raced, and I felt dizzy, my temples pulsating with confusion.

Fuck. Not this again? I let out a huge breath-sigh that maybe sounded a little like a whimper to him and then held my breath. I looked up at him, trying to read his eyes, trying to Read his intentions, which I knew I couldn't.

"Rogue, breathe," Falco said.

I inhaled and exhaled, striving not to hyperventilate. I fucking wanted him so bad I could taste it.

"Look at me. Grab your phone…"

I must have looked confused because he said it again.

"Grab your phone. We need to complete consent before we go any further."

I snapped out of it and nodded.

He must have seen relief cross my face. "I promise I won't run out of here this time." His voice was buttery, eyes fierce.

He grabbed his device from his jacket on the floor. I grabbed my device from where I had knocked it off the dresser. I opened my app, he opened his app, and we swapped.

We each thumb-printed the needed areas, swapped back, and placed our devices back on the dresser in case we needed to update later with a voice-activated request, additional consent, or rescind.

I was shaking and nervous as hell. Maybe I had hoped Falco would run out? Did I really want to go through with this? I had been emotionally fine until just now. I had never fucked someone I'd fallen for, and I'd never fallen for someone I'd fucked. In fact, I'd never fallen. Ever. These were uncharted waters for me.

He must have sensed my angst, so he grabbed my shaking hands firmly and tucked them around the small of his own back. His skin felt like flame-warmed satin, and I stroked his lumbar area with my fingertips, savoring the icy-hot sensation and slickness of his bare skin.

He looked in my eyes and grinned. I melted in his softened gaze, his eyes creamy marbleized dark amber, wholly enveloping me in. I was completely at ease, completely at his beckoning. All was right in the world.

Whoa. I felt like *I* had just been Pushed. He breathed

out in a sigh, and I took him in, mesmerized.

He tilted my face upward, his strong hands partially caressing my neck and lower face, sending sparkling sensations down to my breasts, my lungs heaving up toward him.

He soul kissed me, and I moaned lightly. His tongue moved around my mouth, meeting up and staying entangled, each tongue taking turns leading movement. Our lips were locked, dovetailed together as one breathing and pulsating entity. I could not get enough of his welcoming lips and tongue.

He broke off the mash-up to snag at my lips with his, making a light flicking sound before moving his attention toward my ear, breathing in and out heavily, the sensation sending an instant message to my pussy to get ready.

He grazed his lips and tongue down my neck, meshing his hand with the hair falling out of my bun at my neck. The feel of him touching my hair, slightly tugging it as portions fluttered down, made me juicy hot.

I wanted to see and experience more of him. All of him. I undid his belt and pants and yanked them partway down so he could kick them off. Falco's fingers entwined in my tank, which he lifted over my head and dropped with a swoosh. My breasts and nipples became additionally aroused from the slight breeze that action caused.

He tugged my panty-less sleep pants down. My pussy was moist and ready for action. He caressed his hands over my ass and pulled me in, his aroused cock tight and housed in his dark briefs, beckoning for me to free him. I obliged and swiped his briefs down and off his athletic legs.

He maneuvered me backward to my bed and lowered me down slowly, his weight on top of me. The mattress was a soft cushiony landing for what would come next.

He kissed my jawline, moved down to my neck and to my breasts. He rubbed them, suckled them one at a time, softly biting the nipples, scraping them lightly with his teeth, sending bolts of buzzing sparks down to my pussy.

He kissed below my breasts and down to my stomach. My body pulsating and eager for him to move lower.

He ran his hands down my inner thighs, leveraging his strength to spread them apart, repositioning his head and face inside. His warm skin and breath against my pussy triggered a jolt, making me damp and ready. His wet mouth tasted me for the first time.

Falco's tongue licked up my vulva, zoning in on my clit with enthusiasm. He licked and flicked with force, making me wriggle with intense pleasure, my soft bed sheets muffling my movement.

He first traced his fingers around my lips, teasing me, pleasing me before inserting two fingers, pushing into me. I was so slick from wanting him I felt ready to burst, and I pushed back with my pelvis into his thrusts.

My hands clutched his hair, and my pelvis bucked toward him. He continued lapping my clit while finger-fucking me. I wanted him to slow down the flood, but the gates had already opened, and I couldn't slow down the gush.

He licked my hole and thrust his tongue deep inside of me, making me explode in his mouth, my body gyrating and shuddering. I pushed my hands on his head

Tobin Rayne

to go deeper. I shuddered with multiple climaxes, a loud "oh my God" erupting from my mouth in a breathy gasp.

He started his slow ascent back up, taking his time as he kissed and licked my stomach, rib cage, and breasts, my pussy still pulsating with pleasure, my breath catching.

I wanted him inside me. Needed him inside me.

He arrived at the top and kissed me, and I could taste myself on his lips. His hard cock was just between my legs. I was sopping. He circled his dick tip at the center of my entrance, a mere sample of what he would give me soon, and I shuddered with expectation.

I internally begged for it, but I couldn't Push him to do it, so I had to say it out loud.

"Falco, please." I groaned and broke the word silence of our moaned fucking.

He plunged his dick deep into me, and I came again, harder, moaning out loud. He slowed down his motion and fucked me with long and steady strides, building momentum, snagging at my lips with his lips on the way down while his dick pulsed inside of me, rhythmic and filling.

"Rogue." He said my name, a sigh on his lips, making me come again, hard, taking my breath and turning it into a loud moan back into his ear while he thrust and burst deep inside of me. My body shuddered beneath his, our hips locked together.

"Fuck, Rogue…" he said with a sigh and a soul kiss. I was consumed yet content by his weight on top of me, not wanting to move, wanting to have him between my legs, to keep his full weight on me for as long as possible. Forever would have been nice.

He kissed me, rolled to one side, pulled me in close,

144

and burrowed into me as if we were two parts of a single celestial body meant to fit and piece together as one.

His warmth was intoxicating, and his snug embrace and steady breathing immersed me into an immediate, dreamless sleep. His name on my lips and his taste on my tongue.

I slept that night. Amazingly. When I got up, Falco had already gone.

Chapter Eighteen

I was really falling for this guy. *Had* fallen for this guy. And I felt helpless and exhilarated that my thoughts were completely devoted to him. I had a smug expression that encased my face, grinning wide when I thought of him.

I went for a walk with Lyla and did a couple of hours of rowing machine, stationary bike, and weights at home, trying to stay busy. By noon, when Falco hadn't made contact, I texted him. Once. OK, so I left him three or four texts. Who's counting? He didn't respond.

By the early evening, desolation weighed on me, and doubt sank in like chunky, low-lying fog in the Sound, smothering me—my smug grin had been replaced by *sad face*. I couldn't get out of it so retreated inside myself and to my room to lock the world out. My shining light was Lyla, who rested her head on my back as I curled in a semi-fetal position.

I went through the motions the next couple of weeks. No word from Falco. Besides the occasional client, I found it difficult to get out of bed. One week stretched to two. Two into three.

I could not find a balance between the multiple stalker-like texts and messages I left him and wanting to ignore my feelings for him fully. I wanted to pretend we'd never happened. That night had never happened.

Vee left me to withdraw into myself, which I was

thankful for. I knew she was going to run out of patience soon. Jack came to visit and tried to perk me up. He said he had been seeing spirits less and less and feeling great.

I did get out of bed and out of my house to make sure I took Lyla on walks and did venture out a couple of times to go to the station to speak with Detective Barrow, not about Falco, but to see if he could share any case updates and the latest on Drew.

Barrow told me Drew was out on bail and staying with his folks. He also added that Falco had been out of town on police business. I gave Barrow my best *as if I care* shrug just for dramatics.

I was losing hope of Falco and I ever reconnecting. Typically, I was OK with a one-night thing. I had just been caught off guard by his intensity that night and then nothing after. I was used to knowing what was going on in someone's head. Why hadn't I set expectations with him up front so I didn't feel so dumbfounded and hella embarrassed for being so dumbfounded? I tried to concentrate on my clients and taking care of Lyla, which semi kept my mind off Falco.

I kept physically busy by doing yoga, stretching, and taking Lyla on frequent walks. The walks were especially helpful when I woke up in the middle of the night, not being able to fall back asleep. All because my mind was either thinking about the murders or about Falco. But the walks were also a time when my mind wandered the most, more space to think about him. I was pathetic.

So I might have had one, two, or three self-love nights with a bit of online help. But, hell, I was desperate for some Falco love. Even if it was pretend.

One of those super-late nights, instead of a self-induced sexual release, I took Lyla for a stroll, trying to scrub Falco's image out of my mind.

On the way back, about a half mile from my block, we ran into Falco. Well, not literally. I saw his car and stopped in my tracks. He was sitting in it, and he wasn't alone.

I stepped off a couple of feet to the side to hide behind a touring van so I could observe. Lyla sat behind me and stayed still, which was super cute because it looked like she was trying to hide, too.

Falco was having what sounded and looked like an animated argument, and my stomach fell when I realized it was a female voice he was having a quarrel with.

I was instantly jealous and then uncomfortable because I was eavesdropping on their heated discussion. But then I didn't care as I wanted to know the reason he was ghosting me.

I thought about backtracking and walking the other way as I was only a dozen or so blocks from home, but I didn't want to be seen. Instead, Lyla and I stood frozen, too uncomfortable to move. OK, so I also wanted to know who she was and what they were arguing about.

Of course, this was one of those times when being able to read thoughts really came in handy. Too bad one of those in the discussion was Falco so I couldn't Read shit from him. But *she* was an open book, so I tapped into the woman he was with.

Her thought structure was all jumbled in a mess of emotions and topics and different directions. Something about secrets and conspiracy and murder. She was excited. And afraid. And manic. They were talking about the case Falco was working on. The case *I* was working on. Her inner voice sounded familiar.

She opened the door to get out, and their argument spilled out of the car. The woman was wearing a ball cap, hoody, and dark glasses, apparently wanting to be incognito. But I knew who it was. Olivia Oliver from KING 5. My favorite peppy journalist.

Their voices weren't loud enough for me to hear, so, me being me, I pinged for just a moment so I could Read parts of the conversation.

Olivia had been providing Falco information on a couple of cases he was working on, and she was not happy he wasn't equally providing what he knew back.

"I don't care if it is police business," she said. "I'm putting my career and objectiveness on the line just talking to you. I've provided you some deep background info. I don't know why you can't provide the same fucking courtesy."

He shrugged and shook his head from within his car. His hands gripped and ungripped the steering wheel; his fingers moved up and down in bursts.

Miss Oliver's typical lively, friendly, and very prepared dialogue was angry and pitched. She threw in a couple more swear words. Some of my favorites. Not very professional but probably justified as I could see where she was coming from. I wanted to swear up and down at Falco myself.

"Whatever, Detective. This was supposed to be a mutual information-gathering meet-up, and you keep holding back info. I'm done."

She threw her arms up, tossed a folded wad of paper at him, slammed the car door, and started walking down the block, heading straight for where Lyla and I were hiding. I tried to shrink back even more. She snagged her mobile out of her pocket, looked my way, and caught my eye. She had a panicked look on her face.

I pinged out a *nothing to worry about* vibe, and she looked relieved, blinking twice before she headed toward the corner. She waited about five minutes and hopped into another vehicle that had pulled up.

Falco's vehicle left shortly after. I might have given his car the finger on his way by.

"What the eff was that all about?" I said to Lyla as I steered her leash out of our hiding place and started walking home. I really wanted to know the details of what they'd been talking about. If I could just have another five minutes with Olivia.

Maybe I could talk her into coming into my office for a complimentary Read? But was my curiosity more out of jealousy and wanting to know what was up with her and Falco or about the case? My answer didn't jibe with me trying to avoid conflict of interests associated with a Read.

Lyla and I continued our walk home, my brain firing, not knowing what to do next.

Chapter Nineteen

I reached out to my eff buddy Kel to hook up, hoping he'd take my mind and body off Falco. But when we met, he said it had to remain strictly plutonic. He had followed my Push and was accepted and enrolled into University of Washington's specialized human dynamics coursework with a full scholarship based on a design he'd presented.

He also had met a woman in his classes who he was serious about, so our time together could be only as friends. I got it. I'd have to find myself another eff buddy.

I wondered if I was even in the mood for carnal pursuits as Falco's disappearing trick had me clouded, feeling sorry for myself, and maybe too pitiful and lacking energy to even get laid. He'd literally and figuratively kind of fucked me up.

I could always head to Hatty's or one of my virtual reality online subscriptions or other online options.

Vee forcibly encouraged me to move around and get out occasionally. Now that I could go out in public without getting sick, she tried to drag me around on her daily errands. She also kept me on track with my client schedule. She was the best business partner, roomie, and friend ever.

"What is wrong with me?" I lamented one day when she forced me to make juice smoothies with her for breakfast.

"Well, Rogue," she said while shoving unwieldy celery stalks into the blender, "you have what us mere mortals call *a broken heart*."

"I don't think so." I gave her a weird look and laughed.

"It's true. You can't eat, you either can't sleep at all or you sleep too much, you're depressed, you said you wanna die—and it all revolves around Falco. That's a broken heart...or at least a rip."

I shook my head at her.

"But the good thing about a broken or torn heart," she said, "is that it will fix itself eventually, and you will feel better. It just takes time. And I know because I've been there, many times before."

Fucking wise roomie. I gulped down my smoothie while she was looking online. Probably downloading other terrible healthy recipes to destroy my donut addiction.

"I knew it!" she screeched, surprising me so I coughed up a bit of the smoothie. She shoved her e-reader in front of my eyes. "Look, it's Lyla...or dogs that look just like her. I knew there was something special about her!"

I looked. Vee was right. The dogs in the online photos looked to be the same breed as Lyla.

"Hmmm." I perused the pics.

"And Lyla's breed is Sensitive!"

"You don't say." I looked at the online breed description. I had already known something was amazing about Lyla besides being the most intuitive and adorable dog ever.

Vee read the article out loud as we headed

downstairs. These dogs had been bred to accentuate, distill, and deflect Sensitive powers. I'd noticed a difference in myself being able to block or pinpoint Reads easier after Lyla came into my life. I could go out in public now and not get a serious headache. Lyla had made my ability to *be present* possible.

"And the effect is cumulative—her ability to offset rogue pings aggregates, so this could be a permanent fix for you!" she said.

"OMG, are you crying?" I smiled at her.

She nodded as a couple of tears ran down her cheeks. "That means your life as you've known it is going to change—and..." She stumbled.

"And you can finally stop coddling me?" I finished for her.

"Yes...and no. Rogue, this means you can do anything. You have endless possibilities."

"Uh, OK," I said with a pouty face. "Then I want Falco back."

"Well, we'll work on that one later. Right now we have a morning client, so let's get downstairs and start our workday!"

I rolled my eyes, and Vee put her hand on my shoulder to steer me the rest of the way downstairs so we could get to work.

****

"A party, really?" I said to Jack over the phone later that evening. "Did Vee put you up to this?"

"Yes, but I was going to ask you to come anyway. It's my birthday, Rogue, and I want you to celebrate with me."

"And a hundred or so of your closest friends?"

"Yes, and it'll be fun. Vee said you seem to be OK

153

in crowds now. And you need to get out and *do* something. Plus you can bring Lyla."

"Yeah, but I'm not the party type."

"How do you know? Vee said you haven't been to one…at least not in the last decade or so that she knows about."

I shrugged. I guessed it wouldn't hurt to change out of my pajamas into something nice and drag my sad self out of the condo. "Fine, I'll go, but only because it's your birthday."

****

I was not looking forward to the festivities, as I had become accustomed to avoiding public gatherings most of my life and associated groups of people with being sick. This was a swanky party. Vee and Josie were going, too. So at least I'd have them to talk to and Lyla to hang with.

The party was the following weekend at Jack's place. He lived in his family estate's pool house, which was down the hill from the expansive manor. To call the place a *pool house* was laughable. It was huge and luxurious, almost a mini mansion on its own.

As soon as I arrived, I was overcome with a feeling of ease and joy. I looked around for it and located the sign at the entrance.

Sensitive Emitter(s) in use.

By the weight of the Emits, Jack and his family had spared no expense as they hired a highly powerful Emitter…or two. The fog I'd been in since Falco's absence was becoming fainter, and my outlook was clearing up. It was shaping up to be a great evening.

"Damn, I sound positive," I said. "Gotta appreciate a talented Emitter."

I looked down at Lyla; she seemed to nod in approval. The Emitters were able to work their magic on me with the dog right next to me, which I found curious. Perhaps Lyla only blocked unpleasant or unwanted pings? Or just ones I was averse to? Which was good as I really needed good vibes tonight.

I took Lyla back to Jack's room. Lyla jumped right on his bed and made herself at home, burrowing into his comforter, asleep in seconds. I made my way out to the party.

OK, so the party was enjoyable and had something for everyone. Mesmerizing music, killer dancing, appalling karaoke, amazing food, flowing drinks, party games, enticing legal and illicit edibles, and otherworldly attractions.

Some of the escorts from Hatty's House had been contracted out to keep the party lively. I stayed in the background, still not adapted to being around so many people. Plus, the fact I was socially awkward as hell. Always had been, probably always would be. Luckily, the hired Emitters helped with that feeling.

I was having an amusing time just watching folks. I still received a ping or two, but they were controllable, and I could turn them up or down or off. I was really liking this new capability and protection that Lyla provided me.

My favorite part of the night was the vodka ice luge carved into a quarter-size version of a lifelike, lounging, frozen Jack Knight. The trick was to pour the shot over the frozen canal near Jack's faux neck and catch it near his iced privates. Perhaps the party planners didn't think how that might play out, or maybe they did, and it was all in good fun.

I took several locally distilled icy shots from Jack's faux-ice mechanism and chased them with a Washington Lucy Rose apple wedge dipped in fresh engineered coffee grounds. Only in Seattle.

"How's it going?" Jack asked from behind me.

"Super great, I think I have this down." I turned around with two icy shots in hand. "Probably could get a spot on the Olympics luge-drinking team."

"I don't think drinking's an Olympic sport…yet." He smiled.

I smiled back and handed him one of the shots.

"You look very fucking hot tonight." He clinked my shot glass.

"I know, right?" I appreciated the *fucking hot* comment because I felt pretty good. "It's amazing what you can do with a little makeup and your own personal Healer at home." Both Jack's and my burn scars had healed meticulously. "Happy birthday, Jack—and thanks for dragging me out. I'm having fun."

We both downed our shots and chased them with the coffee-dipped apple slices. He gestured toward me and grinned widely.

"What?" I asked.

"It's just I've barely seen you out of the house, let alone out socially. It's nice to see you having a good time."

"Yeah, I'm sure it's in part due to the amazing Emitters you hired. They really know how to make a gal feel at ease. I'm impressed."

"Glad you're impressed. You deserve to have some fun, you know."

I nodded at him, and we both smiled. The official party photog took that moment to pop in front of us and snap a photo.

"That's bothersome," I said.

"You get used to it," Jack said. "It'll be on the top scan of the gossip section before tomorrow morning."

"Uh, it *is* tomorrow morning." I glanced at my device and read 1:37 a.m. already. Wow. Those Emitters really knew how to make fun time fly.

I checked on Lyla and let her out into the backyard to relieve herself. Such a beautiful, chilly night. I took my shoes off, feeling the frigid turf on my feet. Super soft and silky. At least I think it was. With an Emitter around I never knew what was real and what was emitter-fed.

I called out to Lyla to see where she was. She didn't come back immediately.

I instantly felt uneasy and a bit ill. The relaxed atmosphere I'd just felt the moment before flipped 180 degrees in a flash. Lyla was frozen on point by the yard's edge, eyeing past the pool house opposite of the Knight mansion and down toward the distant lake.

A menacing growl was originating from her throat, and I could see her hair standing on edge from the moon's glow.

"What's wrong girl?" I struggled out. "Whatcha see?"

I looked around, trying to catch where her gaze was. A human shape was standing in the tree line below, barely noticeable and shadowed but seemed to be fixated on the goings-on in Jack's bungalow.

I felt a nauseating presence, a weight on my neck and head bearing down on me until I was physically crouched down, one hand on the ground to steady myself. Then, just as suddenly as it had impacted me, the horrible burden lifted. I was able to clear my head, and Lyla was calm.

I looked back down toward the lake, and the shadow had left. Had to be a powerful force to affect me like that with Lyla around. I was sure she'd blocked what she could, but it had been overwhelming.

There were all types of Emitters, and this one emanated the opposite of feel-good vibes by pinging out negative feelings.

"What or who the eff was that?" I said to Lyla. She shook herself off and gave me a large wet lick as I was still crouched on the ground. I took Lyla's lead as I stood up and shook off the feeling of the watcher, wanting the ominous vibe to erase its presence out of my mind and kick the sickening feeling from my body.

The terrible vibe had a strange and familiar feel. I suddenly thought of Domino, Ms. Brooks, and Drew. I walked Lyla back into Jack's room, shivered off the last of the feeling, and shut and bolted the sliding glass door.

"You and Lyla can feel free to crash here," Jack said, making me lunge out of my skin.

"Criminy, Jack!" I said.

"What?"

"Just jumpy—we were just outside, and we saw someone lurking in the shadows and emitting creepy and sick vibes from below."

"Probably one of my friends wandering around super high or something. I know my aunt and uncle are staying down the hill at the lake house, but they would be asleep."

"It was just weird."

"Everyone else is crashed out all over the place. Vee and Josie are asleep in the bungalow suite…although, by the sounds, they probably aren't sleeping much."

"Sounds like Vee and Josie." I smiled, jumping on Jack's bed next to Lyla who was already comfy. The sickening vibes I had just experienced had muted. Almost as if they'd never happened. Again, props to the hired positive Emitters.

"Gyzmo," Jack said, "play my favorite British cat and dog videos." An enormous wall screen across from the foot of the bed, disguised as an expensive piece of art, turned on. Nothing funnier than dogs and cats with voice-over British accents. The best of both worlds.

Jack settled in next to me and Lyla to watch until we fell asleep.

Chapter Twenty

"So will you?" Jack asked over breakfast the next morning. Vee and Josie had gotten up early and made food for the remaining party attendees in Jack's kitchen.

"Wouldn't you rather invite one of your tabloid gal pals?" I snagged toast off a platter.

"I could." He also snagged and buttered a piece of toast. "Or you could just say *yes*. Plus, then you can meet my family—my dad, my aunt and uncle, they're in town for a bit. You've already met my mom the day of 'The Incident.' "

"Oh, that sounds serious, meeting your family." I smiled at him. "And is that what your mom calls it? *The Incident*?"

He nodded and smiled back.

He had asked me if I would attend the Knight Family Gala & All-Stars the following week. I was still apprehensive about being around large groups of people. Going to the party was pushing it as it was, but another event with even more people I didn't know? I wasn't sure about that.

"C'mon," Jack said. "You're just so…*easy*."

"Well, how could a girl say no to that?"

"I meant *easy* as in *easy* to talk to. I'm comfortable around you."

"Wow, comfortable? Quite the compliment. Are you saying I *get you*?"

"Yes, exactly." He smiled.

I couldn't say no to him. Besides, mulling around the condo and overthinking about Falco was the last thing I wanted to do every weekend.

I had since stopped texting and leaving messages. I guessed I was done with Falco. I didn't have a reason to keep in contact with him, especially since there had been little movement on the case since Drew was out on bail. Maybe I'd gotten it all wrong and Drew did commit murder during one of his fugue states? I wasn't so sure about anything anymore. So a gala sounded like a fun and distracting event.

The gala was the premier fundraising event for the Knight Foundation. The who's who of Seattle and the Eastside would be there. Who knew? Perhaps a good chance to drum up some new clients? And maybe a good way to test and channel my budding ventriloquist-like skill of throwing my Reads to pick and choose pings from a distance instead of getting them all at once. I was in, whether I liked it or not.

****

"You look stunning, Rogue," Jack said when he came to my door to pick me up for the gala.

"Oh, this old thing?" I joked, swinging from side to side in the midnight-blue, alt-silk taffeta dress Vee had ordered for me at a high-end store downtown. The dress had been reengineered and its materials repurposed through a sustainable textile practice. Loved the earth and loved the dress, so it was a win-win.

Jack looked damn amazing himself in his full-blown tux. God, he was a handsome man and had the Knight family's fetching looks. He insisted that Lyla tag along, too, and should be comfortable in one of the Knights' personal security vehicles parked at the event entrance.

"Milo, this is Rogue," Jack said, introducing me to a burly man driving a large, black SUV. "Milo is Knight security detail, and he *loves* dogs." He patted the back seat, and Lyla jumped in.

"I love whatever you ask me to, Mr. Knight," Milo said, smiling, nodding, and tipping his ball cap toward me as we both got in.

"I think your special detective friend is spying on you again," Jack said as we drove away. "There's a patrol car parked across the street."

"So," I said, "ask me if I care."

"Do you care?"

"Pfft, no."

"Yeah, OK, Miss Noncommittal."

The event was being held at the Knight-Seattle Performance Center downtown. Just like Jack said, the SUV pulled right up to the front, no parking app needed. Sweet! Jack and I gave Lyla a pet and handed Milo her leash.

I was OK with leaving Lyla in the SUV with Milo. I had taken notice at Jack's party that I didn't need to be right near Lyla to block immediate pings but could still Read people in a crowd without getting overwhelmed.

Of course, that was until both Lyla and I had gotten the taste of the blatant pings sent out by whatever or whoever was lurking behind Jack's house the night of the party. What a dick move. I did not want a repeat of that feeling tonight. This event was one of those endless opportunities Vee talked about I was hoping to experience.

The venue was beautifully decorated and ritzy as hell. Dozens of humanoids greeted people, served drinks, and ushered guests. I'd never seen so many bots in one place.

The Knight Foundation used events like this to flex their large tech muscles. Jack told me that Knight Industries was a major financial sponsor of artificial intelligence, investing heavily in robotics. I was amazed at how bot movement had evolved in the past twenty years. Human at first glance.

"Welcome, Mr. Knight...and," said the android who had a soft-pitched voice and iridescent robotic metallic shell, pausing at my face, "guest."

My face probably hadn't registered in enough CCTVs around the city to be recognized. That was a good thing.

"This is Rogue," Jack said to the bot.

"Aw, so I'm not just 'guest'?" I said to Jack who gave me a funny look, and we both laughed.

A photographer took a couple of quick snaps of us when a second bot, this one with even more human features, made a beeline to us with a tray of drinks.

"Good evening, Mr. Knight and...Rogue," it said, tipping the tray toward us.

Holy shit, these robots learned fast and relayed info in a millisecond to one another. Oh crap, now I wasn't anonymous anymore. That worried me.

"Two sidecars, perfect." Jack took both drinks from the bot and handed one to me.

The bot knew Jack's favorite drink. I guessed they didn't call them artificial intelligence for nothing.

"I'm Maags and am pleased to meet you. I'll show you to your seats." The robot bowed, and the drink tray automatically flipped down and stored at the robot's side.

We followed the androgynous bot into the grand room, which was enormous, luminous, and set up like famous awards ceremonies I'd only seen broadcast online. Folks were taking their seats.

Maags sat us at a large table with Jack's siblings and Knight Industries executive staff. All of whose names I would never remember. I was bad with names, however, good with Reading, so I called it a draw.

I sat down as the robotic usher pointed to my phone, which pinged, sending me the program for the evening. I had trouble trusting machines that acted human, probably because I couldn't Read them. I quickly scrolled through the night's lineup.

The foundation was presenting awards for public health, including to its NoODxone partners. The drug, heralded as a true cure for drug addiction, helped quell the burgeoning addicted population nationwide. It was said to alter brain chemistry to completely reduce multiple drug cravings and provide a solution to a handful of mental illnesses. A true lifesaver, I believed.

I continued to scroll down the night's itinerary, took a sip of my cocktail, and sputtered the drink down my chin as my gaze stopped on one name. "Are you serious?" I said louder than I'd meant.

Folks seated at and near our table looked my way. My bad. Still not used to being in public.

"Did you know?" I whispered to Jack, pointing to a name on my reader.

"I had no idea." He looked at the program and shook his head.

Detective Greg Falco was listed on the evening's roster and was being honored by KING 5 and the Knight Foundation for his community contributions. I looked around the room. The tables were packed as the program was about to begin. I located Falco who seemed to be just getting to his seat.

He was sitting at the *Right Place, Right Time* recognition table and wearing his police blues. He was one handsome, devoid-of-feelings, prime-time asshole. But he looked so hot in his uniform he made my panties wet. I Pushed the twinges I was feeling in my emotional cortex and in my most delicate places down and Pushed them out of my mind.

Falco was next to Olivia Oliver from KING 5, that peppy broadcast journalist I'd once admired. My admiration for her had cracked a bit after I witnessed their secret street meeting the other night.

And that admiration continued to plummet as it currently looked like she was chatting Falco up. And he was smiling. He could eat a dick. Wow. I was surprised my anger bubbled up so viciously. I sent a piercing thought his way.

He looked right at me. I kept his glance for a moment, shook my head, and looked away, then the lighting dimmed. The night's program was beginning.

I started to feel peculiar about twenty minutes in. I looked down at my drink, which was only half finished, so I knew I wasn't buzzed. Then I was overcome with queasiness. Sweat beaded on my upper lip. I had to breathe in and out deeply.

I waited for a long applause in the program, leaned in next to Jack, told him I was going to the ladies' room, and made a beeline toward an exit. I was so close to hurling I didn't think I'd make it.

As soon as I was out of the Great Hall, the feeling died down. Weird. A familiar weird, though. Similar to the bullshit sensation that had been thrown my way from the shadowy stranger at Jack's pool house party. Why would an Emitter be sending out feelers like that? That's a shit thing to do at an event where multiple people could have a negative reaction.

Establishments sometimes hired negative Emitters as additional security at public events to break up crowds or threats. However, I was no threat, so I had no idea why I was being targeted. Maybe it had something to do with me being there with Jack? Or maybe it was nothing but a coincidence.

I used the restroom to splash water on my face and look in the mirror. I still looked a little green from the exposure, but my color was perking back up. I applied lip gloss and slipped it back into my dress's hidden pockets. A big score on the hidden pockets, as far as evening dresses went.

I made my way back out of the bathroom, took a right down the hall, and ran into Falco. I was immediately embarrassed. And angry. And I still had feelings for this guy. So I just stood there like a dumbass, looking at him, shoving my hands deep into my hidden dress pockets out of discomfort. My face grew warm.

"Are you OK?" he asked. Hot as ever and mesmerizing in his dress blues.

"Am I *OK*?" I looked at him.

"I just saw you leave suddenly and wanted to check." His eyes sparkled with amber intensity.

I knew better than to stare into those eyes for too long. "Don't I look OK?" I sneered at him.

"You do. You look amazing." He reached over and touched the hair on my shoulder.

I was wearing it down for once, in its full crazy

curliness. I was taken aback, but that didn't stop my body from wanting to take his clothes off. He confused me. I shrugged him off.

"Thanks, I guess." I didn't want to open my mouth to talk anymore because I felt a crying spell churning its way up my chest. I was afraid this feeling would make its way to the surface to blubber up in front of him. I was not going to let Falco see me cry about him. So I just shut up. He looked at me like I was going to continue the conversation. I didn't.

"So…how have you been?" he asked.

Of course, I couldn't stay silent and felt myself switch to bitch mode. "Well, you know, weather's rainy, and Seahawks made it to the playoffs, *again*," I said in my best *fuck you* monotone. I'd always been a blurter, even when sarcasm wasn't appropriate or appreciated. "And I definitely haven't been avoiding my last fuck while secretly meeting my next lover to hook up and argue in the streets near the last conquest's home. And yourself?"

He looked at me, his eyes glinting a darker brown. "First of all, I have no fucking clue what hookups you are talking about, and secondly, I've only been a *tad* busy clearing Drew's name and trying to solve multiple murders. So sorry I didn't *personally* take time out of my crime-solving to check in with you." He dished the sarcasm right back.

"I know, right? Too bad there wasn't a quick, easy, and convenient way to message someone so you don't have to talk, right? Heard of texting or IM?" Oh shit, my eyes started watering. And to think of all the times I'd masturbated to thoughts of this guy. *Calm the fuck down, Rogue.*

He looked at me. Then his tone changed, and his eyes melted to a baked molasses color. "Rogue, I'm not sure how to explain it so you'll understand." He shook his head. "This is a longer conversation we need to have…that I…don't have time for right now."

"Oh, yes, please mansplain my feeling away, or better yet, go back and get your reward, or award, or whatever the hell you're getting tonight and go fuck yourself…and your new tablemate."

He gave me a confused look, then must have realized who I was talking about. He laughed. "Pffffft, really, Rogue? She's a reporter. That would be quite the conflict of interest with me being a cop. And I could say the same. Better go back and sit with your *we sleep together but don't fuck* pal, Jack, now that you two are *engaged*."

Now was my turn to be confused. What the fuck was he talking about? Falco didn't give me time to respond but abruptly turned and headed back into the Great Hall. I gave myself five minutes and then headed back in.

Ten steps in and I started feeling sick again like my insides were turning out. Who was this Emitter, and what was their beef with me? I couldn't go in. I texted Jack that I was feeling like total shit and had to leave, making sure I sent him five customized barf emojis to emphasize.

Chapter Twenty-One

I went outside and breathed in some crisp Seattle air. It was raining sideways, which felt soothing on my hot face. I felt amazingly better the farther I got from the venue, so I walked back to the SUV and knocked on the window. Milo popped the lock and let me crawl in the back.

"Sorry, I got sick—but I promise I won't yack in your rig."

He nodded to me in the rearview mirror while Lyla wiggled her butt in greeting. I sat next to Lyla, leaned back, and dropped my shoes, curling my legs onto the seat, one hand on my unsettled stomach.

"She's happy to see you. I had to take her around the block a couple times," Milo said. "She was circling and pacing and whining like crazy. Must have known something was up with you."

I smiled at him, happy that he was there with Lyla. Happy she was there to help ease whatever or whoever was Emitting the foul feelings. I took in a couple of breaths, still a bit queasy.

I thought about it for a hot second, but I knew the nausea wasn't due to being pregnant, thank the gods. I hadn't used additional protection with either of my last fucks—stupid, BTW, as I could never be too sure what new venereal bug could pop up on the STI continuum— but I had a ReadiWhen implant, which was foolproof.

Kel and I had pretested before we started down the libidinous path, but Falco and I hadn't. At least I knew I wasn't with child; I had only fucked someone who communicated like a child. I laughed at that out loud. But I guessed Falco could say the same about me.

In the scheme of things, I was thankful that there was finally a birth control method that was perfect, eliminating human error, preventing babies and STIs, with little side effects, and available free to anyone who couldn't afford one. *Thank you, Knight Industries and other leading sponsors.*

Felt great to be outside and close to Lyla. While she hadn't been able to completely block whoever had been hanging around Jack's pool the night of the party or the Emitter from tonight, she really had made a difference in my life and being able to be in the world and around other people.

And I guessed I'd fallen into that world with two larger-than-life outings, first Jack's party and now the Knight Industries event.

That reminded me of something Falco had said to me tonight. I searched my mobile for "Jack Knight engaged" to see if I could shed light on what in the hell he was talking about.

Several photos of Jack popped up, including three photos of us. Two from his birthday party and one was just taken tonight, all with various captions.

Damn, the paparazzi really moved fast, even faster than tonight's bots. One caption mentioned hearing wedding bells in the Knight family's future, and another listed me as Jack's fiancée.

Hmmm. Didn't know I'd marry so well. I chuckled out loud, causing Milo to gaze back at me, one eyebrow raised.

"Says here, in this e-zine," I said to him, "that Jack and I are *engaged. S*omehow, *I* missed the memo."

"Miss Rogue," he said in his deep voice, "from what Jack tells me, if it *were* true, the Knight family would be privileged to have you." He winked at me in the rearview.

"Aw, thanks, Milo." I wasn't sure what Jack had said to him about me.

I fell asleep at some point and woke up when I heard activity outside the vehicle. The event must have been over.

Jack opened the SUV door. "Hey, Rogue, I'd like you to meet my aunt." The door of the SUV was still open. "This is Monterey."

I popped my shoes on quickly and slid down off the seat by the door outside.

A formally dressed, middle-aged woman bowed. Jack must have told her I didn't shake. I could see the family resemblance right away. She looked like his mother.

"So nice to meet you, Rogue, Jack has been *silent* about you." The woman smiled at me with a side glance to him.

Had she seen any photos of him and me with captions denoting our engagement? "Nice to meet you as well." I stepped out from the door and bowed back.

"Great. Looking forward to getting to know you *better*." She gave me a wry look.

"Yes, me, too." Then something she was wearing caught me off guard, making my breath hitch and chest thunder.

She gave a quick smile, walked away with Jack, and

they were greeted by another group on the sidewalk.

I slumped against the SUV and dragged myself back in with considerable effort, barely making it all the way in before a burst of wind slammed the SUV door closed.

I rolled down the window and could still see the glint emanating from Jack's aunt's collarbone—which was what had caught my attention. She was wearing an elongated pink gemstone. Domino's missing crystal.

I kept my stare over where Jack, his aunt, and others were standing, the crystal flickering, beckoning. I tried to ping out a Read to her and a separate one to Jack, but something blocked me.

Lyla was standing on the seat, stiff beside me, her fur standing up, a guttural growl vibrating off her. I froze as Jack walked back up to the SUV's window with another person.

"Rogue, this is Robin, my uncle," he said. "He's married to my aunt Monterey."

His uncle stepped to the window. He reached in, and I instinctively drew my body back, but not before seeing the watch. The same Vitruvian watch Domino's killer had worn. Lyla's growl intensified, and I grabbed her collar to hold her.

Then the scent hit me. The familiar woody vanilla of Mortis Lux.

"You know, on second thought," Robin said, drawing his hand back when seeing the dog, "I'd better not; I think I'm coming down with something. Wouldn't want to get you *sick*." He exuded a discomforting state. "So nice to meet you, Rogue, I'm sure we'll *bump* into each other again *soon*."

I nodded, swallowed a gallon of bile, and rolled up the window, which couldn't close quickly enough. The urge to throw up was overwhelming. Robin and Jack walked away from the SUV. I was uncontrollably terrified of that man.

"What the fuck?" My body shook in a noticeable shudder. Cold sweat ran down my back and the side of my face. I eased my grip on Lyla's collar.

"*Never* liked that guy," Milo said, moving his fingers in the shape of a cross near his body. "He unnerves me."

"You're telling me."

I had no idea what had just happened. All I knew was Jack's uncle was a powerful Emitter that no one had thought to mention, and that his uncle and aunt were involved in Domino's murder.

His uncle must have been the one who'd made me sick tonight in the Great Hall and probably the one leering at Jack's party. He was so powerful that Lyla's blocking abilities could only block portions of his power. I didn't know much about his aunt and uncle, only that they spent most of their time traveling nationally and internationally for Knight Industries.

OMG, Robin *was* the murderer. It all became clear. I thought. It was difficult to concentrate, and my head was booming with searing pain. What was going on? I felt like I was going to black out.

The image of the crystal bouncing on Jack's aunt's neck kept flashing, replaying for me. Was I in a dream sequence?

I tried to call Falco but got no answer. I texted him to call me asap and that it was urgent.

As soon as I hit *send*, the SUV door opened from the outside.

"I'm going to ride home with my aunt and uncle,"

Jack said, making me jump as I was lost in my panicked texting. "Driver, take the girl home." He sounded off, not like himself, and he didn't say bye. And he called me *girl*.

"Will…do…Mr. Knight," Milo said, but it sounded more like a question with a slight pause after each word.

Wait. There was something I was supposed to tell him. What was it? I was so confused. What was wrong with Jack? What was wrong with me?

Jack had already shut the door. Milo pulled away from the curb, heading to my house. He shook his head. I felt a bit better and clearer as we drove farther away.

"OK," I said, breathing in and out slowly, trying to catch my breath, "did that just get super weird?" I couldn't stop my voice from quivering.

"Not sure, Miss Rogue." Milo shook his head again. "It was odd. I've been with the family twenty years, and he's never called me *driver* before."

I was drained and wanted to sleep right there in the SUV. I was still fighting the urge to vomit. Maybe I had been drugged? I know I hadn't drunk too much. I needed to put my thoughts together and tell Falco about seeing the crystal, but it was hazy already. Had it really happened?

I looked down at my phone. It was dead. Had my last text gone through?

Getting home was foggy. Somehow, I trudged up my steps, unlocked the door, and waved to Milo. A tuckered-out Lyla crumpled onto my bed. We were both too beat to bingo. I took my arms out of my dress, tugged down, and it dropped to the floor. Lyla let out a monstrous yawn.

"I feel the same way, Lyla." My words slurred. "It

takes a lot out of us girls to fight such…uh…such negative Emits…" I curled up next to Lyla and crashed. I heard my phone ping and echo from miles away. Maybe it wasn't dead anymore? Moments later, I must have passed out.

Chapter Twenty-Two

"Are you going to sleep all day?" Vee said, the bright hall light shooting through my doorway. "It reeks in here."

"What time is it?" I pulled my head up, my face sticking to my pillowcase.

"Shit, Rogue, looks like your face hemorrhaged. Nasty." She headed into my bathroom.

I could hear the water running. I rubbed my arm on my face, and chunked bits of gelatinous, semi-dried blood smeared down my arm. I'd had a doozy of a nosebleed. And a doozy of a headache, a rough, metallic taste in my mouth like I'd eaten raw meat.

Vee came back with a warm washcloth, wiped my face in spots, and handed it to me. She picked up last night's dress I had dropped on the floor. "It's two p.m. Are you hungover?"

I shrugged at her. I couldn't quite piece together the fuzzy evening. My brain hurt. Maybe the very first part of hanging out with Jack and seeing the bots was fun. But it went downhill after that.

"I'll make you a juice smoothie." She touched my head on her way out.

The blurred parts of the evening left me uneasy. Anxious. Terrified. I wasn't sure all the reasons, but it felt like something bad was going to happen...or did happen...or...I didn't know.

I remembered seeing Falco. Had I told him to *eat a dick* or *go fuck himself?* Or both? I then remembered I'd gone out to Milo's truck; Jack hadn't come back with us.

Oh fuck. The revelation of the crystal swinging along his aunt's neck popped into my mind's focus. *Fuck. Fuck. Fuck. Fuck.*

I grabbed my phone and noticed the last text to Falco had not gone through, so I re-sent.

I texted Jack, too. A message came back that my number was blocked. I tried again. Blocked. I called. The recording said I was blocked. I scrolled up and read Jack's last text. The ping I'd heard from last night.

—*We're done being friends. Don't contact me, or I'll have you arrested.*—

What the fuck? Lyla scurried up and ran out of my room with a bark.

"Rogue, there are two cops at the door for you," Vee yelled from the kitchen.

I looked down and was just wearing my bra and underwear from the night before.

I pulled on clean sweat bottoms and a top. Falco's sweats. I was hoping that's who was at the door with a thousand apologies and flowers or better yet, donuts.

Vee was pointing to the door from the kitchen. I nodded, and she turned the blender on high and headed to the back of the condo, probably to toss my sweaty dress in our Robo-dry cleaner.

I opened the door a crack. "Yes?" *Sad face*, it wasn't Falco. But Vee was right. They looked like cops.

"Are you Rogue?" one cop said.

I nodded and stepped partially through the door so I could hear better, the blender still whirring. Confused pings shot at me.

"Ma'am, we have a report about a vicious dog on your premises."

"What?" I smiled back at Lyla sitting by the door. "You must be mistaken."

"No, ma'am." He grabbed the doorjamb. "We are required to take the dog."

"No way," I said without a second thought. "That's not going to happen. May I see some identification?"

"Look, we're just here on orders to grab the dog and go," said the guy in the garb that looked more like an animal control uniform. "Don't make this difficult," he added.

The cop adjusted his hold on the door with one hand and then grabbed my wrist with his other and pulled. "Stop resisting." He twisted my hand and jerked it forward hard, catching me off balance.

He lost his grip, but I Read him already.

Oh God. He wasn't a cop. I lunged back and struggled to slam the door, wishing I had never opened it. I smelled burning, and my thoughts went blank.

****

"Rogue?" I heard a voice echoing, then louder. "Rogue!" It was Vee. "Are you OK?"

An awful smell kicked me out of my daze. Vee was waving smelling salts in front of my nose. Goddamn Healer.

"What the fuck just happened?" she asked.

"Oh God." I looked around. "Where's Lyla?"

She shook her head, looking very confused.

I reached down to touch my stomach where I felt a searing sensation. I looked down at the red welt that had formed there. "The fucker tased me and then took Lyla." I struggled onto my knees and stood, still wobbly.

"Tased you? Why?"

"I tried to slam the door so I could lock it. They weren't police, and they wanted Lyla."

"What do you mean they weren't cops? Who the fuck were they? Where'd they take her?"

"I don't know. I don't know. I don't know." My voice was high pitched and panicked. "We gotta find her."

Vee drove me around the neighborhood to look for any Lyla sightings and then to the police station to make a report. I had already left Falco multiple texts as she pulled up.

I didn't know what I was going to say to him. I had no idea who the pseudo-cops were or why they took Lyla. I just knew they had bad intentions. I knew all the weird stuff going on was all connected somehow.

Falco met me in the lobby. I started in immediately about Lyla, trying to tell him the details of the morning, but it came in sobbed blurts.

"Slow down, Rogue," he said. "What's going on?"

I told him about the two cops, who weren't really cops, who tased me and took the dog.

He nodded at me. I said we needed to find Lyla soon because the swift Read I'd gotten from the cop impersonator was not good—whoever they were, I knew they wouldn't think twice about hurting Lyla.

"Listen, Rogue," he said, "Drew has disappeared as well. His folks said police came and got him for more questioning. I've called around, and no one seems to know where he is or who picked him up. His disappearance may be related to Lyla's. I'm headed out there now to talk with them. Come with me?"

I nodded, and we headed out. I let Vee know that I

would be riding along with Falco. She let me know she would start a viral crowd search for the dog and assured me everything would be OK. I wasn't so sure.

Falco plugged in the address, and the car drove. I was trying to stay calm but was panicked about Lyla and now about Drew. We needed to find them. Falco radioed an APB with a description of Lyla and the men who took her.

Oh crud. A fuzzy, demanding thought popped into my head. There was something else I needed to tell Falco about the night before. Something urgent about the case. It was there at the tip of my recall. Thought bubbles were popping all around my head. Then they were gone. I shook my head to clear it. What was going on with me?

"You OK?" Falco asked.

"I'm OK. I think." I then felt eerily calm. "How long until we get there?"

"You will reach your destination in twenty-two minutes," the car's robotic voice said.

Falco looked at the vehicle's directional map as the car continued to drive and gave me a reassuring glance. Then he started humming, I was assuming to fill the quiet space.

"You know," he said, nodding down at me, then slightly tugging at the tied ribbon drawstring hanging from the hooded portion of the sweatshirt around my neck, "you can go ahead and keep those. I like them on you." He returned his attention back to the car's operational dashboard.

I looked down. There I was, wearing his sweats again. I had tossed them on when Vee said someone was at the door earlier. I'd already planned on keeping them. They reminded me of him. OK, so I might have touched myself wearing them on occasion.

"How the fuck can you be so calm?" I blurted.

"I just know we'll find them."

And all of a sudden, I believed it, too. We sat in silence for a few minutes. It was too silent.

"Falco. Look, I'm sorry about last night, at the Knight event." I slowed my breathing, trying not to sound like an emotional wreck. "I was feeling like shit...and I was surprised to see you...and I was jealous."

He nodded.

I kept talking. "I hadn't heard from you. And I'm OK if you just want to be friends, even friends with benefits or whatever. I just can't play games. You ghosted me big time."

He glanced at me but didn't say anything.

Was he the strong, silent type or a coldhearted one-night stand? I wasn't sure which one.

He started to say something, then stopped, paused for a moment, and started again. "My intention wasn't to ghost you, Rogue. When I get on a case and I'm following a lead or a hunch, that's all I can focus on. I get *wholly* fixated, like tunnel vision. I've always been this way. That's why I don't do relationships."

"I get it; you're a cop, and finding murderers should be your top priority. But not even a text? And then I see you at the dinner being social when you couldn't even IM? What was I supposed to think?"

"Rogue, I was afraid to complicate things, and you stopped leaving messages a couple weeks back. I saw that photo of you and Jack. I assumed you were a couple. What was *I* supposed to think?"

I nod-shrugged, not at all excusing his behavior.

"Well, we're not a couple. I thought I made it clear that Jack and I are nothing but friends."

He gazed down at me, smiled—and was that a look of relief?—and then put his gaze back on the dashboard, continuing to let the car do all the driving but tapping his fingers on the steering. "So you were *jealous*?" He grinned.

"Yes, jealous. And if I can be honest, I was crushed."

His grin disappeared. "Shit, I'm sorry, Rogue. I had no idea."

"Well, now you know." I glanced out the side window as a warm tear formed, then I brushed it off quickly with my sleeve when it rolled out. "So what did you find out?" I choked back a minute sob, changing the subject.

"What?"

"About the case. What did you find out? While you were out ghosting me?"

He smiled at this. "Well, I followed some strong leads, and there is evidence that our murderer has done it before, not just Domino and Sophia, not just in Seattle."

I looked at him, surprised. "Really?"

"Killings throughout the Pacific Northwest and other states, dozens of women and trans with similar, questionable deaths, all Sensitives, most of them sex workers over more than two decades."

"What do you mean 'questionable'?"

"Most made to look like accidents, overdoses, or suicides, so no one looked too deep, and most with a trail of cover-ups and disappearances."

"But that doesn't explain Domino or Sophia.

Domino's strangling was not made to look like an accident, and Sophia was brutally stabbed—and she wasn't a Sensitive *or* a sex worker."

"Who they were and the way they died *was* different. Everyone at the station thought it was a separate killer. I didn't agree. The killings *felt* the same."

I looked up at him and nodded. "They did *feel* the same. Jack felt it, too."

"Where is he anyway? I thought you two were attached at the hip."

"I don't know." I pouted. "Jack broke off our friendship last night. No idea what I did. He told me not to contact him or he'll have me arrested. Maybe I embarrassed him in front of his family?"

"I did notice a whole slew of Knights there last night."

"Yes, there were…" I trailed off. I remembered what I wanted to tell Falco about Domino and meeting Monterey.

"This is Drew's folks' house," he said. The car, on auto-pilot, made a perfect parallel park in front.

And just like that, my brain scrambled, and I forgot what I needed to tell him.

Chapter Twenty-Three

We got up to the door, and Falco introduced me. I already knew Drew's parents from Reading Drew when I touched him at the police station.

I had Read that Drew felt immense love for his parents and they for him, even if they didn't understand him all the time.

"Thanks for coming, Officer Falco. Like we said on the phone, two officers showed up to take Drew in to the station for more questioning," Drew's mom said, "but we haven't heard anything since, and we are worried. It just didn't feel right."

"I appreciate the call, Mr. and Mrs. Baltimore," Falco said. "I'm sure it's a misunderstanding with one of the precincts. Rest assured I'll find him."

Drew's folks nodded.

Falco had a way of reassuring people that was uncanny, but a slight twitch in his body language made me think he was more concerned about Drew than he was letting on. I guessed I could Read him, a little.

"I also came to let you know I followed up on a couple of the insights Drew had shared with you—the ones you wanted me to look into. I wanted to provide an update."

"OK," Mr. Baltimore said, grabbing his wife's hand.

"What Drew told you was correct. He was acquainted with Sophia Brooks from the past."

Drew's parents gave each other apprehensive looks as Falco continued.

"While he was working at Arkane Army Outpost, he served security detail for Ms. Brooks who was running a virus vaccine trial for villagers—the same virus Drew contracted, the long-term side effects causing his fugue episodes and his eventual discharge from the army."

Drew's parents nodded; Falco continued.

"I *was* able to track down the information I could validate, but I can't wholly verify Drew's account, as that information remains classified and not releasable."

"We assumed Drew's ramblings were just one of his spells," Mrs. Baltimore said. "His rants about drug company conspiracies and weaponizing viruses were…true?"

"I can't confirm specifics with you yet, Mr. and Mrs. Baltimore, but my source repeated much of the same information Drew provided to you." Falco nodded. "I know it sounds farfetched, but there may be some truth to it. I will be investigating to see if this history may have something to do with Ms. Brooks' homicide. That's all I can tell you for now, but I wanted to assure you I am leaving no stone unturned. As far as your son's case goes, we're still investigating. I'll find the truth, and we'll work through it, whatever that is," he assured them.

He shook hands with Drew's parents. The relief on their faces was apparent even though he hadn't really told them anything. I was getting ready to bow but instinctively reached for both their hands, squeezing each one slightly. I saw just enough, then smiled at them reassuringly. Falco and I walked out to the car in silence.

"So what'd you see?" he asked.

"Drew's in trouble. The same pseudo-cop who took

Lyla took Drew, and they left in a—"

"Black e-van," he finished.

I nodded.

"I was afraid of that," he said. "The vehicle description matches a dark van shown in CCTV footage picking up Drew the night of Ms. Brooks' killing after he'd passed out behind a business."

"Wait, I thought Detective Barrow said there wasn't any footage, that it had all been damaged by a power surge or something."

"Right, apparently, we missed a spot. I fell into some video that clearly shows Drew stumbling by and passing out right in front of the camera and later being picked up, all occurring during the same time as Ms. Brooks' murder. So this newfound video alibis Drew."

I chewed on his statement a bit as he instructed the car to return to the station, then changed his mind and told the car to take me home.

"OK, so Drew's disappearance, the murders, and whoever is trying to frame him…it's all connected somehow?" I asked.

"I don't know. What I do know is whoever is setting Drew up can simultaneously destroy CCTV feeds. Someone fizzled camera footage that would prove Drew's alibi." Falco shook his head. "That's hours of footage, gone. You'd need a major electrical power surge or deliberate network tampering for that to happen like it did."

"So what else did you find out about Drew and Ms. Brooks?"

"I found a blog caster willing to talk to me off the record. I verified most of what Drew told his folks and was shown evidence of Knight Pharmaceutical's attempts to release a bioweapon and its connection to an expedited vaccine in the making. Ms. Brooks was deployed onsite to manage the virus with no idea that Knight Pharm was behind the virus's release in the first place. The conspiracy goes all the way to the top."

"So what does this have to do with her murder?"

"That's what I'm missing," Falco said, "the critical pieces that tie Ms. Brooks' murder and Domino's murder and the others all together. I know you don't want to hear this, but Drew did know Sophia Brooks. I know you want to believe he's not involved, but he may be. The Knights, too.

"Whatever is going on has the Knight family name written all over it. There are just too many surrounding coincidences," he continued. "Sophia Brooks was scheduled to speak to Knight Industries board members this month after recently reconnecting with the family, so maybe all of this has something to do with whoever took your dog, too."

"What about a powerful Emitter?" I spat out abruptly, interrupting his thought stream. All the past events from the night before shot out of my deep brain repository and plummeted into my current thoughts.

"What do you mean?"

"Emitters can manipulate people via their brain chemistry…and those are just electrons, right? Could a powerful Emitter cause an electric pulse that could destroy CCTV feeds in multiple locations, even on the cloud?" I was having trouble talking, my brain still trying to swallow my thoughts whole.

Falco eyed me warily.

"So hear me out. Jack's uncle Robin is a powerful Emitter," I said. "Maybe the most powerful Sensitive

I've ever run across. What if he is somehow involved in Ms. Brooks' murder and deleted footage to set Drew up and to cover his tracks?"

"OK, I'll bite. But with a strong accusation, we need motive, which we don't have."

"I don't know, but you said Ms. Brooks was involved in vaccine trials for the virus Drew contracted before he was discharged." I sounded a bit crazed. "And Drew and Domino have a connection and…and…and…" I spluttered at recalling what I wanted to say next, choking on my words, trying to sift them out through taffy-like threads in my brain.

"That's just not enough."

"What if. What if. What if," I said, choking, making Falco look worried. I shook my head, swallowed hard, took a deep breath, and looked inside myself, visualizing reaching inside my brain, picking out the stanza I was trying to say and boggling the words out.

"Jack's aunt, Robin's wife, was wearing Domino's lost crystal," I finally spurted out, followed by a surge of relief as I let that little chunk of knowledge backflip out of my brain.

"What?"

"Yes, I saw her wearing the crystal last night after the dinner." I felt elated that I could describe what I saw to Falco.

That revelation made a pressure-pop sound in my brain and my nose tickle.

"That's fucking huge, Rogue." Disbelief scrolled across his face. "Why didn't you say something earlier?"

"I couldn't. I'd been trying to remember that I had something critical to tell you, but it kept disappearing from my recall. My thoughts have been mushy. When I saw the crystal around her neck last night, I was freaked, then I met Jack's uncle immediately after, and he Emitted his negativity all over me, and my knowledge of the evening literally slipped into the soft spot in my brain somewhere."

He shook his head, then handed me a tissue from the car's console and pointed to my nose, like my nasal hemorrhage was the most normal thing ever.

I wiped the trickle of blood coming down that I could also taste was running down my throat. I tried not to gag. "I told you he was powerful—potent enough to target me directly and fuck with my memory after the fact." *And probably calculating and evil enough to kill someone.*

He was quiet as if he was thinking. "Do you think it has something to do with Jack's changing attitude toward you?"

"I wouldn't be surprised. Jack started acting strange as soon as he met up with his uncle."

"I'm going to figure this out, Rogue. But why the dog, too?"

I shrugged. "Maybe because the dog blocks pings?"

"The dog?"

"Yeah, the dog is a special breed, and maybe having Lyla allowed Sophia some memory release or something, and that is why Sophia wanted to talk to the board. Maybe something to do with Drew and the work they had done?"

He nodded and seemed to take it all in. "I can see pieces and parts falling together. I just need a bit more time."

He made me feel like everything would be OK.

"How do you do that?" I shrugged at him.

He gave me a questioning look.

"How are you able to put me and other people instantly at ease?"

"As you told me when you first met me, I'm Sensitive." He smiled at me just as we arrived back at my place.

"I wish I could talk to Jack. Maybe if I got close enough to him, I could at least Read him or someone else from his family and find out what connections we might be missing." I opened my door to get out of the car, already planning out the questions I was going to ask Jack.

"Didn't he text he'd have you arrested if you contacted him?"

"Technically, yeah, if I *contacted* him, but he really didn't say anything about *visiting*."

Falco grabbed the sleeve of my sweatshirt so I couldn't slip completely out of the car. "Listen, Rogue, don't go anywhere near Jack or the Knight family. I have a bad feeling, and if that Uncle Robin is as powerful as you say he is and what I've drummed up about the Knight family is true, that's dangerous ground. I don't think the Knight family fucks around. Stay away from them."

"But…" I blurted.

"Promise me. Promise…" he repeated, looking up at me, still holding my sleeve.

I held up my right hand like I was being sworn in and nodded. "I promise I won't go to the Knight mansion to track Jack down," I said robotically.

He let go of my sleeve and grabbed my hand instead. "I'll be at the station if you need me." He squeezed my fingers and gave them a soft tug. "Probably all night…going through the Ms. Brooks evidence again, so please call me if you think of anything else. I promise I'll find Lyla and Drew, Rogue." The look he gave made me feel like he could solve all the world's problems.

"OK." I squeezed his hand and dropped it. I knew somehow that he would get them both back. "Do you want to come up first?"

"You know I can't, Rogue," he said firmly but without explanation.

Well, it was worth a try. I shrugged. Then felt guilty about thinking about sex at a time like this. I seriously had a problem.

I waved and climbed up my stairs, the pistons in my brain firing on how I could accomplish what I needed while keeping my promise to Falco. He waited until I was in my door to drive away.

Chapter Twenty-Four

So, OK, I'd promised I wouldn't track Jack down at the Knight mansion. Good thing I'd said nothing about tracking down Jack at his pool house or the boathouse that his aunt and uncle were staying at. The hard part would be getting past security.

I retreated to my room to do a bit of online research for accessing the Knight residence. I had already been virtually to the boat house's beach and docks vicariously via the horrendous vision the first time I Read Jack.

I knew that the boathouse was contained on the lower lot of two hundred and some acres the Knight family kept after purchasing the former Saint Edward Park from the state in 2027 to help reduce the state's deficit after the pandemic and resulting bankruptcy.

The entire property was secured, even two hundred fifty feet off the lake water, with thirty-foot fencing, top-of-the-line security, and armed, former special-ops personnel. An impenetrable force.

I tried calling Jack again. My call bounced. I'm sure his uncle had something to do with his radical behavior change.

Like his uncle had made me forget Domino's crystal hanging around his wife's neck and that he was a powerful Emitter, Jack had forgotten we were friends. Good friends. Now he was just ghosting me. I laughed out loud at that. Jack could see ghosts, and now he was ghosting me. OK, so it wasn't that funny. Maybe I just needed some sleep.

I went to check on Vee. She was asleep on her computer with the e-flyer she'd made for Lyla still open on the screen. I could see she had boosted the post all over social media and offered a reward. I moved the laptop aside and tucked her in, lightly kissing her hair. I loved my roomie.

I went back to my room and looked around. It would be lonely without Lyla. I had become so used to her being there. I settled back on the pillow and looked at the multiple photos we had taken of Lyla.

I fell asleep aching for and dreaming of my fur baby and hoping she was safe and that she was with Drew, keeping him safe, too. My dreams answered me.

Lyla and Drew are sleeping near each other in a dark place. It is the boathouse. There is a surrounding buzz. It feels heavy. I can feel the dense weight of tragedy. I feel the sickness of past sacrifices. Suffering. Unmentionable dark deeds the dead can't even talk about. Death. Unforgiving cruelty. Spirits screaming out, lashing out. Wanting to be heard. To be noticed. To be found.

I am suddenly in Drew's thoughts, his dreams, and he knows I'm there.

"Hey," he says. "It's about time you went to sleep and showed up—I needed to reach you while you were dreaming. I want to show you something."

I take Drew's hand, and we are in Robin's thoughts. Robin is not conscious of Drew or me being there. I am Reading Robin through Drew. I Read him. I see what he sees. I see what he does. I see what he is. Then Robin sees me.

I sat up in bed with a start. I now knew how some of the pieces fit together. I knew Drew and Lyla were in danger, and I knew Robin was connected with it all. He was a killer.

I jolted out of my skin as my phone pinged on high volume. Jack was calling.

"Rogue, I'm sorry I've been such a shit. I need your help," he pleaded. He sounded like he was having trouble breathing. "Lyla's here."

"You have her? Is she OK? Are you OK? Where are you?" I sounded desperate, irrational.

"Yes, she's here. I sent a car for you. It should be there soon." And then he hung up.

I tried to call back, but my calls were still blocked.

I hopped up and started to change out of sweats, but that little voice inside my head stopped me. I needed to hurry. Instead, I pulled on my track shoes, scooped up my coat, which had fallen from off my dresser, and tightened my hair bun.

I checked on Vee one more time. She was snoring softly.

I went outside to wait for Jack. It was a crisp evening, frost had formed on the turf across the street, and I could smell snow. My breath billowed puffs of steam as I shivered to keep warm.

I pulled on my thick wool coat, and something soft fell onto the grass. It was Falco's silk tie. Somehow, I must have picked it up also when I snagged my coat off the floor.

He must have left it when he came and went. Literally. I'd have to give it back to him someday. My hope was that he'd intended to leave it so I would bring it to him. I could hope, right?

I folded the tie and shoved it in my jacket pocket, hugging myself in my coat. The thick wool was heavy and warm on my frame, in my favorite icy-blue color and soft, no-itch blend.

I had bypassed fall, and I hadn't been paying attention to the season change, probably because I had been too focused on Falco. It was probably time to break out the fuzzy boots and gloves.

As I waited, that uneasy feeling folded over my brain like a mist and enveloped it. A gazillion thoughts winding around my head, conflicting what-ifs. I had to go, didn't I? Jack needed me, and he had Lyla. He's my friend, right? I should stay home, just like Falco said, right?

Of course, I needed to go. What was wrong with me? *Get it together, Rogue.* My brain fired live rounds of better judgment, but I didn't allow them to hit my intuition warning target enough to stop me from doing something stupid.

I was shaky but relieved when I saw the black e-SUV pull up. I opened the door. The driver wasn't Milo. And no Jack. I hesitated.

"Jack asked me to come and get you, Ms. Rogue," the driver said casually. "He told me to tell you he was having quite the meltdown and needed your help." That sounded like Jack. "Plus you need to pick up your dog," he continued. His voice was calm.

"Where is she?"

"It's a long story, Miss Rogue. Jack will tell you all about it when you get there."

I couldn't specify what, but something was off about the driver. But I pushed my better judgment down past my throat, back into my acidified stomach, and got into the SUV anyway.

I knew it wasn't a great idea, but I couldn't talk myself out of what I had already decided. At least visiting Jack could get me on Knight family property and take me to Lyla. I knew Drew was going to be there somewhere, too.

We drove in the direction of the Knight mansion. I texted Falco.

—Don't get mad, but I'm on my way to see Jack. He has Lyla & called me for help. Have to go. R—

As I waited for a response back from Falco, I noticed the driver slowed and pulled to the side of a road by a large parking lot. We weren't there yet.

"What's up? Why are we parked?" I asked.

"Not to worry," the driver responded briskly.

His voice now sounded weird, and my neck hairs stood at attention. I leaned over and quickly grabbed the driver's arm. He didn't pull away. I couldn't Read him but felt a slight electric surge. I then noticed what was odd about the driver. He wasn't human but an extremely advanced bot, wearing a shit-eating grin while turning his neck at an odd angle.

"Oh fuck." I scrambled out of the large vehicle.

Just as I swung my legs to hit the pavement, Jack's uncle came toward me. Frozen in place, I felt a wrenching sharp pain in my eyes. I was too late to counter his forceful ping. My phone tumbled from my hand.

I reached up to touch my face. A warm sticky stream of blood burst from my nose. Or my eyes. Or both. I could taste blood and tried to scream, but the only thing that came out was a frothy blood bubble. Then I felt myself dropping.

Chapter Twenty-Five

I woke, shivering, my clothes damp with sweat. I was somewhere dark and musty, and my body felt numb. As I got used to the blackness, I saw a line of light under what looked like a door. I could immediately hear Lyla whining, her nails lightly clipping against the door in the background somewhere.

"Hey, girl," I said under my breath, and she seemed to quiet down from afar. I struggled to sit up in the dark.

My wrists and ankles were bound in front of me. They felt loose. I had been lying at an awkward angle, so my hands were asleep, and I had to wait until the pins and needles stopped and I had feeling back in them to fumble around with the ties.

The ones around my wrists came undone easily, as if they had been tied hastily around my thick jacket instead of my actual wrists. Once those were off, I worked out the knots and undid the ties around my ankles.

I concentrated and sent out a slight ping directed to Lyla and picked up another presence. Drew was here, too. Thank the gods.

I knew Jack was there, too, but I couldn't ping him directly. Where was he?

I could also sense Jack's uncle Robin upstairs but was not about to send a direct ping as he might Emit a powerful mental stab directly back at me into my eyeball like he had done earlier. I could tell Robin was not in control and seemed preoccupied.

His thoughts were a word cloud I could read. The word "predicament" and the old-fashioned phrase "in a pickle" popped into my head. I snickered as I haven't heard that idiom for ages. Something was seriously wrong with my sense of humor.

I did not want him to know I was awake and thinking. Keeping him distracted was a must.

The slight Read I got from Robin made me visualize him pacing back and forth upstairs. In fact, I could almost hear him pacing, and…was that the sound of him tossing and breaking shit?

I crawled toward the light under the door and used the door handle to pull myself up. I felt up the wall for a light switch, and when I snapped it on, I had to blink multiple times to get accustomed to the bright light.

I felt gross and smelled and tasted iron. The front upper half of my sweatshirt was pasted with blood, making me retch a couple of times, the rusty smell overpowering my sensitive nose.

At least it was my own blood. I touched my face, which was sticky. I used my sweatshirt sleeve to wipe it as best I could. Robin had punched my brain with his thoughts to knock me out. His power was incalculable.

I looked around to assess my situation.

The room was an office setup, with a marbled desktop and executive chair. I pulled aside a set of blackout curtains, revealing glass blocks with lighting behind them, giving the illusion of sun-filled windows.

I couldn't see an out besides the door. The largest fixture in the room was a semi-floating desk. I envisioned the walls pushing in on me, so I knew I was underground someplace, perhaps a bunker or underground shelter. Jack's uncle Robin was weird enough to have a secret fortified hideout.

I could sense water and movement, so definitely by the lake. I was at the lake house. And from the energy of the waves outside, I could sense a storm brewing.

The desk chair faced a wall with a mounted big-screen television and a gathering of frames surrounding it. The frames contained several dozen shadow boxes. Each hosting a variety of items.

I looked at the frames intently and then realized what I was looking at and sucked in a breath, jabbing my lungs in a painful hitch.

My earlier dream about evil, sacrifice, and suffering came to light. Each frame memorialized Robin's murdered victims. I scanned them, looking for some familiarity, the majority of which I didn't recognize.

I recognized the last two, which were at eye level beneath the screen. These last two represented Domino and Ms. Brooks.

In Domino's frame was their picture, taken in front of Hatty's House, smiling, their eyes shining. The pics were surrounded by a mesh sachet of dried herbs, what looked like underpants of some sort, and a lock of hair.

Ms. Brooks' case showed an older photo of her, a UW sticker, a restaurant napkin drizzled with something like wine, and the words *I know* written in a script font. The box also contained a large, rust-covered knife and Lyla's missing collar.

On second glance, the rust on the knife was not rust. It was dried blood.

My head was spinning as I looked at the other frames. I started counting them.

Forty-two.

I had already seen inside Robin's head during my earlier dream, so I knew what he was capable of. I just hadn't expected such butchery. How had he gotten away with it with all the advances in DNA and crime scene analysis? Why hadn't he ever been caught?

Then it occurred to me. He'd been using his Emitting skills this entire time to deceive everyone, even the cops.

"He's a Sensitive mother-fucking serial killer," I said out loud. Maybe too loud, as I heard the pacing upstairs stop.

Shit, shit, shit. With nowhere to hide, I needed something to defend myself. I yanked Ms. Brooks' shadow box off the wall, cracked the glass on the corner of the marble-top desk, and fished in to grab the knife. I also took Lyla's collar and zipped it in my sweatshirt pocket.

"Think, Rogue." How would I get out of this? I then realized I hadn't checked the door. I turned the handle, and the door clicked open. Again, too easy.

Perhaps Robin was getting careless. I knew he was being absentminded because of his flustered state upstairs. I was curious how I could Read him when I wasn't trying to.

I looked through the door.

The industrial-looking hallway had strip lighting on the walls and a handful of closed doors leading to a dimly lit stairwell. I walked quietly, listening for any sound behind the doors and up toward the stairs for any movement.

The pacing and thrashing around upstairs started up again, along with some guttural sounds. Robin Knight was not a happy camper in the least. In fact, he sounded pretty pissed off, talking loudly. I didn't want to be around when he decided to come downstairs to check on his captives.

I pinged again and found the door Lyla was behind. Drew was in there with her. I could hear her having a sniffing frenzy under the door. I tried the door handle. It was locked. I tapped lightly.

"Drew, can you open the door?" I tried to keep my voice down, but I needed him to hear me through the door. No answer. "Drew…can you hear me?" Louder. I heard nothing.

I pinged a Read directly to Drew. He was in a deep sleep, or trance state with a direct connection to Robin's activities upstairs. That was interesting.

I could see Robin pacing through Drew's eyes as Drew slept and as I Read him. That's how I picked up what Robin was doing upstairs even without pinging up. It was as if Drew were keeping tabs on him, leaving him in a state of perpetual pacing.

"Lyla, wake up Drew," I urged the dog half out loud, half Pushing. I had no idea if she understood what I was saying. I heard muffled activity from inside the room and then the sounds of Drew waking up.

If Drew was keeping tabs on Robin in his dream state, I needed to be prepared for if and when that monster came down the stairs. Pinging out a Read toward Robin was too risky as I couldn't chance he'd sense me. But he already knew I was down here. He and his psycho bot had put me here.

I heard exertion sounds behind the door. Loud shuffling and a couple of thuds.

"Back up," Drew said from behind the door, and part

of the door by the handle seemed to give way, cracking and splitting, then nothing. Then the door snapped open.

Lyla rushed out and greeted me with a wiggly tail and circling fur body, with Drew right behind her.

We headed cautiously, quickly, up the stairs. Once out of the unlocked door at the top of the stairs, I wasn't sure where to go.

I followed Drew to the right and kicked something on the floor. My mobile phone. Robin must have picked it up when I dropped it. My phone's screen was shattered. I turned it on, hoping for the best. My little starfruit icon flashed.

I texted an alert to 9-1-1 for tracking and tucked it into my sports bra for safekeeping. We headed through what looked like a living room toward a huge wall of glass doors.

A large storm had developed outside, bright decking lights showing lake waves crashing onto the dock, water splashing high, making the lights flicker and strobe.

Drew slid one of the glass doors open to leave. Out of the corner of my eye, I saw Jack lying on the couch. He looked dead.

I backtracked and went over to him. He was still breathing but cold AF. *Oh shit*. I motioned and nodded for Drew to help me carry him out. I rolled the knife I'd snagged from the shadow box in my too-large sweatshirt and shove-tucked it into the top of my sweats.

Robin was nowhere in sight. Not knowing where he was scared the fuck out of me. Never liked jump scares.

Jack's dead weight was difficult to carry. I should cut down on the donuts and work out more. Again, I giggled lightly. What was wrong with me? Drew gave me a weird look and shook his head.

We got Jack out the door with Lyla in tow. Drew was strong, so he was bearing most of Jack's weight. I was strong, too, but mostly my strength at the time was motivation and fear. I didn't want Jack to die. I could feel eyes on me, and that unnerved me enough to uncontrollably ping out wide. I heard Robin in my brain.

There you are. His virtual voice just as disturbing as his real one.

Fuck. The only appropriate word I could muster up. Then I blocked him out.

We carried Jack near the driveway under a carport and laid him down.

Drew checked him again. "Rogue, he's stopped breathing."

My heart skipped out of my throat. I looked at Drew. I felt helpless. He started chest compressions immediately, and I grabbed my phone out of my bra and dialed 9-1-1 for an ambulance and law enforcement. Dispatch told me officers were already near that location with more on the way due to my earlier alert to them.

They asked me to stay on the line. I looked down at Drew and Jack. Drew's military first aid training provided Jack a good chance, but his lips looked blue. I knelt and Pushed a stay-alive ping toward Jack. He was hanging on. Barely.

Thunder smacked overhead, sending Lyla bolting. I whistled for her, but she was gone, heading up the road toward the mansion. Scaredy-cat.

I remained on the phone with the dispatcher but ran back to the open glass door we'd come through. I had seen a Pendleton wool blanket on our way out. It was nice, and I noticed it had matching pillows. Again, what was wrong with me?

I snagged the blanket to cover Jack and was running out the back glass door.

Glancing toward the lake, I noticed that the storm had really picked up. I could smell something funky, like a dead animal. I went to cover my nose from the putrid smell, and I was instantly knocked off my feet and tackled hard.

Fuck, that hurt. The force was enough to shatter the breakaway glass door and dangle it out of its frame. My phone shot out of my hands somewhere.

I struggled to get back up, trying to catch back the wind that was knocked out of me, but Robin was on me, slithering up my body's core in the wet conditions, trying to grope his hands around my neck. He was seething and spitting.

I remembered the knife and yanked it loose from the bottom of my sweatshirt tucked into my sweatpants. The knife clattered out onto the deck closer to the water, and I lunged forward. He saw what I was lurching for and shot for the identical target. We pounced at the same time, falling together in a heap.

I had my hand on the knife and grabbed mostly the blade. I felt it slip, and that's when he grabbed the knife. He was trying to inch his way up and over me with one hand and was half straddling me with his knees and had the knife in the other hand. He grinned at me, and I struggled with every bit of my strength. He was going to kill me and enjoy it.

I bridged my body, arched suddenly, and swiped my legs to one side hard, making him teeter over. *Thank you, Vee, and the hours of yoga you insisted that I do.*

Robin toppled to one side but was hanging on to my sweatpants leg, and I felt a sharp slash on my bottom leg.

I snatched my legs back and crawled, clawing my way forward and away from him.

The storm was now delivering a torrential downpour, making the deck extra slippery. I was close by the water, and Robin was on me again.

He slashed the knife down, stabbing me in the lower stomach, and then the blade sliced into a soft part of my arm. He was going to kill me, and I felt like he was succeeding. I pinged and knew that he was having fun. He lived for this. He wanted to subdue me and kill me slowly.

As he tried to stab me again, I held his arm back with mine, the injured one not doing so well. I was losing my momentum and power. The blade was dark, I think with my blood, and he just grinned like a crazy fuck.

He slashed forward, and I moved out of the way, but he caught the back of my thigh. I was tired, my adrenaline running out of me like my blood and the nerves in my arms and legs succumbing to this murderous fuck.

At his close presence, I could feel every unmentionable thing he had done, every horror. He was getting in my brain, which was exploding. My eyes felt like they were on fire even in the cold night temperature.

He was savoring the moment. I relaxed and took a breath, letting him flow through me, Reading him completely. The pain, fear, and uncomfortableness dissipated. I could hear echoing and voices. From beneath. It was hollow. Oh God, was I dying?

Robin's eyes stayed focused on mine. He was waiting for the life to go out of them.

Suddenly, his weight was lifted off me as he tumbled to one side.

Detective Falco had tackled him, and they were rolling in a big pile on the wet deck. I couldn't tell who had the upper hand in the darkness and pouring rain. The deck lights were not bright enough to see details.

Loud thuds came from where Falco pummeled Robin. At least I hoped that's the way the fight was leaning. The slick deck allowed neither to gain footing. I scrambled to my feet.

Robin still had the knife and lunged forward, slicing out at Falco, snagging his forearm with the blade. Robin sprang at him again, and I lunged forward, wedged my unhurt arm between them, and grabbed Robin's wrist that was holding the knife, tight. Once I had it, I wouldn't let go until I Pushed him. Hard.

Echoes of the voices I heard got louder.

His whole life flashed out before my eyes, and I knew at that moment he wasn't going to quit and he'd keep killing and would get away with it. He had to be stopped.

So I Pushed harder. Harder than I'd Pushed anyone before. He stopped struggling and trying to kill us and looked dazed. His eyes snapping back and forth from what I could see through the lightning flashes above. I gave him a large final Push and let go of him.

The deck lighting was illuminating him in slow motion. He stared down at the knife and looked around blindly. He started mumbling and screaming. Screaming so loudly. He stumbled on the slick surface but remained standing.

The echoing voices were louder. I knew he could hear them, too. He could also see them. Jack's ghosts. All around. I saw them, too.

He looked at me, looked at them, looked at Falco,

and then looked at me again before he plucked the blade against his throat and swiped it across his neck. His face frozen in confusion.

At first nothing, then a sucking, spurting sound emanated from him as he started hemorrhaging below his head. It was a lot of blood.

The knife slid from his hand, and as soon as it did, his body collapsed on the wooden deck, making a hollow thud.

Falco grabbed for the nearby wet wool blanket I had dropped before Robin attacked me, and used a folded part of it and his hands to put heavy pressure across Robin's neck to stop the bleeding.

Voices reverberated in and around my head. My mind was light, wanting to lift away. I had tunnel vision of a bright light illuminating a portion of the deck ahead of me, waves splashing over it. Water sparkling with bits of light in the dark air.

The back of my leg was bad. It hurt but was numb, too. The blood trickled from the gash, warming my leg. I fell to the ground and almost off the deck.

I yanked the wide laces out of the sweatpants and hoodie I was wearing. They slid easily from the quick-dry fabric, making a smooth slurping sound on the way out.

I paralleled the shoelace-like ties and fed them under and around the top of my leg, making a close-fitting loop.

I dug the dog collar out of my pocket, fed the leftover combined loop edges around the dog collar, and tied it. I twisted and turned the collar multiple times until it was painfully and almost unbearably constricted around the top of my leg. I then attached it tightly around itself.

I managed to lose feeling in my leg, which was a good thing when trying to stop blood.

I fished Falco's necktie out from my pocket and strapped it above the gash in my arm, using my teeth to tighten it in a knot.

It was hard to breath, and I couldn't stay focused. I had lost sight and sense about what was happening on the deck. I used the last bit of adrenaline to stand up.

I visualized Pushing my own blood flow to slow down, but I was so tired. I could hear ambulance sirens, heading closer, making their way down from the main mansion. The sound was so far away. Resounding. Bouncing off the waves.

I looked at Falco who was trying to save that murderous fuck-nut who'd tried to kill us. *Let him die*. I was filled with unadulterated hate for Robin. Hate at a level I had only felt for one person before in my life. And like that time and this time, it was well deserved.

I hadn't been sorry then either. Maybe that made me just as bad? To knowingly take someone's life out of hate and desperation.

I was tired. I had to let go. Of it all.

My weightless body could feel the snap of the wind on my skin, and when I looked up, the rain hit my face, making splattering, plinking sounds. Hollow and echoing. I looked back down. Broken glass chips sparkled on the deck by the smashed back door. So pretty. Shiny like glitter. I had always loved glitter. I grinned with the energy I had.

My extremities were numb, and I had no control over them. I saw myself suspended, right above my body. I didn't feel myself give way but saw a body fall back onto the deck, lose balance on the slippery boards, and plunge into the stormy waves.

My aura floated above, providing me some perspective on what was happening on land.

Falco was still holding tight to Robin's neck, and I snatched a glance at Drew and Jack upfront. The paramedics had arrived. Lyla was lying right by Jack. I somehow knew she was feeding him life force.

The water was frigid when I first hit, but I felt relief, almost as if I were sheltered from it. *There*, but *not there*. Knowing the water was bitter cold but only feeling half of what I should be feeling.

I remembered I was wearing Falco's sweats and felt comforted. They were a quick-dry, wool blend. *Cotton kills*. I laughed at that. Again, what was wrong with me?

I sank and could hear muffled voices. My thick wool coat pulling me down. Murmurs. I knew they were spirits. Spirits long connected to the lake house and Robin's murderous past.

They were putting their hands under me for support. I was hovering on water. Keeping me afloat but partially submerged. Lowering my body temperature, slowing my pulse and my heart rate.

Yet I was still floating above it all, watching everything going on down below. Jack was with me. A spirit, too.

I looked around. The paramedics took over for Falco, trying to keep Robin alive. That fucker couldn't even end his own pathetic life, what a narcissist. I laughed at myself from far away.

I watched Falco plunge into the water, lurch around, and find what he was looking for. He dragged a partially submerged body out of the lake and set the body down on the deck. The figure had no resistance left in its limbs.

I realized the body was mine.

I felt cold and detached. I watched him watch me. I heard him say my name, telling me something, but it was muted. Inaudible because of the storm surge and the echoing and feedback.

I could sense impending nothingness. I had floated a bit farther up. So this was how it ended? I just floated out and up into what? Where would I go? I was sad for the end of me. But relieved Robin would stop the killing.

I could feel myself jolting back down to earth, a few feet at a time. I looked down.

Falco had started chest compressions and emergency breaths on my body. It felt a little like a goodbye kiss. It wasn't enough, and I began to float back up and out.

He was quickly replaced by paramedics and machinery. I was flitting away, higher. Then I stopped short. Hands around me. They were pulling me back. Dozens of hands. Then nothing.

Chapter Twenty-Six

I knew I was alive because I felt pain. And intense discomfort. And I smelled hospital smells. Sanitizer, alcohol, heating unit, saline, floor cleaner, cafeteria rice pudding. *Yum*. Rice pudding.

My extremities ached and pulsed. I was not ready to come out of it. I did not want to face the fact Jack could be dead or the horror of what Robin had done.

I had wanted Robin dead and was OK facing the fact that I had killed him with every intention and every part of my being. I don't think anyone could have faulted me for that.

I had always been afraid my past would come back to haunt me. I had murdered before. Vee was the only person who knew about that, and my secret was safe with her.

I opened my eyes, hoping to see a familiar face. Vee was there. I gave her a big smile, and she slid over in a rolling chair to grab my hand. Luckily, my hand closest to her wasn't injured.

"Let me guess," I said, my voice cracking and hoarse. "We're in the Knight Critical Care Unit?"

She nodded. She looked exhausted. I mouthed *I'm sorry*, and she mouthed back *I know*.

A tear rolled down my face.

I couldn't feel *him*, so I just blurted out, "Is Jack here…somewhere?" I didn't know if he was alive.

"Yes, he's alive. They have him in a medically induced sleep to continue flushing his system of toxicity," she said. "His uncle tried to poison him."

I blinked back more tears, relieved Jack was still with us.

Vee told me what she knew, that Jack's uncle had meant to kill him and turn the blame on Jack's jilted ex who stalked and killed him. Apparently, that jilted ex was to be me, and Robin had written an elaborate murder-suicide note in which I stated I was going to consume the same poison. How romantic. How tragic.

"Lyla is fine, too," Vee said. "Josie's dog-sitting. And I guess Lyla was quite the hero." She broke me out of deep thought.

"Oh, yeah?"

"She led Falco down to the boathouse and the ambulances through the thick trees during the storm. That's one smart effing dog."

Hmmm, and I thought Lyla had hightailed it because she was freaked about the thunder.

"She wouldn't leave Jack's side and tried to go with him in the ambulance," she added. "That detective friend of yours had to lock her in his car until I could get her later."

"Falco?" I couldn't hide the pitch in my voice when I said his name.

"No, the other one…Baron-something?"

"Barrow."

She nodded. "They were both here earlier, Barrow and Falco—they were in the hall with a group of suited-up, serious agents, sunglasses and all."

"Oh, I wish I had my mobile."

"Yeah, I tried to call it." She gave me a sad face, lip

turned down. "I'm thinking it's about seventy-five feet down in the lake somewhere. I'll get you a new one."

I nodded. I was *dying* to read the news. I laughed. Too soon? Probably.

I was also exhausted, starting to feel pain intensify, so I let Vee know I was fine and was going to catch some z's. She leaned in and hugged me, making me wince. She smiled, blew me a kiss, and left.

When I woke up from my nap, Barrow was sitting in my room, scrolling through his hand tablet. He looked up and smiled.

"Can I see that?" I asked him, pointing to his e-reader. He handed it over, and I Gyzmoed quick headlines. The news on what happened was hella easy to find and not in short supply.

Lake House of Horrors. Knight Mansion's Hidden Secrets.

Knight Family Conceals Secret Killer. Multiple Bodies Found.

Bodies Found at Knight Manse. Potential Serial Killer in Family.

Serial Killer in Seattle. Multiple Bodies Found at Knight Lake House.

Seattle Sensitive is Prolific Serial Killer from Prominent Family.

The captions went on. I needed to process, so I scrolled through multiple accounts, gathering details. The storm surge near the lake had been powerful enough to break apart portions of the boathouse deck, uncovering multiple bodies tightly wrapped and taped up in black plastic sheeting.

Some of the dead bodies had been wedged under there for decades. The reports had mentioned the potential for even more carnage due to evidence found in the shadow boxes being tied to multiple missing person cases.

Then I read the words I was not expecting.

Robin was alive.

"Robin's not fucking dead?" I said out loud to Barrow, and my voice choked up. He shook his head.

I scrolled down to read more.

Robin was alive and being held in the hospital unit of a high-security prison. A prison unit fortified as a Sensitive-free zone to prevent the prisoner from using any Emitting powers. I had no idea there was such a thing. But then again, I had no idea that an Emitter could be so powerful and so dangerous.

I put down the reader and looked at Barrow. "Why hasn't Falco been here?" My voice cracked.

He looked uncomfortable, like he wanted to say something but stopped himself.

"What?" I was curious about what he was holding back.

"Just that he's been busy working with the government agency in charge of Sensitive misconduct."

"Yeah, I know, he's always *busy*...at least too busy for me," I snapped, then stopped. "Wait...*that's a thing?*"

He nodded. "Yeah, FBSI—Federal Bureau of Sensitive Investigation. They have a keen interest in this case because of Robin Knight's power, plus are highly intrigued by the fact Falco can't be influenced by Sensitive powers."

I looked at him suspiciously.

He leaned toward me. "He hasn't said anything about you, Rogue...or...your *gifts*, and he asked me not to offer up anything either." His voice was low. "He's well aware of the additional scrutiny this case will be under and anyone who may have been involved."

I nodded.

"They will do whatever they need to do to find out how a Sensitive serial killer murdered dozens of people over three decades right under the noses of multiple law enforcement agencies and no one knew a thing."

I nodded again and shrugged. "What about the Knight family? How are they doing with all this?" I was thinking of Jack.

"Well, I'm not involved since FBSI took over, but media reports state they are crushed with the realization that someone connected so closely to their family and Knight Industries could have carried out such horrific crimes for so long. They have already set up a fund with two billion dollars for the victim's families and to help pay all funeral costs. When forensics are done with the physical evidence, that is…. That's going to take months."

I shook my head. "I meant to kill him, you know? I put all I had into that effing…"

"Um…I'm sorry, I didn't hear that." He got up with a start, shaking his head, talking fast. "So I'm just going to leave the room, and maybe you should sleep on it and think about how and when you want to talk with the authorities about that evening's events?" he finished.

Falco must have already told him how it went down at the lake house. How I'd Pushed Robin to slice his own throat. I reached out my hand to give Barrow the reader.

"You keep it for now," he said. "I heard you lost your mobile."

I was relieved as I wanted to continue perusing the

multiple online story threads. Barrow waved and shook his head on the way out.

One article quoted an FBSI agent, saying that Sensitives who perpetrated illegal activity with the intent to harm our citizens needed to be tracked and held accountable for their crimes.

The agent said having dangerous Sensitivities was like holding a loaded weapon. And just like a weapon, *Sensitives* needed to be located, accounted for, and registered. The agent alluded to national legislation to force this concept to protect more innocent lives from being lost because of dangerous and, unfortunately, lethal Sensitives.

A shiver went through my core. What the fuck was happening? Registered and licensed? As Sensitives, we'd always had to deal with the religious right demonizing us into something evil and threatening. But laws requiring all Sensitives to be registered? Requiring signs when Emitters were being used was one thing, but needing a license was a whole new order.

Robin was dangerous, but he was the only Sensitive I knew who had killed. Well, besides myself.

I had intended to kill Robin that night, as I had meant to kill once in the past. But surely, both could be considered self-defense? I had no choice. Right?

I put down the reader to force sleep. I dreamt of storms. I dreamt of my past. I dreamt of Jack.

Summer at the lake house. Jack's there. He's young, just a kid. I follow him as he walks on the deck. The planks are hot on my bare feet. Jack runs and jumps off the dock into the lake. Sun's rays shoot through the water splashing up, flashing the air. The water's chilly and so dark. Deep and murky. Jack splashes around. Buzzing.

Whispers. Then voices. Louder. More voices. The scent of grungy water. The putrid smell getting worse. Voices too heavy in his head to hold it up. Then panic. Jack panicking, screaming, hands reaching for him from the waters. Jack's glare on the deck pleading for help. A much younger Robin looks on. Watching the boy struggle. No emotion. Robin moves his hand up to his face, his finger to his lips. "Shh. Shh. Shhhhh," he says. Jack goes under, gulps water. Jack is drowning. Hands are reaching for him. Ethereal bodies. Floating. Just under the water. They grasp at him. Try and float him up. Screeching in Jack's underwater ears. Robin fishes Jack out of the water, places him on the deck, breathes life back into him, Emits straight into his soul. "Shh. Shhh. Shhhhh," Robin says into Jack's depths. I stand stupefied, in terror, watching Robin Emit so forcefully into Jack's minuscule frame—the moment Jack's Sensitivities and his gifts burrow deep down to hide.

Then I'm flung forward in time. I'm at the Knight mansion, and Detective Falco is there. He's there to interview family members. He's talking to Jack's mom about the event the night before, then he meets Robin's wife Monterey, sees the crystal around her neck, and asks her about it.

"Anniversary present," she says.

Falco is trying to kill time until the search warrant arrives. The one he wants for the lake house. Judge is going out on a limb for Falco on the warrant, knowing that serving any kind of legal document on the Knight family could be professional suicide.

Fast-forward again with a yank. I'm on the deck of the lake house, Pushing Robin. I am outside myself. I see myself. My eyes are black, not my eyes. They are like

Robin's eyes when he killed Domino. The eyes of a killer.
Then Falco looks right at me as he is trying to save
Robin.

"You're no better than him," Falco says.

I woke up with a start, wincing with pain.

Falco was sitting in my room, scrolling through an
e-reader. He looked over and half smiled. "You OK?"

I nodded.

"Glad you're back."

"Good to be back." I cleared my raspy throat, still
thinking of my haunted dream. Did Falco think I was no
better than Robin? I hoped not. I looked around, curious
where his FBSI colleagues were.

"They're gone," he said, "at least for now."

I nodded at him.

"Your roomie, Vee, was here and said she'd be back
later—but not before giving me the evil eye. I'm
assuming she blames me for this?" He gestured to my
hospital bed.

"Yeah, Healers are like that, always cursing people
with their *evil eyes*."

He moved the chair close to my hospital bed and
looked at me. He was not smiling. The small space, the
silence, was awkward. He leaned in closer, speaking in a
low tone. "We need to get the basics of our story straight,
Rogue. Parse out only need-to-know info, give the police
the main events and the timeline details only vital to the
case. Nothing more." He enunciated the last two words.

My brow furrowed with concern, and he continued.

"I'm just asking you to filter some details and not
overshare."

I had an idea what he meant by that. I assumed he
meant for me to talk about what happened on the surface

only. What could be seen only from the outside looking in. Nothing about thoughts or dreams or ghosts. No talk about Sensitives. Nothing about my Pushing Robin.

I thought for a moment, then spewed out, "So what am I supposed to say?"

Falco raised his eyebrows at me, shrugged, looked like he was going to say something, and then stopped.

I, of course, filled the silence with talking. "So…I say…what exactly? That Lyla was dognapped by Robin's henchmen, I reported it at the station, took a field trip with you, got a call from Jack, and was headed to help him when a robot kidnapped me, took me to the lake house where Drew and Lyla were being held prisoner, we escaped and found Jack comatose, called 9-1-1, then Robin tried to kill me, you arrived just in time…a struggle ensued, and in his madness, Robin slit his own throat, you rendered aid, and I fell in the lake and…and…" I took a breath.

"And nearly died due to injuries sustained after Robin Knight attacked you," he finished for me. His voice choked up.

I was surprised that Mr. Unemotional had such a reaction to me almost dying.

He nodded. "Yes, stick to *that* story, to those events, and we'll be golden."

"But there are so many holes in *that* story. Even me being Robin's scapegoat for Jack's death and Drew for Domino and Sophia's murders doesn't answer the questions. Won't they want to know how we're all connected? How do we explain the gazillion coincidences that fell into place for all of this to occur?"

He shrugged, and I continued.

"They are going to want to know after all these years

how Robin stayed beyond their radar—how he ticks. They are going to want to know the multiple glued and unglued pieces and parts that needed to be put together for Robin to finally be caught. Right? Won't they? They are going to want details so they can know if there are others like Robin out there. Right?"

"FBSI's in command, and I want to believe they are concentrating efforts on investigating the bodies found under the dock, not getting sidetracked by ancillary details of the living," he said. "Matching the DNA from the shadow boxes to the victims and linking them to Robin takes precedence. At least for now. They are going to want to know all that other information, too. You will get questioned in detail, and I want you to be prepared."

"You want me to lie?"

"Not exactly…"

I cringed, remembering the moment I recognized what was housed in the shadow boxes. "Telling the story without details sounds farfetched—all the critical chance and circumstances get missed. I don't understand why I can't just tell the events as they happened."

"This is why." He handed me the e-reader.

I took the reader from him and read. Headline after headline accompanied by disturbing video simulations popped up as I scrolled. Some deepfake shit.

Sensitive conspiracy theorists were crawling out of their hidey-holes, making headlines in popular vlogs and streaming media, all thanks to Robin's homicidal wrath.

From planted alien beings, cults, brainwashing, and taking over the world to "accidental" deaths, demons, disasters, and cult leaders. At any other time, I would have found this humorous. It wasn't funny now.

Each headline more egregious than the next, but all

based on a clear and unanimous conclusion: Sensitives were dangerous, had been uncontrolled for too long, and society had to police this mounting malevolent force in our society. They should be registered. They should be regulated. They should be locked up.

"But that's not true…and that's not real," I said to Falco, pointing to a deepfake photo showing a Sensitive looming over a pile of dead bodies, a mist emanating from the Sensitive's body. "Am I the only one finding this ironic? Sensitive gifts are the whole reason Robin was finally caught."

"Rogue, you and I know that, but the government's job—and FBSI, specifically—is to protect the public, and the public needs protection from monsters like Robin."

I cringed at the thought of more Sensitives like Robin out there. That was an unsettling picture. What if there were a lot more?

"The public is out for blood, so I need you to keep your gift on the down-low." Falco tilted the e-reader, his hand brushing by mine, sending a spark through my body.

I couldn't Read this guy, but his presence, his touch, did sensitive things to my body. "So what do we do about it?" I felt deflated.

He shook his head. "Not sure, just be cautious when talking to the FBSI, Rogue."

Whoo. I loved when he said my name. He put his hand on my arm and looked like he was going to tell me something. I hoped it was something about us spending more time together.

"I need to…" He trailed off as a medi-bot activated my door and rolled into my room.

"Good morning, Rogue," the medi-bot said. "Here to take some vitals."

Fucking robots. Falco lightly squeezed my arm, got up, gave a wink, and left my room. At least I got a wink, which made my skin jolt with warmth.

I was dying to know what he was going to say and put a pin in it to follow up with him later. I was also dying to get out of the hospital and back home to my roomie and Lyla.

I let the medi-bot take my pulse, BP, and scan my extremities.

Chapter Twenty-Seven

Whiny pleas to my doctors that I was ready to go were met with eye rolls. I was still weak but was no longer on a drip. I could do some light stretching and walk around.

I was def on the road to recovery thanks to medical science and Knight Industries.

Being at a Knight hospital made me think of Jack. I needed to know how he was. Falco had told me he was no longer in a medically induced coma but had not woken up yet. The hospital wouldn't share any of his info with me because of health privacy laws.

"Well, if the hospital won't tell me," I whispered to the medi-bot after it scanned my vitals, "I will just have to find out myself."

The robot didn't seem to care. "Have a nice morning, Rogue," it said while rolling out of my room, "and make sure to get some rest."

I took the robot up on its advice. I fell asleep thinking of Jack, hoping he was OK. But like most of my sleep sessions, this one turned into another hellish dream sequence.

I am floating above, observing the goings-on below. Sophia Brooks and Robin are sitting in a covered outdoor eating area. It looks like Sophia has just sat down as she is still adjusting her raincoat on the back of the chair. She has Lyla with her. The dog is sitting nicely to one side. The two seem to chitchat for a bit. Sophia writes something on a napkin and pushes it toward Robin. He reads it. Looks up at her with piercing eyes. Miss Brooks folds her arms across her chest and shakes her head, giving a shrill laugh. The two start arguing.

"That's not going to work this time," Sophia says. "I know you sabotaged my drug trials; I know you brought the virus into that village, so instead of helping them, you made them sick. You killed people."

"You have no idea," I mutter to myself as an observer in my own dream.

"After all these years," Robin says with a smug smile on his face, "not sure how you found me out. I've been fucking up your trials and testing biological weapons for most of your career. How is it you're just figuring this out now?"

"You have no influence over me anymore," she says, "and I know what you are. You're a monster."

I know right away why Robin's Emitting no longer has power over Sophia. Sophia has Lyla, her secret weapon. Lyla absorbs all Robin's Emits he is using to control Sophia's thoughts. For some reason, Lyla has not been able to fully absorb his Emits for me or for Jack or Drew. Maybe because Sophia isn't a Sensitive, the block worked differently? But Robin has no idea that it is the dog who possesses the power to block his pings. Or he would have killed Lyla the same night he killed Sophia.

"Your time at Knight Industries is over," Sophia says. "I've already written an official memo to the board and have contacted the media."

Ahhh, *I think.* That was peppy reporter Olivia Oliver's insider that Falco had mentioned when he was talking with Drew's folks.

"*You should bow out gracefully,*" Sophia says, "*and turn yourself in before it gets even uglier.*"

Robin just stares at her.

"*You infected dozens of our own service members who either died or are still recovering from lifelong side effects. You implanted your own DNA into the bio-virus, connecting you right to it. What kind of person does that for control?*"

He seems surprised she knows this tidbit of information. "*You're right.*" *He looks up.* "*I didn't mean to take it all that far. It got away from me. I was doing it for the greater good...sacrificing a few to help the masses.*"

She looks shocked at his confession.

"*Please, just give me until the weekend. So I can tell my wife and her family. Then I'll resign from the board. Then you can do whatever you want with the information.*"

Oh God, he is convincing her to wait. I want to scream, "*No,*" *to get her attention, but I am frozen, watching the conversation unfold from above and not being able to control it even in my own dream. Fucker. I know what comes next. In two days, Sophia will be killed. Gruesomely stabbed and slashed by this powerful fuck-nut.*

At that moment Robin turns and looks right up at me, grinning, his devilish lips taut against his teeth, and winks.

I woke up with a start and knew why Robin had killed Sophia and why he wanted to frame Drew. The fact that Drew had been infected with the virus that contained Robin's own DNA was the reason Drew could connect with Robin in his dreams.

Drew knew what a killer Robin was, but because of Robin's power over him, he'd spent most of the last fifteen years in a fugue state.

Robin couldn't let either of them survive. He couldn't let any of us survive. He knew I knew and Jack as well, so he was going to off us in one fell swoop and tie it up with a perfect little bow.

The one he didn't see coming was Detective Falco. Falco's ability to not be affected by Sensitive powers made the ensuing discoveries possible, allowing it to unfold and be seen, allowing Robin's perfect bow to unravel.

How many other Knight Industries staff had he been able to fool to keep running his dangerous trials? How many detectives had he gotten past to keep killing Sensitives? Emitting into everyone he encountered to make them think the opposite of what they should.

That's also how he was able to keep his family in the dark. Made them think he was the greatest. That's why he had to Emit so forcefully into Jack. He knew Jack saw ghosts of the people he had killed, and he knew those ghosts could tell his secrets to Jack.

Robin couldn't have his nephew blowing his cover by telling people what he really was. A murderer.

God, I hoped Jack was OK. I missed him. I looked at the clock. It was after midnight, and I decided there was no time like the present to try and find Jack.

I got up and slid open my room door a bit so I could ping out. Two night staff were down the hall but too busy arguing over Seattle Storm's season point spread to notice me, and most of the medi-bots were secured at their charging ports.

I was in a secluded section in the hospital that was still being modernized and remodeled.

I slid stealthily out my door, down a long corridor to my right, and peered around a corner, sending out another ping. I found who I needed and slowly followed him down the hall. I Read him without his permission, but I had to find Jack.

The custodial tech's name was Chuck, and he was a long-time Knight Hospital hire and four-time employee of the month, I found out from my brief Read. He was just finishing his mid-rounds, checking in on a cleaning-bot that had malfunctioned earlier this week.

I kept a constant Read as he ambled next to the mop-bot, looking down at it with ire. Chuck and I seemed to have the same issues about robots—they were not to be trusted.

He said something about trusting robots as far as he could throw them, which made me picture him picking up the mop-bot and chucking it down the hall like a bowling ball. I had to stifle a laugh with my arm so I would not give myself away.

Chuck had Jack on his mind as he badged himself into a corridor, and I quietly surfed in on his access, just missing the mop-bot's erratic bob and weave. Again, fucking robot.

Chuck headed left, but his gaze lingered to the right farther down the corridor. *Bingo.* His thoughts showed me a picture of Jack's hospital room. Jack was just down that hall.

Chuck had scoped out Jack's room while finishing tech-rounds one night because he had been tempted to take and leak a photo for a quick payoff.

He knew the e-tabloids would pay a hefty price for

a pix of the Knight golden boy. But Knight Industries had been good to him, and he was not about to throw away his lifelong pension for a quick buck. *No siree, Bob*, thought Chuck. I hadn't heard that expression for a while. I'd have to use it someday.

"Thank you, Chuck," I said silently to him, turning in the direction of Jack's room.

This hospital corridor was extra lux with fine Northwest artwork on the walls. I stopped at Jack's door, tried the handle, and slid the door open. I was surprised it was not locked. Someone's head would roll for that one.

I went in and closed the door slowly behind me until it clicked.

The Knights had spared no expense. This room was swanky and modern, decorated as if my roomie Vee had designed it. It even had calming mood lighting.

I walked toward Jack, who was centered in the room in a large plexiglass tent, probably intended to keep out bacteria and viruses often associated with hospitals. I unzipped the tent, ducked underneath, and zipped it back up.

The pod was fitted with top-of-the-line everything. Jack was wearing a full-face oxygen mask and had wires and tubes all over and what looked like a contraption to exercise and massage his muscles so they wouldn't atrophy while he was unconscious.

"Jack?" I whispered. "Jack?" Louder.

I looked around for an opening to touch his skin. Through the medical contraptions I saw a free arm. I grasped his wrist, wrapping my hand around firmly.

I breathed and went in, trying to Read him lightly at first.

Nothing. I went in deeper, calling his name cerebrally while I delved.

I walk through a dense, kaleidoscope fog with multicolored distant lights, a hum all around. My ears pop as I descend. It is murky and difficult to wade through. I can feel Jack and swear I see a glimpse of him farther in the mist. Then he is gone. Then I can see him again. I can't quite reach him. The murmuring is loud and scattered and bounces around. I feel myself move backward for every step forward, and Jack seems to be moving farther away. Whatever I am wading through is sludgy and tiring, and I begin to struggle. I don't want to get stuck in Jack's head, but I can't turn back. I slosh through the muck and fog. Then I see Domino, a bright lavender light coming toward me, bringing Jack. I grab Jack in a huge bear hug and lunge backward. I can hear swooshing, and the murmuring gets farther away.

I fell, landing hard onto my butt in Jack's hospital pod, careening into and then bouncing off the opening flap. I scrambled up and grabbed his wrist again.

"Jack? Jack?" I called out to him. Nothing.

I heard a commotion at the door.

Eff and double-eff, I had forgotten to Push out an *all-clear* to hospital security so I would be undetected. They probably had me on all over CCTV, sneaking down the hall and into Jack's room.

Security came into the room and struggled to unzip the encased plastic. I double-downed my hold on Jack's wrist. I yelled his name, directing my voice inside to his cranial core, trying again to connect.

Two guards grabbed me, yanked, and I tumbled out of the pod while they wrestled me to the ground and zip-tied my wrists. They pulled me to a sitting position. I did not want to Push someone in anger, so I just breathed. I had already learned my lesson on that one; Pushing someone out of anger or desperation could be deadly.

"Stop," someone said with a raspy voice, as the guards worked to get me into a standing position. "Stop!" The voice was louder. It was Jack.

The guards looked at each other. They eased their grip on my shoulders, and I fell back down onto my butt.

"Un…zip-tie…me." I breathed out. "Please…"

The guards cut the tie, and I half crouched, half lunged up to Jack's bedside.

"Jack…Jack?" I said to him as he slid the full-face mask off.

"What took you so long?" His voice was dry and cracked.

"OMG, you have no idea." I tried to hug him but had difficulty with all the machinery he was encased in.

"I have some idea."

I freaking missed you, Jack.

I said this silently, not wanting to share our conversation with the guards or whoever else might be listening in. Jack answered silently, and we continued to carry on in secret.

Yeah, me, too. Thanks for getting me. I wasn't sure I was going to get back.

Of course, that's what BFFs are for. I knew you were still in there somewhere. I hesitated as I wasn't sure what he knew about what had gone down, but he encouraged me to continue.

I'm not sure how to tell you…

Just spit it out, Rogue.

OK, so your uncle is a serial killer responsible for dozens of murders. He tried to kill both of us. It's all over the news, and now the government and right-fighters want to license and control Sensitives.

He paused and swallowed a couple of times. *How is my family? How are they taking it?*

I can't get them to talk to me. They blame me for all this...for almost getting you killed.

We kept our silent conversation going. He said he didn't remember anything from that evening. Last thing he did remember was having a cigar and toasting with his uncle earlier in the evening.

I shared the details of what had happened at the lake house, how I'd gotten there, what I'd found in the underground bunker, and how Drew, Lyla, and I had escaped and found him unconscious.

I told Jack how Robin had attacked me, and Falco had shown up and intervened, and how, after Robin cut his own throat, Falco had tried to save him and I fell in the lake.

Jack nodded. *I kind of remember that—I was up there, floating. With a bunch of others.*

Ah, yeah...you were there, weren't you? I think that's why I thought you were dead. I thought we were both dead.

I shared details on how the storm had broken apart pieces of the deck, which led to the discovery of two dozen bodies triple-wrapped in black plastic sheeting and industrial tape.

I informed him about Falco's involvement with the FBSI and relayed what Falco had told me about not talking about being Sensitive, especially due to the recent anti-Sensitive rhetoric all over the news.

I told him to tell the FBSI just the basics of how we met, and told him to keep to surface information. Jack acknowledged what I said with multiple head bobs, then paused. His eyes were teary.

I hate that my uncle was part of so much horror and sadness for so long, he thought. *God, I hurt for the families. I felt all the victims' pain...the details of how it went down.*

Yeah, I felt it, too, when I was trying to reach you, Jack. You know it was Domino who helped me find you?

He nodded. *Yeah, I felt her presence the most. She is a fierce person in death as much as she was in life.*

We paused our silent communications and just looked at each other.

I hugged him again just as his care team rushed in and shooed me out. I gave Jack a slight wave. He raised his eyebrows and gave me a smile.

"OK, OK, I'm going," I said to his impatient medical team. I was so relieved that I was able to help peel Jack from his coma, with a lot of help from Domino. He was going to be OK, and I had Domino's fortitude even in death to thank for it.

Security escorted me back to my room, and I think I heard the door lock behind me, which was fine now because I knew Jack was OK. I went back to sleep with peaceful dreams for the first time in months.

Chapter Twenty-Eight

I was awoken by activity in my room, but I feigned sleep and pinged out. Couldn't make out direct internal voices, something was muting them with additional noise, but I could sense at least two people, and I received a variety of garbled info from both.

I sat up, rubbed my eyes, and then stretched my arms above my head in an exuberant yawn.

Two FBSI agents dressed in matching suits were sitting across from my bed, their badges affixed to their lapels.

I glanced over at my phone. It was six fifteen a.m. For the love of everything holy. Much too early for answering serious questions.

"We figured if you were well enough to wander the halls at night, you were well enough for some questions," the one on the left said. "Thought we'd get a jump on the day."

I looked at them. I could tell right away that the one on the left, the one who'd spoken and had a perma-scowl, was Bad Cop. The one on the right, smiling reassuringly at me, was Good Cop.

"Mind if we ask you a few questions, Rogue? May I call you Rogue?" Bad Cop said.

I answered both questions with a nod and glanced down at a black-and-silver box perched between them, emitting white noise and a high-pitched tinny sound, giving me a slight headache.

The machine looked like a souped-up mind-jumbler apparatus, probably why my Read on them was unclear. Listening to the sound, I was hoping that the FBSI had a higher-caliber contraption in the prison Robin was staying at. One stronger and more effective than this one at blocking Sensitive powers as it didn't hinder all my abilities, just muted them a bit.

"Oh, this," Bad Cop said sardonically, pointing down to the box I was looking at. "Typically, we'd bring interviewees to our offices for questioning, but now that we have this handy-dandy Sensitive blocker small enough to haul with us, we've taken our show on the road."

I nodded at them, assuming they just used the machine as a standard tool. Maybe they knew something about me?

"Why didn't you just wear foil hats?" I said, making Good Cop look surprised and Bad Cop roll their eyes.

"We don't like to play games, Rogue," Bad Cop said.

Then I couldn't help myself. They walked right into it! "No? Not into playing games?" I said facetiously, pulling a bit of the Read I had gotten earlier when I was feigning sleep and combining it with something I'd observed Good Cop wearing. "Then which one of you got wasted on glitter beer while dressed as a bunny…or was it a dog…at the furry convention last weekend and threw up in transit on the way home?"

This brought a startled gawk from Good Cop and an unimpressed gaze from Bad Cop.

"I'm just messing with you," I said to Good Cop. "I'm not psychic. I'm just observant." I pointed down to their wrist. "You are still wearing your event bracelet."

Both agents looked down at Good Cop's wrist, then back up, Bad Cop with another eye roll and annoyed exhale and Good Cop with an awkward shrug.

"I'm sorry. I talk too much when I'm nervous," I said.

"Why would you be nervous?" Bad Cop said. "Do you have anything to be nervous about?"

"No siree, Bob." I nodded, smiling despite myself. "I know your name isn't Bob, but I promised some old guy at this hospital I'd use his idiom the soonest chance I got. I nailed it, right?"

I got blank stares from both agents. This was going to be a long sequence of questions that I had to be careful in answering. Especially difficult because they were not impressed by my joking around to ease the mood.

So I did just like Falco advised me. Only answered questions from the surface, not elaborating or adding any Sensitive flair or details that could give me away.

I told them I had met Jack through his mom when providing life coaching and found we both were interested in true crime, and I had met Detective Falco after looking into Domino's murder, and I had mentioned I loved dogs, so he called me to take care of Lyla.

I told them that we hadn't intended to, but we got embroiled in solving the case and got way in over our heads, nearly paying with our lives. Blah. Blah. Blah. Blah.

I did not share anything about my Reads or Pushes or Jack's proclivity to see ghosts. And I didn't mention anything about hooking up with Falco or my ongoing fixation with him. I stayed calm, being thoughtful about each answer and tidbit of information given.

I didn't remember checking the clock, all I knew was they were there for what felt like several hours, and I was exhausted, having to readjust my sitting position multiple times while they were there.

My brain hurt from concentrating on making sure I did not share too much and that I told the same pieces of info the same way even after multiple times asked.

They thanked me for answering their questions and said they would be in touch soon, but that if I thought of anything else, I could call them.

Bad Cop started walking out of the room while Good Cop leaned in.

"It was a dog," Good Cop said, handing me their business card.

"Pardon?"

"I was dressed as a dog with long ears, at FurryCon, not a bunny."

I smiled at them. "Good to know." And nodded as they left.

I couldn't recall the last time I had spent more than five hours awake, so I was mentally fatigued and physically drained. Even skipped the lunch that was brought. Skipping food was a first for me, so I knew I was worn out.

I had one of those vivid nap dreams. The ones that seemed so real. I dreamt of Falco. And yes, we were fucking. This time, I was on top. But then when I looked down, it wasn't Falco but a fucking robot. I didn't see that coming. I tried to shake it off and switch up the dream. I dreamt of a lake and floating. I heard whispers of ghosts past. When I woke up, Falco was there.

Chapter Twenty-Nine

"Welcome back," Falco said, smiling.

I just nodded at him, trying to shake off sleep. I had been in a deep-as-shit, total REM dream and was trying to remember it. I'm sure I looked a mess and was at least hoping for looking like a hot mess since he was there.

"How'd the FBSI interview go?" He looked handsome and hot, as always.

"OK, I think. It was awkward, but at least I don't think I overshared."

He nodded, then rolled the visitor chair he was sitting in so he could sit closer.

I suddenly remembered my dream, making me flush, the heat moving up my neck, past my face. His touch and his velvety voice saying my name. The taste of his lips on mine. *Whew*. OMG. This man's presence did things to my brain and body I couldn't even begin to explain. What the hell was it about this guy that made me feel like I had lost brain cells?

He was cold and distant when I needed him, didn't like to share, and I had no way to Read him. So totally not my type. But so totally my type.

I had no idea what he wanted from me. Were we friends? Friends with benefits? God, I hoped it was the latter because I wanted multiple repeats of our one night together. I wanted to live out the dream I'd just had about him.

He leaned in closer. OMFG, his smell was intoxicating. Couldn't even describe it. He reached over and touched my arm, sending prickly skin from my head to my toes.

"Rogue, I was hoping you'd let me explain..." He looked at me.

I leaned closer, thinking he might be about to share something about himself and tell me he wanted to be my boyfriend. A bit childish in the overall state of things, but a girl could dream, couldn't she?

"So you said I ghosted you, and I want to tell you why," Falco said, sounding serious. "I've been chasing disaster my whole life. I've been in the right place at the right time for so many crazy things...so much so, there was a point where I thought I might have been causing them. Others thought so, too, so I was in and out of legal trouble as a juvenile."

He continued. "I was not in a good place in my life...spiraling and thinking I wanted to end my life, so I started driving, thinking I'd head into the mountains and either drive off a cliff or just start walking and not stop."

I nodded with attention as I'd been there a couple of times in my life as well.

"During that drive, I took a right when I planned to turn left and found a stranded driver with a flat tire and no cell service. That happenstance meeting with a stranger and random course change pivoted *my* course. I helped the woman fix her flat, and at the next truck stop, she repaid me with a meal and a life-changing conversation.

"This woman, a professor at Western teaching a course in, get this, *chaos and coincidence*, told me that some people are drawn to chaos—some are magnets for mayhem, some with happy endings, and some with not-so-happy endings. I shared a handful of stories from my recent events, and she smiled and said I was lucky. I was gifted with the good portion, being in the right place at the right time to save others.

"She said *it was no coincidence* I took the detour and found her stranded. I was meant to learn from her that disaster didn't follow me. Instead, I was innately attracted to it, that it wasn't my fault, and I couldn't avoid it. She told me to choose my future carefully."

"OK." I was trying to take in what he was putting out, but I was perplexed.

Falco grabbed my hand. As if that would help me concentrate on what he was saying.

"So here's a recent example of an uncanny coincidence. You knew that initially we had no CCTV footage of Drew, so he had no alibi, right?"

I nodded at him.

"The planets literally had to align for Drew to be cleared—a string of small unrelated chance encounters and timing that fell into place to happen at the exact moment for the outcome needed." He nodded at me.

I nodded back. I was definitely intrigued and leaned forward with interest.

He continued. "I was at the North Seattle precinct, following up on a lead, when I walked by a screen and saw footage of Drew. It was the footage I was told didn't exist. The video wasn't even brought to the station for any case I'm working on. The shop owner had been trying to catch illegal dumping near his business and brought the footage in to show police. That's the string of events that had to play out at the exact right time.

"How did the exact evidence I needed to clear Drew

fall into my hands at that exact moment when I just happened to be at that precinct? Why did that shopkeeper just happen to have an old-school format tape that couldn't be fried, and how was it playing on a screen at that exact time I looked up and knew that man lying near the gutter passed out was Drew?"

Wow. That's all I could think. Just *wow*.

"Call it luck. Call it fate. Call it whatever you want. But that is how I engage with life. I can't even go with the flow because the flow goes with me. That's the whole reason I decided to get into law enforcement, so I could continue to help people…rescue people in trouble. When I met you, I was instantly attracted…so I was not sure if it was real or just a—"

I cut him off. "A disaster waiting to happen?" I finished for him.

He shrugged at me. Oh God, he felt sorry for me. Saw me as a victim. I got that the last handful of months had definitely been no picnic, but my life was hardly a disaster.

Outing a long-time serial killer who'd had everyone fooled was a positive outcome, even if it had created chaos along the way.

"Sorry," he said, "that didn't come out sounding like I thought."

"I think it came out exactly how you thought it would sound. You think you were here to rescue me from my doomed disaster of a life?"

He didn't say anything, just looked at me and then down at his hands.

"And now your part's done?"

Again, silence from him. OMG, we hadn't even officially been together, and now he was dumping me.

So instead of waiting for an answer from him, I, per usual, filled the silence void with incessant talking. "Well, I didn't need and don't need to be rescued, and I sure as fuck don't want to just be part of your chaos theory." I didn't even try to hold back a small sob. "I thought it was as simple as I liked you and I thought you liked me…no turmoil or coincidence involved…"

He remained silent. And at that point I made it easy for him and gave him an out so he did not have to tell me if he had any feelings for me beyond pity. I was not going to ask him for an answer as I most probably didn't want to hear the truth outright.

I couldn't continue talking as I knew it would turn into sobbing, and then it'd be an ugly cry, and I was not in the mood for Falco to see me ugly cry.

"I'm actually feeling sick," I said matter-of-factly so it wouldn't come out in one long sob. "Can you close the door on your way out?" I rolled over in my hospital bed, faced the windows, and hoped he would just leave quietly, which he did.

Chapter Thirty

I was overwhelmed and feeling sorry for myself, so I counted deep breaths, as Vee would have suggested, until I fell asleep. My sleep was restless and unsettling and, much like a streaming show, had multiple episodes all night. I dreamt of the legal proceedings in Robin's court case.

There I am, sitting in the court audience, and my mind-sequence keeps hopping from his legal council's questioning of witnesses to the prosecution's trail of evidence.

"The evidence will substantiate Robin as a sociopathic, methodical killer, hell-bent on checking boxes down a premeditated path of terror," one prosecutor says.

For the scenario, I conjure all the lawyers wearing dark robes, white-collar ties, and powdered wigs. I'll have to do something about my British TV addiction because it is leeching into my dreams. I laugh in my dream. I am disturbed.

The prosecutor continues.

"Robin used his Emitting abilities to deceive his family and the authorities by hiding bodies, fabricating and destroying evidence, and choosing under-the-radar victims with questionable lives and no family. He killed them and stashed them away beneath the dock like human trash no one would miss. He thought he was

above the law by using his scientific knowledge in DNA and forensics to make any deaths he couldn't clean up or hide look like overdoses or suicides. But he was wrong. All those victims had families, and the decades of suffering he has caused needs to be reckoned with."

This prosecutor really has the dramatics down. Almost like I am watching one of my favorite vintage cop shows play out before my eyes. The prosecutor looks right at me in the crowd, and I sit at attention.

"For his most recent rampage, Robin left thousands of pieces of evidence."

A plethora of slides are being displayed up front. I recognize a couple. Robin's draft e-post, pretending to be Drew and apologizing for murdering Domino and Ms. Brooks, and my forged note, of my intention to kill Jack as his jilted ex-fiancée, still fresh on the laptop found at the scene.

I see slide pictures of injuries projected for the jury. I recognize my multiple healing injuries in photos. I recognize Falco's. Still hot, even injured. They even show photo proof that Robin had trace evidence of the poison he used on Jack in his kitchen and on his skin.

The shadow boxes are part of the slide show juxtaposed with victim photos and showing DNA sequences matching some of the dead bodies found. A series of grotesque unidentified remains are clicked through. The prosecution holds nothing back. I want to vomit and gag in my sleep.

I'm sure Robin never thought the bodies would turn up, but the reinforced lake-house deck was no match for a fifty-year storm and Robin's recent bad luck.

He killed so many people he had to stop caching them under the dock. There was no room left. That's *when he set up his murders to look like suicides or overdoses.*

"From the perfect storm of coincidence to the weather storm that walloped the lake house with enough power to unearth the lost bodies, left to rest, but not forgotten by their families.

"Robin left all the physical evidence needed to put him away for good just in the shadow boxes he kept as trophies memorializing his murdering spree. His DNA was found intermixed with the victims found dislodged under the lake house dock. But Robin couldn't hide from the truth any longer."

The attorney continues and adjusts his wig, which has now turned a turquoise blue.

"Robin bypassed life undetected until fate intervened in a big way. And it took a slew of chance encounters that, combined, were no match for even his strongest Emitting skills.

"A mix of chance. A quarry of coincidence…"

The blue-wigged lawyer exclaims this last part, making a swooping point gesture with his hand and pointing to me and Falco. And to Jack and Lyla. And Drew. We are all there in the courtroom and now front and center.

Lyla on a hot-pink dog bed with a cat graphic and me sitting on a neon-orange Adirondack chair and Falco, Drew, and Jack sitting on bench seats. Fuck, I have weird dreams.

"So, Your Honor and members of the jury, how exactly did two amateur sleuths kick up all this dirty laundry by chance and bust this decades-old murder spree wide open?" The lawyer gestures largely and walks around the courtroom, looking at multiple people

straight on to increase the dramatic flair.

"I'll tell you. A quinfecta of Sensitive powers, the perfect combination to bring this serial killer down."

I turn to Falco. "I thought we weren't supposed to talk about Sensitivities!"

He shrugs at me.

The attorney continues, his wig morphing into a longer style, the color a blue-black. He gestures to us again, pointing to each of us as he speaks. "The Ghost-Whisperer, the Pushy Reader, the Canine Bouncer, and the Chaos Detractor with his alter-ego Mind Trap."

The lawyer scrolls through these titles like they are our superhero names. Stupid names. I hope they don't stick.

"The evidence is undeniable, Your Honor. Robin's true intentions were to continue killing and deceiving people with his Sensitive powers."

Then my dream takes a twist, as they almost always do.

"But, good people of the jury, Robin is not the only one who killed and deceived with their Sensitive powers. We have another murderer amongst us."

Suddenly, the whole courtroom turns to me. I am no longer part of the witness list or courtroom audience but the one on trial.

The judge looks right at me with a scowling face, his eyes the size of a stop sign. A bright-red spotlight beams on me. I can hear the entire courtroom taking in a breath and seething at me. I can feel hate and disdain from the judge, jury, attorneys, and the audience.

"Rogue, you have been found guilty beyond a reasonable doubt by a jury of your peers for using your powers to kill. You will be immediately remanded to

prison for life without the possibility of parole."

I awoke with a shudder, a frigid chill wafting throughout my body. My room phone rang, and I jumped out of my skin.

It was Jack. "What the fuck, Rogue? I just had a helluva dream; we were in court, and I was getting questioned by the prosecutor, asking me about your past. Then he said that I don't really know you and to ask you about Route 66 through Arizona."

"OMG, Jack. Are you serious? We're still having the same dreams?" I hoped he would ignore the other part and not prod me about my past. Not so lucky.

"I guess so. So tell me about Route 66."

"That, my friend, is a discussion for when we are both out of this joint." I tried to make light of the question. "Although I'm not sure it means anything at all."

"All I know is that dream seemed so real. Except for the lawyers. They were all wearing blue wigs and spoke with English accents."

"We are so on the same planet with our weirdness." I smiled through the phone. "And on that note, I'm going back to bed. Good night, Jack." I hung up the phone and silenced it so it wouldn't ring again.

I didn't want Jack to know I was responsible for trying, and almost succeeding, to kill his uncle or that I had already taken someone else's life what seemed like ages ago. I had purposefully left out the part that I Pushed his uncle to slit his own throat. I wanted to tell him. Needed to tell him. I just needed to wait for the right time.

Chapter Thirty-One

I was happy to finally go home after my docs gave me the thumbs-up to leave the hospital. What did not make me happy were the FBSI agents waiting for me when I got there.

"Hello, Rogue," one agent said. It was Bad Cop.

I nodded a greeting. "Hiya." I tried to sound enthusiastic. "What's up?"

"We'd just like to ask you a couple more questions," Good Cop said. "Can we come in?"

I punched in the code and motioned for them to enter when I opened the door. I looked around for Lyla, remembering she was still at the dog park with Barrow. He had become a pretty good dog sitter and loyal friend to me.

"Have a seat." I gestured the agents to the couch in the living room.

They sat down, and I pointed while walking toward the kitchen.

"Do you want coffee?" I asked them. "Or something stronger, like a vodka and soda?"

They both shook their heads. Bad Cop rolled their eyes at me but smiled. I knew they were warming up to me.

I took my time making my signature coffee-flavored beverage. I was nervous and wondering if this was it. If the agents were here to ask me questions they already knew the answers to. If they'd be arresting me for lying to them and trying to kill Robin. I brewed my cup, cradled it in my hands, sauntered over, and sat down across from the agents.

"Soooooooo…" I said, drawing out the word for several seconds, then taking a nervous drink, looking down into my cup. I was jittery, but the smell of coffee and vanilla calmed me.

"Rogue, we wanted to chat with you again today and do some follow-up," Bad Cop said.

"OK." I tried not to sound apprehensive, but I was. I gripped my cup tight, to try and keep from visibly shaking. The smooth cup was slick, making it hard to hold on to with my clammy palms.

"So we met with Robin in jail, and he shared some interesting information about you."

"Oh yeah?" I said with a nervous laugh, a prickly sensation running through my body. Oh God. I needed to compose myself.

"You mentioned you weren't a mind reader when we met, but it seems that you are one," Bad Cop said, "and a pretty good one, at that."

"Hmmmm." I shrugged, knowing that I was just about to do what Falco always told me not to do. Share too much. "I've been known to dabble in the mental arts a bit."

They just looked at me.

"Am I in trouble? Uh…like are you here to arrest me?" I was half joking, half serious, but because of my nervousness, I sounded neither.

"Did you do something to be arrested for?" Bad Cop asked.

I shook my head, knowing that wasn't quite true,

especially since I had been practicing my Reading and Pushing with folks at the hospital without following the newly passed law requiring me to be registered and licensed. My bad. I did not plan on ever registering.

"Actually, Rogue, we've come to you with a proposition," Bad Cop said.

What on earth would they propose? I looked at them with a questioning gaze.

"We were hoping you'd consider coming to work for the FBSI as a special-duty officer."

I was not expecting that. I gave them another questioning glance.

"Yeah," Good Cop said, "we think you would be valuable when interviewing or assessing people…like a human lie detector."

Bad Cop gave Good Cop a wicked side-eye.

"What exactly did Robin say about me?" I asked.

"Enough," Bad Cop said, nodding and leaning toward me. "*Enough* for us to know he hates you with a passion, totally outed you about your Sensitivities, and tried to get you into trouble…so we think you might be a good fit for the investigations we do."

"I'm not sure that's quite ethical. I don't typically Read people without their consent, and I don't think a criminal would give…me…that…" I trailed off and shrugged. I felt bad since I hadn't been forthright in getting consent on all my Reads lately, including the slight Read I'd taken from both agents the other day.

"Well, you'd be just another tool in our kit," Bad Cop said, "like the noise-cancelling machine we use. Just like businesses are supposed to post they have Emitters or other Sensitives in use, we'd tell the people we are interviewing what you can do, and they can either agree to have you present during the interview or not."

"That way if they say *no*," Good Cop joked, evoking another side-eye from Bad Cop, "we know they are guilty of *something*."

"Anyway," Bad Cop said, shutting up their partner with a snapping closed-finger hand gesture, "we'd like you to think on it and let us know."

I nodded and breathed, and they continued.

"Any offer would, of course, be contingent on an extensive background check and some formal psychological testing, but that shouldn't be a problem since you probably already know how we want you to answer on the tests."

My neck hairs rose at that. The good news was that Bad Cop had made a joke and smiled. Bad news was the background check could be a problem. I had no idea what they'd rake up on me.

Also, I guessed if I was thinking of joining their team, I'd have to learn their names and would have to stop calling them Bad Cop and Good Cop. I'd probably also be asked to register as a Sensitive. I really wasn't keen on that idea at all.

The agents hadn't yet brought up the fact that I had Pushed Robin to cut his own throat. Maybe Robin would never admit I was just as powerful as him? Maybe Robin *had* told them everything and they didn't believe him?

Or maybe Robin didn't even realize that I had so easily gotten in his brain. Maybe because Robin was that narcissistic. Or maybe because I was *that good*. I laughed out loud at my internal confidence statement, which garnered questioning looks from Good and Bad Cop.

"So you'll think about it?" Bad Cop asked.

I nodded.

We conversed for a bit longer, and then they took the hint to leave when I stretched my arms way up in a boisterous yawn. I was hoping the agents would leave soon so I could take advantage of a nap to help me get my mind straight.

My high-level napping capabilities were often cathartic, and some of my best thinking was done asleep. I lounged on the large gray couch where the FBSI agents had been, still warm from where they had been sitting.

I was hoping sleep could help me think, and I had a lot to think about, my brain on fire with decisions needing to be made.

I was hoping the FBSI offer meant I was out of trouble. At least for now.

I needed to talk to Vee about the job offer. And to Jack. He'd be getting out of the hospital in a few days. And Falco. I needed to tell Falco. Fuck Falco. He hadn't consulted with me when he joined forces with the FBSI. I had heard they had offered him a lead agent position.

Although to his credit, I'd been incapacitated at the time he decided. Still, he'd probably just want me to do the opposite of what I would think about doing. I just needed to get over him, shove thoughts of him way down deep, and keep the relationship purely in the friend zone.

I Pushed myself to think about Falco as just an acquaintance and not to be so infatuated with him. I figured if I could Push myself to slow down my body fluids physically to prevent blood loss when Robin tried to kill me, I could do the same for my heart, right? Slow it down. Reset it, maybe? Fingers crossed.

I was sure a long nap would provide me some time to think as I dreamt. My dreams were windows to my soul. They showed me the good, bad, and the scary and often showed me paths to take. Sometimes my dreams brought me some deliverance, atonement, but sometimes just more unfinished business.

I dreamt about Falco, definitely some unfinished business there. And it was a good one, too, unapologetically. Also, a bad one, unapologetically. A good, bad one. But I forced myself to lucid dream directly into that bullshit so I could Push Falco out of my thoughts and out of my system. Of course, not until after. After I'd finished.

I also dreamt about Robin, who, of course, was the *scary* part of the dream equation as well as unfinished business.

I am floating above an FBSI interrogation room as a silent observer. Robin is there, physically contained with e-cuffs attached to a counter. The counter housed in a protective pod encased with some kind of specialized coating that looks like layered cellophane. I hope they cut holes in the top so he can breathe. I laugh out loud at that.

Falco and two other agents I don't recognize are interrogating Robin.

My attempt to Push Falco out of my thoughts must be working because I only feel a minute twinge in my groin from seeing him.

He is asking Robin questions and repeating each one in a slow and steady fashion. Telling him small stories about some of the evidence the authorities discovered. Robin seems frustrated and starts peppering all three of them with some hefty mind pings without answering any questions. I grow a tad nauseous in response, so I'm thinking the protection pod Robin is in is only partially effective. I am able to quell Robin's pings before they get too overwhelming.

The other two FBSI agents aren't so lucky. They have to vacate the pod, one retching and grasping onto the other as they stumble out. Falco remains steadfast. Robin has met his match. He can't get into Falco's head, and that is pissing him the fuck off. I just laugh from my perch as I float above. Falco's calmness under pressure makes him even hotter. OK, so I pushed myself not to have a strong emotional reaction about him, but I didn't Push myself to feel nothing. I mean, geez, I'm only human and don't want to take away all the physiological pleasure of having someone like him in the same room. Even in my dream I justify feelings for Falco.

Falco turns off the recording mechanism. "I guess we're done here for the day." He gathers up some items and starts turning off a couple of lights from the e-touch console.

Then Robin speaks. His voice is raspy and broken. Probably due to the fact he cut himself shaving. And by shaving, I mean when I made him slice through his own throat. I laugh. It sounds more like a maniacal guffaw.

"So you know that head-game of a bedmate of yours?" Robin says, trying to get Falco's attention. "She's a killer, too."

Falco looks up at him, unimpressed, and continues to gather up his items.

"She'll kill again, you know." Robin's voice is getting scratchier the louder he tries to talk. "You'll need to lock her up before she does."

Falco shrugs at Robin, looks down, and then looks directly up at me as a not-so-silent observer.

"Is that true?" he asks.

I awoke with a start. My breath caught in my throat,

my pulse going a gazillion miles per hour. Rolls of sweat easing down my hairline, making my pillow moist, sticky.

I rolled over to shake the dream out of my head. My eyes were blurry, so I wiped them forcefully, trying to focus.

Domino was floating beside my bed. She was smiling at me. Not a creepy grin but a hopeful one. I knew why she was there. I could Read her instantly.

"Lemme think about it," I said out loud to her. I reached for my phone and called Jack.

He told me he was still being visited by several of Robin's victims. That they all had unfinished business and they wanted Jack's help. I told him that Domino came to visit and was asking the same thing. For help to contact the living.

He said that was what we should do. Make amends for the departed who couldn't do it on their own but who needed closure for themselves and their loved ones. We talked for what seemed like hours, Jack going over the idea in his head. He had obviously thought it all out, and it seemed like a solid plan.

I hung up from our call. I had so much to think about. I was def intrigued by the FBSI's offer, but I was also drawn to Jack's proposal.

I was worried about not being able to pass their background check or even their psychological tests. What would they even find out about me?

I didn't want the FBSI digging into my past. I had skeletons that lived there. Well, at least one, although he was not a skeleton the last time I'd seen him. Nor did he live any longer. Just an ex-asshole-boyfriend flattened by a truck after wandering onto a lone country road.

I didn't want them digging more into my present. I had tried to kill Robin, and I still wanted him dead. I was not sure anyone would fault me for that. The FBSI would most likely rule that it was in self-defense, but I couldn't chance it.

I was reluctant to register as a Sensitive, which would make my business more legal but less anonymous for my clients, so I had to make some career decisions. And some emotional decisions. I had to stop pursuing Falco. Stop thinking about him. Stop wanting him.

Chapter Thirty-Two

My car auto-parked and switched into its energy-saving mode. I had twenty minutes before my scheduled time with the FBSI regional director and a couple of interview panelists. I wondered if Falco would be there. I hoped not. Or I hoped so. I still liked looking at the guy.

I had already disclosed to the FBSI more details about my Sensitivities and that Falco and I had had an intimate yet short-lived, no-strings encounter with no plans to rekindle.

I had to remain focused on fizzling its memory out of my cortex as a meaningless tryst, although I did use him as a job reference, so there's that. It was important that I let them know the nature of our relationship since Falco had been offered and accepted employment as an FBSI agent.

He had provided a positive recommendation, so I guessed something good had come out of our coupling. He'd said many favorable things about my work ethic and at least that I seemed competent to hold a job, anyway.

The FBSI team had notified me that I passed the background check and psych tests already, so today was just a formality. The final job offer. I guessed my past was hidden better than I'd thought. I was relieved that some parts hadn't come back to haunt me.

I already knew what my answer was going to be at

the interview and was still mulling over what I was going to say to the FBSI about their offer.

I was looking forward to something new and was hoping I was making the right decision. My roomie had said it was up to me and she didn't want to sway me one way or the other. She was too busy making wedding plans with Josie.

I heard a loud honk and looked out of my driver's side window, breaking me from deep thought.

When I looked back, Domino was there, smiling at me, translucent in my passenger seat.

"OK, OK," I said to her. "You win."

She just sat there; her head tilted in my direction.

The FBSI could wait. I'd call it a gap year if they'd still have me when I came back.

Jack and I were going on a road trip. And what a trip it could promise to be. Traveling to find the families of Robin's murdered victims to provide them some closure and maybe even some comfort sounded like something we had to do. More pressing than working with the FBSI or remaining a life coach. At least for now, anyway.

Jack had talked me into committing to the trip with a little help from our friend Domino who had been visiting me often in dreams and in person the last couple of weeks. I had a feeling she wouldn't leave me alone until I said yes to the trip. For a ghost, she was persistent.

I'd miss randomly running into Falco but had to move on. If he really was a magnet for disaster and we were meant to keep tabs on each other, perhaps we would run into each other again while I was out traveling. I was sure the FBSI had field offices and had to investigate all over the country, so it was possible. Or he'd still be back at the Seattle FBSI office when I returned now that he was a full-time agent.

Either way, he'd have to make the decision to stay friends or lovers or both or nothing, I guessed. It didn't seem up to me. His aloofness pushed me away, and the emotional coaster he had me on was too draining to continue.

I was looking forward to seeing the states and providing closure to folks with my best friend Jack leading the way, Lyla in tow to block pings, the Knight family footing the bill, and Domino sitting shotgun. What could go wrong?

I looked over at Domino again. God, they were always smiling now. I nodded at them, opened the car door, and walked across the parking lot, knowing what I would tell the FBSI, hoping they'd still have a job for me when I got back. If not, oh well, I'd see where the road took me after that.

It was going to be a wild, weird adventure, to say the least.

A word about the author…

Tobin lives, loves, and laughs in Seattle's Mapleleaf neighborhood with her spouse of many moons, dog Hazelnut, and cat Finnegan (her two kids are grown). She works in the public sector, is a retired Navy Public Affairs officer, and has always found fantasy a nice escape from reality. Fortune Giver is her first novel. www.seattlerogue.com